He finished the
boxes, making sure copies went in the billing tray and giving the rest to Natalie, who ran the little store they'd recently put in. The "a few items behind the reception counter" area had soon outgrown itself.

"You need help stocking the shelves?" He hoped to hell she said no. Rock had left at lunchtime, and Dick had spent the ensuing hours imagining exactly what was going on back home given that Rig was home on a Saturday. It'd left him horny and wanting his men.

"I don't think so, no. Saturday afternoons are dead. I'll be happy with something to do." She grinned at him, hefting a tub of protein powder. "Besides, this is a workout."

"Yeah, it sure is. All right, you know the number if there's any problems. See you on Tuesday." Dick gave her a wave, made sure the office was locked, and headed out for his car, eager to get home.

Traffic was good—most people were heading into town not away from it—and in no time at all he was pulling in behind Rock's truck.

The mutts welcomed him home, and he spared a pat for everyone before looking for Rock and Rig.

Not in the kitchen. Not in the bedroom. He headed upstairs, where he found them at last on the big couch Rig loved. Naked, asleep, Rock holding Rig close. Dick would bet they hadn't even eaten. He was torn, for all of two seconds, as to whether he should go fix some food or wake them up.

Naked men won out over food every time.

Kegs and Dorms
TOP SHELF
An imprint of Torquere Press Publishers
PO Box 2545
Round Rock, TX 78680
Haven Copyright 2008 © by Lee Benoit, House Call Copyright 2008 © by Jane Davitt, In Sickness and Health Copyright 2008 © by Sean Michael
Cover illustration by Alessia Brio
Published with permission
ISBN: 978-1-60370-628-5, 1-60370-628-3

www.torquerepress.com

**If you enjoyed Bedside Manner,
you might enjoy these Torquere Press titles:**

Bad Case of Loving You by Laney Cairo

Drawing Closer by Jane Davitt

Tempering by Sean Michael

Three Day Passes by Sean Michael

Wild Raspberries by Jane Davitt

Bedside Manner

Bedside Manner
by Lee Benoit, Jane Davitt, and Sean Michael

Torquere
Press
Inc.
romance for the rest of us
www.torquerepress.com

Bedside Manner

Table of Contents

Bedside Manner

HAVEN
by Lee Benoit

Chapter 1
In which Haven attends the ballet

You're making a spectacle of yourself, Tucker."

I make a show of inspecting my ornate, antique opera glasses. The Love Doctor must be peeved to hiss in my ear during a performance. I'd have thought that was a breach of propriety worse than my using opera glasses. I shrug, grin as charmingly as I can at my date, and go back to watching the Buenos Aires Ballet's staging of Carmina Burana.

With my opera glasses covering my face, I shut out the Love Doctor and resume slavering over the male principal.

The Love Doctor, predictably, raises another objection. "No one uses opera glasses at the ballet." There's a definite, disapproving 'hrmmf' in his voice.

Just because he's sponsoring me in his new nurse practitioner program doesn't mean he can boss me around when we're out playing "mentor and protégé." I may be new to town, but the Love Doctor knows I have connections, or I wouldn't be working as a nurse outside the VA. My newly minted LPN isn't enough, and we both know it, but if he pulls this high and mighty shit too often I'll pull some of my own that'll leave his bourgeois, white-bread head spinning.

I indulge a smirk and picture myself as the female principal, spun this way and that by the lean, male dancer, lifted, turned, and brought up snug against his taut, delicious body again and again.

Alberta at the hospital would have laughed at me for being faggy, and believe me she's the only person alive—besides Daddy, maybe—who could do so and keep all her teeth. My army buddies? They'd have needled me for my stupid, romantic fantasies right before pushing me to my knees. We all knew way too much about each other in 'Nam. Hell, they'd have had a field day at the sight of me all gussied up. The Love Doctor had hinted about buying me a tux, but I'm fine—more than fine, and I know it—in my dove-gray Nehru jacket and snug, black trousers. Half of those mugs had never heard of the ballet anyway. Which was why I was here with the Love Doctor. Who wouldn't shut up.

"We're in the fourth row, Tucker. For God's sake!" He's pissed because I'm being low-class, not because I'm telegraphing queen vibes. That particular danger never occurs to him; he's untouchable by public opinion, or so he thinks.

I wrap my fingers more tightly around the brass barrels of my opera glasses and sink back into my fantasy, banishing Alberta, my army buds, and most emphatically the Love Doctor, who has another think coming if he expects his customary good-night blowjob.

The male principal spins alone now, My mouth goes dry as the man's dark red tights flash basket-ass-basket-ass in eye-watering, cock-hardening, heart-pounding repetition until I have to squirm just a little to readjust things down below.

I watch for the same dancer in each of the scenes that follow and get such a deep fantasy going that I hardly taste the wine the Love Doctor buys me at intermission. As we take our seats for the second half, he yammers about how just as we were celebrating our Bicentennial last year, Argentina experienced a military coup, and now these dancers were part of a repressed population. I've heard of the Dirty War, sure, but it doesn't seem too different from other wars. I shrug him off as the curtain rises, looking for my dancer. Watching him is better than listening to the Love Doctor any day, and I'm so aroused by the time the curtain falls I forget my promise to punish the Love Doctor for being a bossy old priss.

If there's one thing I hate about living in Boston, it's knowing where I can be out. Nowhere, that's where. In New York, I know the score, and at least there's a game to play. Bars like the Ramrod have their uses, but after New York they don't really appeal. I've found two bath houses since coming here, one of which is too skanky for words, and that's saying a lot considering some of the places I've sucked cock. So, one bath house and one doctor's in-town flat. That's the sum total of la vida homosexual in my new hometown. Still beats Coal Ridge to hell and back, though, so I guess it'll do for now.

I'm a world class sucker of cock and seldom pass up an opportunity to show off my hard-won skills. Having given up on punishing the Love Doctor by the time we're back in his downtown pied á terre, I coax his pale, reluctant prick to enthusiastic stiffness using only my tongue, all the while reminding myself that the Love Doctor has a name: Stephen. I mentally chant it over and over so I won't forget to use it after I swallow. The Love Doctor—Stephen, Stephen, Stephen—likes to believe what we do is a different animal from anonymous, back room gloryholing because we work at the same hospital and attend cultural events together. Idiot.

Now me, I don't mind back room sex or cultural events. Both have their place. But I was beginning to think that maybe I minded Stephen.

I put the thought out of my mind, for now, with that mental shrug I perfected in the army, and haul my own prick out of my pants. Stephen finds handjobs distasteful and probably won't offer to finish me off. As it happens, I come before Stephen; the image of tonight's dancer leaping and extending, arching and bending, is all I need to blast to the finish. It's only after I swallow, dust off the knees of my good trousers, and catch a cab home—the Love

Doctor never invites me to stay the night—that I realize I forgot to grab the program from the performance. There were pictures of the principal dancers in it, and their names, too. I'll admit it: I wanted to know the name of the dancer who'd captured my…imagination.

The next night, I go back to the ballet, alone, same Nehru jacket, but over jeans this time. I bring my trusty opera glasses and my student ID. The latter gets me a night-of-performance seat in the nosebleed section, and the former would give me a glimpse of the object of my desire. I'm betting I can even finagle my way backstage if I set my mind to it.

Except the man isn't there.

The ballet is as sensual and beautifully staged as before, but without Tadeo Neyen—even a student ticket gets you a program—the whole thing's flat. I'm almost relieved when intermission comes. I leave the theater, hop on the train, and head home to jerk off to the grainy picture beside the name.

Chapter 2
In which Tadeo meets death in a strange land

My boarding school English is good, but it is completely unequal to the American hospital staff. I can't understand a single word from the stricken-looking young doctor, and when the harried young nurse takes over it's just as bad.

"Mr. Neyen...your wife...," they say, and I know the numbness of my heart looks like shock when they peer into my face. They even test my eyes with that little pinprick light of theirs. Maybe I look like I'm about to pass out.

For a moment, every death I've ever known crushes me.

"Your baby...intensive care..." They're still talking, but their words are no match for the one death that's risen to the surface.

Josue. Why must the name of my old lover be forever coupled with death in my mind?

Lena's death should mean more. On a selfish level, it does. Her death will remove the protection of the dance company, which only tolerates me for her sake. Her uncle, the director, and our manager, her cousin—what will I tell them? These are pressing questions, but neither they nor the distant hollowness of Lena's death are enough to silence the screaming, clawing horror of Josue's murder.

We were still students, enraged by the Junta's incursions and foolishly certain of our own immortality. We were invincible revolutionaries, like Che. Don't remind me— Che had been dead for years, butchered in the Bolivian jungle. Willful idealists that we were, we refused to remember. Our studies, our politics, even our furtive couplings, all were driven by our cause, elevated by it. It seems laughable now.

When the purges came, student leaders were among the first to disappear. Their followers, often, were merely tortured. I, who had followed Josue into leftist politics like a puppy follows a butcher, all hope and ignorance and provincial naïveté, was left alone while he "disappeared."

My "anti-government" activities didn't force an end to my studies, nor my career as a dancer. I wasn't important enough to disappear, nor well-enough connected for anyone to try to turn me into an informant. So I became one of many examples of the Junta's clemency. I couldn't have cared less in those first days after Josue went into an unmarked and unconsecrated grave.

Then, like sunlight burning away fog, there was Lena. One of those clean, earnest "supporters" of the cause of democratic reform, she knew about Josue. I mean to say, everybody knew about Josue, but she knew about Josue and me, and she married me anyway. She befriended me and resolved to make me safe, or safer than street runners or trade unionists or poor students, anyway. My plight was, to her, romantic. She got her indulgent colonel father and company-director uncle to turn a blind eye to my past, to cast their circle of protection around me. As her husband, I was out of reach of the Junta, able to work. But I was also cut off from my old life. In those early days, I told myself I didn't care. I convinced myself I'd been a revolutionary only for the sake of my love for Josue. A whore, my old friends called me, on account of Josue, and on account of Lena. Yes, I told myself, better a safe whore than a dead revolutionary.

I was easily one of the best male classical dancers of my generation. Some said the very best, but that compliment usually came right before they came in my mouth. Lena, my savior, was a mediocre dancer on a good day, though no one could match her when it came to choreography or dance history and theory. She had designs on production and management, but had to legitimize that claim with a stint en pointe. In any company besides one run by her uncle and financed by her father, she would have been lucky to land a place in the corps.

In me, Lena had everything she needed: a principal role without the work, the marriage her family craved, and, almost immediately, the child that would get her off stage for good without losing face.

By the time she was pregnant, she was my best friend. My only friend, if I were to be honest. My old friends—Josue's friends—had abandoned me when I joined the Buenos Aires company. The dancers didn't trust me, though they had no choice but to accept and respect me. Her family, especially her uncle and father, hated everything about me but my dancing. But they loved Lena beyond reason, and she loved me, so they put up with me.

For a short time, we were safe. So I thought. But there was no safety for Lena from that oldest predator of women, was there? She was dead, like Josue, and my baby with her.

Bile stings the back of my throat as the world flickers crazily from past to present and back again, over and over. I smell the despair on my clothes, like stale fear.

Words the young nurse had spoken filter through my panicked reverie.

"...intensive care..."

I raise my head, ready to find someone to ask if I'd heard correctly, and meet the bluest eyes I've ever seen.

"Tadeo?" the white clad young man asks, an inexplicable note of amusement in his voice.

"Tadeo Neyen? I'm Nurse Haven Tucker, and I'm here to take you to meet your son."

Chapter 3
In which Haven becomes a
stalking-horse

If I'd known how the day was going to go, I'd have taken more care with my appearance. Not that there's much you can do with the boxy, white scrubs that pass for a uniform for male nurses.

I arrive at the hospital about a quarter hour ahead of my oh-seven-hundred shift, later than usual, but I just had to start the day with another jerk off session in honor of the gorgeous, absent dancer from the Buenos Aires ballet. Had to do something with the extra time between coaxing something like coffee out of my old stovetop percolator and waiting for the shower water to warm up to something I could stand. The second I mustered out from my tour in Vietnam, I swore two things: no more olive drab and no more cold showers.

I rush through my routine in the converted supply room male nurses were assigned as a changing and storage area. I call it the boys' closet, just to drive my roomie crazy. Swears he's straight. Yeah, and I'm Jimmy Carter. The tiny room has a chipped porcelain sink, but no toilet. According to Alberta, female nurses even get showers, but hey. I get my gear together, looking into the little, spotty, unframed mirror to check everything's straight, so to speak, and make my daily pledge to my silver-framed picture of Walt Whitman from his years as a nurse during the Civil War. Beats the Nightingale Pledge all to hell, if you ask me, but that was thumb tacked to the wall, too, courtesy of my counterpart, the only other male nurse in Boston, as far as I knew. Little prick, but that's another story.

I hum the "O Fortuna" bit from the ballet—pretty

damn catchy even if I don't know the words. I have just enough time to say a quick "hey" to Alberta over in maternity before clocking in. My hand is on the door handle when someone knocks.

"Got something for you, Haven." I open the door. Speak of the devil and the devil appears, if the devil is an imposing black woman in nurse's whites starched within an inch of their life. I grin, knowing it'll have to stand in for the hug I'd rather give. I know Alberta loves me best of everyone at St. Sebastian's, but she only calls me "honey" when we're away from the hospital.

"Get your David Bowie ass to the NICU. They asked for you special." The smile she gives me with the order tells me everything I need to know.

"The fuck?" I say. The powers only let me near the babies when something's gone seriously pear-shaped. "Call down to the ER for me?" Something is up, for sure, but I don't want my supervisor, who I lovingly call "Nurse Ratchet", to have any reason to get on my case later for being elsewhere than my assigned ward.

"Language, Nurse Tucker," Alberta says with her trademark stone-faced wink before peeling off back to Maternity. "I'll clock you in."

So, instead of heading down to the ER and facing down Nurse Ratchet like usual, I head up to the Intensive Care Unit where the snazzy new neonatal care ward sits within its shield of glass and steel. I hate coming up here—or going to any of the regular wards—without knowing what's going on. See, down in the ER, all the nurses know my history, and know I'm studying in the new nurse practitioner program, so when things get dicey, most of the gals on the ward cut me some slack when I cross the line and set an IV or jot care plan notes on a patient's chart. But that's the ER, where they're used to me, where my particular talents are valued.

Anywhere else in the hospital it's a daily battle to do much more than the work of an orderly, and the ugly uniforms don't help at all since they looked a lot like the orderlies' scrubs. Heavy lifting, shifting patients and cleaning up, all that's fine with me as long as the other LPNs do it too, but mostly they don't. Too many of my fellow nurses see me as some kind of invader from Planet Man and go right along with it, never mind that I'm just as qualified as they are. More so, if we're being honest, 'cause no more than one or two of them ever saw anything more serious than a bad traffic accident in their lives.

I push into the ICU wondering what sort of disaster has forced them to swallow their ever-loving pride and call in the cavalry. Now, I don't flatter myself it's anything medical—the docs would never ask a nurse to advise, and the nurses would never ask me. No, it's something more... combat related.

See, I have a reputation. Don't know how it got started, though I suspect Alberta had something to do with my legend. But somehow the docs know about my stint as an army medic. None of the young ones were in 'Nam, but some of the older guys had been in Korea or even the Big One, and they get it. Maybe they talk about it with their buddies on the golf course or wherever the hell doctors hang out when they aren't getting in nurses' ways or counting their money. However it happened, the docs know who to call when an accident victim is bleeding out or an emergency c-section goes south. The nurses, for all their insistence about being autonomous and all, follow the doctors' lead.

Everyone agrees, even if they never say anything, that no one is my equal when it comes to running interference on the really bad cases, when tempers heat up and a different kind of triage is required. I'll never forget the new dad, spluttering and making threats when he met his baby daughter, who was just a few shades too dark to be his. I thought he was going to gut the OB just for delivering her. Talked him down, though, when no one else could get near him. Yeah, man, battlefield psychology sure comes in handy sometimes.

I wait to be buzzed into the NICU and wonder if

today's crisis will be something like that.

The orderly on duty points me toward the bank of incubators, one on the end in particular, and I peer over while I scrub up. Baby seems fine.

"He is fine. A little underweight, but otherwise fine," says Matron. Matron isn't her real name, but she reminds me so much of an old-fashioned British nursing sister— like the ones in Hemingway books, the ones the hero never falls in love with—with her faultless posture and severe air, that I usually have to cast about a bit before I remember her real name.

"Reading minds, now, Miss Elliott?"

"You've got a glass face, Tucker."

"There aren't any lines in, no bili lights, no oxygen. Why's this little fella here?" Why am I here? I want to add.

"Special circumstances. You'll meet the father soon."

Ah-ha. Here it comes, I think.

"Not the mom?" I bite my tongue. Of course not the mom. The high-and-mighty NICU battleaxes would never have called a lowly emergency ward LPN for a healthy baby with a healthy mom. They need me to run interference on the dad. Because the mom is…

"…dead," Matron is telling me. "Uterine rupture."

"They couldn't stop it?" Cynical as I am about doctors, I'm always amazed when they can't stop something as tragic as a young mother's death. This is supposed to be the most advanced medical system in the world, if you believe the hype, but I have my doubts sometimes. Like now.

"The father hasn't seen the baby yet," Matron is saying. "There's some question about…legal issues." She makes a face that tells me exactly what she thinks of administration wonks keeping a man from his baby.

Now, here's the other thing about me. Me and the wonks? Do not get along. They don't like my 'anti-authoritarian attitude' and I don't like their officious prickishness. A good day at St. Seb's is a day with no admin interference. This? Is not shaping up to be a good day.

I take a look at the baby. Skinny little guy, dark hair, little frowny face. I take a look at Matron. Hefty gal, blond, glowering frown. I may have been a match for whatever the Viet Cong threw at our guys, but I'm no match for the two of them. They need a special recon mission, one that won't backfire on Matron and will get Baby Doe what he needs, namely his dad. I'm their man. Hey, I never said I don't have romantic hero aspirations, did I?

I tip Matron my cheekiest grin and don't say a word as I exit the NICU.

"Where's the dad?" I ask the orderly on my way into the main ICU.

Fuck me sideways, they have the guy waiting right outside the OR where his poor wife died. Ghouls.

I head down that corridor, eyes peeled for wonks.

I turn the corner into the makeshift waiting area and skid to a stop. That's how I end up face to face with Tadeo Neyen.

"Tadeo!" is what I start to say, but I'm a pro at hiding what I'm really feeling, even if what I'm feeling is a very weird combination of lust and sympathy. That name accompanied my two most recent ejaculations, after all, so you can't blame it for being on the tip of my tongue. It's an act of will, but I pull up just as his eyes rise up to meet mine.

Fuck if he isn't as stunning off stage as on. Pale, disheveled, eyes a little wild, showing white all around and practically glowing over dark circles underneath. My focus does that freaky thing it used to when things got hot in-country, or when things get hot in the bars or baths: it gets real narrow, quiet, and nothing matters but my objective. My objective, right this minute, is to make everything okay for a guy whose world just shattered five thousand miles from home. Hero complex, remember?

I'm having a hard time deciding if my day just got a

whole lot better or a whole lot worse. My fantasy life is intruding uncomfortably on my real one, and I'm not sure how to handle that. But I'm a pro, and in the end I go with doing my job and seeing where things lead from there.

"Tadeo Neyen? I'm Nurse Haven Tucker, and I'm here to take you to meet your son."

If there's a patron saint of screamingly fucked-up situations, let us pray to him.

Chapter 4
In which Tadeo confronts acquaintances new and old

S it there; I'll pull the curtain."

Everything fades away when Nurse Tucker reaches into a brightly lit glass coffin and extracts my son. He settles the warm weight in my arms.

"You ever held a baby before?" This Tucker seems curious rather than critical.

"Never," I whisper. No point explaining that indio kids like me who grow up in state boarding schools never learn the first thing about being part of a family. I have no idea what to do besides hold on and not drop him. I can't even bring myself to touch the impossibly soft-looking dark pinkness of his forehead.

"He won't break, you know," Tucker is saying. I spare a second to glance at him. He's smiling broadly, as if I've done something terribly clever by having a small part in bringing this tiny creature to life.

The baby squirms and screws up its face, and this time I have a reason to look at Tucker that doesn't include figuring out why he looks at me as he does.

"You want to feed him?"

Before I can answer, Tucker walks over to a machine that looks like an iron lung and takes out a glass bottle full of something milky-looking. He puts it in my hand. It's warm.

Then he runs a gentle finger along the baby's cheek, causing him to turn and open his mouth. I stifle a gasp, but really, it's like magic.

"Now tickle his lip with the nipple, see if he'll take the

bottle from you."

I do, and the baby grapples a bit before settling down to a rhythmic suck. I earn another of those proud smiles from Tucker.

"You got a name?"

"You know my name," I remind him.

He rolls his eyes at me, and for a moment he's a man my own age and not the efficient, competent nurse who delivered my son to me. "For the baby, man."

I smile sheepishly and watch the baby suck until he drops off to sleep again, bubbles of milk popping between his perfect, wet lips.

"Suyai," I say, startling myself. I had expected to hear "Fernando," the name Lena had chosen for a boy. I'd left all such decisions to her.

"That's not Spanish, is it?" Tucker helps me turn the baby slightly. "So he can burp if he needs to." I shouldn't, but I relish the warm press of his fingers on my arm and chest as he tucks the little white blanket in.

"It's an Indian name," I say. "My mother's people, they were Mapuche."

Tucker nods like that means something to him and just watches me hold my son. The moment stretches between us for far longer than should have been comfortable, until with a slight shake and a sheepish smile, Tucker says, "You, um, you want some privacy? I can make sure no one bothers you until it's time to check his vitals."

I shrug, oddly reluctant to see the man go. "You have things to do, I'm sure," I say, giving him a way to leave if he wants to.

"Just...running interference," he says cryptically. "You got anyone I should call? Someone who needs to know about your..."

"Lena," I provide, looking into Suyai's now sleeping face rather than risk showing this American nurse my tears.

"I'm sorry," he says. "Really. Anything I can do...." He trails off.

"My company should know," I say, thinking of the host of unsaid perils involved in bringing Juan Carlos into this, but knowing at the same time how inevitable it is. "Our touring director is…was…Lena's cousin. I don't know if the doctors called." I don't remember anyone asking me who to contact, though I was so distracted I suppose it's possible.

Tucker nods and stands. "Look," he says. "There's going to be issues, you being a foreign national. Probably some consular stuff, I don't know. Just, before you do anything, let me know, okay?"

"Why?" It's a disingenuous question, I know, but surely such matters are outside this man's purview.

"'Cause, well…." Tucker sounds awkward for the first time since he came to find me. "The hospital administration can make things more complicated than they need to be. I'll help if I can."

I have no idea what he thinks he can do, but I nod anyway and return to my baby-gazing.

"You dare to suggest I have no rights to the child?" Juan Carlos' outraged, accented voice sounded strangled, as if he were shouting through clenched teeth.

The sound of his voice shatters my reverie. I know the nurses in the main area won't be able to hold my in-law back for long, and I want to meet him standing up, only I don't want to jostle the baby.

As if he'd read my mind from wherever he'd been, Nurse Tucker slips through the rear edge of the curtained area and grins conspiratorially at me.

"Showtime," he says, and deftly relieves me of Suyai's tiny weight. I'm surprised how cold I feel without him there, how empty my arms.

Tucker stands by me, cuddling the baby as we listen to the angry barks and placating murmurs through the curtain.

24

"They won't let him in here," Tucker assures me. "Matron would throw a fit if they did. It's bad enough I got you in here."

"Should we leave?" Much as I hate to leave Suyai, I don't want to cause Tucker trouble, and I think we might be able to draw off the dogs.

"Maybe so." Tucker looks thoughtful. "Kiss daddy," he says, and I have to think fast to understand what he means. He's addressing Suyai, not me. I almost blush. But I dutifully lean over Suyai's sleeping face and place a soft kiss on his velvet forehead. It's my first touch of his skin, and it's electric. Equally electric is the look Tucker gives me when I straighten up, slightly flustered by the close contact, though I couldn't have said whether Tucker or new fatherhood unsettled me more.

Tucker deposits Suyai back into his glass box, and I wish it was softer and more welcoming.

As if he reads my mind again, Tucker whispers, "He's healthy, won't be there long, promise. Matron won't let anything bad happen to him. Ready?"

I sigh and follow Tucker across the small unit, glancing back more than once.

My usual tack with Juan Carlos is to avoid him when possible and to be impeccably polite when forced into his presence. This was a moment for impeccable politeness. I steel myself as Tucker leads me out of the baby room and around to the front of the unit via a service corridor. He walks like a soldier, purposeful and loose. A frisson of fear and—can it be?—desire slithers up my spine. Tucker turns at the doors and pushes through backward, winking—winking!—as he ambles through.

As he said: show time.

Juan Carlos is alone, which is a small mercy. I don't think I could have faced any of Lena's friends just then.

"Nurse Elliott!" Tucker's voice snaps, and Juan Carlos and the mannish, blond nurse who is evidently in charge of the sick babies both quiet down and look at him.

"I'm sure this ruckus is unnecessary." His voice is

disapproving, but I see the nurse quirk a little smile at him before schooling her face.

"I'm Nurse Tucker, in charge of Mr. Neyen's case. You are?" He holds out his hand to Juan Carlos, who shakes it meekly before remembering to glower again.

"Juan Carlos Gutierrez. I've just been told my cousin is—" he can't say 'dead' "—and her baby is being held here."

He tries to peer around the big nurse and catches sight of me in the process. Predictably, his face darkens. "¡Asesino!" he accuses, and lunges at me.

I stand firm. I'm no killer, no matter what Juan Carlos says. Tucker steps into Juan Carlos' path before he can reach me. "I know you're upset, Mr. Gutierrez, but please don't make matters worse by forcing me to call hospital security."

Even Juan Carlos, as well-connected as he is in Buenos Aires, comes up short at the mention of involving agents of social control. I see his clever little mind change directions.

"Are you my cousin's doctor, or this man's gorila?" He points rudely at me with his stubby thumb.

In an admirable tone of professional affront, Tucker says, "I'm Nurse Haven Tucker, and I'm at your service." I watch Juan Carlos process the idea of a male nurse, and take the moment to translate "gorila" in case Tucker thought the man was calling him an animal.

Without taking his eyes off Juan Carlos, Tucker says, "Oh, cool. I don't dig being called a gorilla, you know? But 'bouncer'? Okay." He's using colloquial language with me and official tones with Juan Carlos, but Juan Carlos' English isn't good enough to pick that up. Still, I gather it means Tucker is on my side.

I'm grateful someone is.

"Nurse Elliott," Tucker says, smoothly cutting off whatever Juan Carlos was about to say, "Please let the maternity nurses and whoever else needs to know that we're in the doctors' conference room."

He steers Juan Carlos and me away from the door of the baby room.

Another man approaches us from farther down the corridor. Juan Carlos seems to know him.

"Barnes!" Tucker hisses as if the name was a dire curse at the same time as Juan Carlos booms, "Señor Barnes!" as if it was the answer to his prayers.

I decide my years of knowing Juan Carlos are as nothing to my minutes' acquaintance with Haven Tucker; I know right away that this Barnes is a threat.

Chapter 5
In which Haven justifies his reputation

This Gutierrez dude is bad news; I can tell by how Tadeo is reacting. He's got all the signs of shock, and who can blame him after the day he's had? I walk beside him and try not to be obvious, but honestly, who can blame me for slowing down a little so he gets ahead of me and I can appreciate his lathe-turned waist, disproportionately muscled thighs, and that high, round ass I'd framed in my opera glasses two nights ago?

We get to the conference room, where Barnes makes us all sit down. Any second now he'll notice I'm still here when I've got no reason to be. But for now I'll just sit here wishing I could hold Tadeo's hand, maybe rub his shoulders, help get rid of the fine tremors I can see all up and down his arms.

Barnes lays a blue cardboard folder on the table and folds his hands over it.

"Mr. Neyen," he says, as insincere as you please. "Let me say I speak for the hospital when I offer my condolences on the loss of your wife."

Tadeo nods tightly, and Gutierrez looks murder at him.

"This is an unusual case, as I'm sure you realize," Barnes goes on. "Mr. Gutierrez has assured me the ballet company has made all the necessary...arrangements." He's talking about money, the bastard, and I can see by the way Tadeo's eyes glaze over that he has no idea what kind of medical coverage his bosses have for their dancers.

"I've consulted with our legal department...." Oh,

here it comes, I think. "The baby is healthy and should be released later today. Mr. Gutierrez, as the mother's closest relative, will receive custody of the infant."

Tadeo's English must be better than I'd thought, because before I've even registered what Barnes said he shoots up from his chair, all feral grace, and wheels on Gutierrez.

There follows a torrent of Spanish where I catch maybe one word in three. My Spanish is pretty good for pillow talk, thanks to that second summer I spent as my leather daddy's boy on the Cape when we shared that delicious Puerto Rican boy, so I keep up okay. Tadeo and Gutierrez trade insults like "hijo de puta" and "pendejo," and I almost laugh to think that sweet Boricua from the Cape taught me more inventive cuss words than "son of a whore" and "asshole." Then Gutierrez spits out the kicker:"pinche maricon." He shoots Barnes a slimy, triumphant look when he calls Tadeo a fucking faggot. Tadeo takes a deep breath—I can see his nostrils flare and fuck if I don't want to lick them—and turns to Barnes.

"Mr. Barnes," he says, as cool as you please. "I insist my son be released to me."

"I'm sorry, Mr. Neyen," says Barnes, not sorry in the least. "Can you produce a legal document declaring you were Miss Fernandez'S husband?" I notice the "Miss," and so does Tadeo. "In the case of foreign nationals taking custody of an American citizen, which this baby is, a blood relation with proper documentation is our first choice. I'm afraid there's nothing I can do without some countermanding proof of paternity." He shares an oily smirk with Gutierrez.

I brace myself for another freak out from Tadeo, but it doesn't come. I can't say as I understand, but I know whose side I'm on. Barnes and Gutierrez are up to something. Well, there's nothing to prevent me from being up to something, too. Tadeo, I can see after five minutes with Gutierrez, has no one. I do love an underdog.

I sit there willing Tadeo to fight back, to tell them he

has his marriage license in his luggage or something. I want to tell him there's new ways of proving he's related to the baby, but he has to know to request a tissue-type test. I doubt they have those in Argentina yet. I need five minutes with the guy to bring him up to date on his rights.

If this Juan Carlos knows Tadeo's queer and using it against him, I can see why he's afraid to speak up. But I get the sense there's more to it than that. Tadeo's scared of Barnes, and he's terrified speechless of Gutierrez.

I'm just starting to get a plan together when Barnes notices me. "Nurse Tucker. Are you here in an...official capacity?"

Of course I'm not, you limp-dicked wonk. I think it, but I don't say it. Technically, I'm still on duty in the NICU, and that suits me fine.

"I'll just be getting back to the unit," I mutter. "Just trying to help." I go for affronted and underappreciated, which Barnes seems to buy because he shakes me off like rain. When he does, I shoot Tadeo what I hope is a speaking look and incline my head very slightly toward the door.

"Excuse me a moment while I thank Mr. Tucker for his care of my son," Tadeo says with definite emphasis on those last two words, and gets up to follow me into the hallway.

He closes the door behind him and turns desperate eyes on me.

"Look man," I say. "I don't know what they're up to, but I have an idea or two of my own."

"Juan Carlos is the son of a very powerful man," Tadeo says. "You know of our...troubles in Argentina?"

I remember the Love Doctor's screed on the night of the ballet, something about a military coup and torture of citizens and shit like that. I nod.

"Lena's family will take Suyai and make him part of all that. Now that she's...gone, they'll claim the baby, and it will be even easier in Buenos Aires than here to deny me."

I get where he's going. I wait for the other shoe to drop.

"I'm only alive because of being married to Lena. Without the latter condition, I fear the former is temporary."

Where'd he learn to talk all flash like that? I'm about to get lost in those dark, intense eyes when his words sink in.

"You think they'll keep the baby and get rid of you?" It sounds crazy when I say it out loud.

"I will disappear," he confirms, all bleak and defeated.

"Good idea," I say. He frowns at me.

"Listen," I say. I know any minute Barnes or Gutierrez will come see what's taking him so long and haul him back in there to get jerked around some more. As fast as I can, I tell him about the tissue test and make sure he's gonna be a good little soldier and follow orders, at least for now. "You got your papers on you, your visa and passport and shit?"

He nods. Thank heaven for small favors.

"I'll do what I can," I say, wheels spinning. "You go back in there and stall as long as you can. Remember the corridor behind the NICU, the one we left by?"

He nods again.

"Meet me there in an hour. Get lost in the hospital for a while if those two finish shitting all over you before then."

I hate to send him back to the jackals, but there's nothing for it.

"What are you going to do?" he asks.

"The less you know..." I trail off. I'm guessing he knows just what I mean, and I don't want to admit how flimsy my plan really is.

His hands land on my shoulders, squeezing almost too hard. "You, Mr. Tucker, are a gentleman. Thank you."

I almost laugh, but he's so serious, it would be mean.

I'm a little flustered, though, so I let myself go all queeny for a sec. "Oh, honey, a gentleman is the last thing I am." He looks confused and drops his hands.

I drop the camp and look into his eyes. "Please, call me Haven." And with that—oh, all right, with one glance back at that magnificent ass as he returns to the conference room—I'm off.

Chapter 6
In which Tadeo takes a chance

I understand this Haven Tucker has been assigned to handle me while Carlos and the hospital administrator work out how best to take my son from me, but I admit to bewilderment at his fierce reaction to their machinations.

I fear I have made a mistake when we meet at the appointed hour. I tell him as much and he wheels on me right there in the corridor. I'm still raw from Juan Carlos' betrayal, and I admit I don't anticipate his anger.

"Listen here," he growls, blue eyes blazing like gas flames. "Those suits back there are trying to do you a bad turn, and that would piss me off no matter what. But it seems to me one of their blades at your throat is you like cock, yeah? I heard that Gutierrez guy call you 'maricon.' He wasn't just blowing smoke, was he?"

I try not to quiver or look away as I jerk a nod. I can't tame the blush, though, and I know it makes my face look bruised.

The flinch when he turns my face to him is involuntary, but I see it register with him. "Hey now, man. I'd be the worst sort of hypocrite if I held that against you. Got something else I'd rather hold... nah, bad joke, not the time." He trails off, talking more to himself than to me. I process his words.

"You're..." I don't know a word in English that won't offend.

"Queer as a three-sided penny, yeah."

I notice his fists at his sides.

"Ain't ashamed, either, just can't be too obvious about it here, you know."

I know, and say so.

"So that's another reason I'm helping you."

"What do you propose?"

"I propose we call in some bigger guns than me." He leads me into the neonatal unit, only to learn Suyai has been transferred to the regular maternity ward.

"That's good news," he says to me, but doesn't elaborate, so I don't know if it means good for Suyai or good for me. "Nurse Elliott, could you please page Dr. Carr to maternity?"

"Stat?" the big blonde asks with a smile.

"Yes, please." He bats his eyes at her, and she laughs delightedly as she raises the steel microphone to her lips and presses a button.

We're up and down corridors fast enough that I wish I had breadcrumbs to drop or twine to unwind to get me out again. At the doors to the maternity ward, Tucker takes a moment to straighten his uniform and run his fingers through his hair.

"Ready?"

I don't have time to answer as he sweeps us right through the double doors and up to the nurse's station, where a formidable black woman of indeterminate age greets him with a tight smile.

"I don't know what you're thinking, Hay—Nurse Tucker, but you got me worried and no mistake."

"Don't fret, Nurse Robinson," he says with exaggerated deference. "This here's Tadeo Neyen, proud papa. Is little Suyai here?"

"Baby Doe from NICU?"

I frown at the designation.

"Not for long," Haven says, more to me than to his friend. "Stephen's on his way."

"I wondered why a cardiologist was getting paged to Maternity. You're not making me any less worried, here, Nurse Tucker." She turns to me like a frigate in a canal. "Why don't you come with me, Mr. Neyen, and we'll check on your baby."

I thank her cordially and follow, taking a look back at Tucker, who turns away without meeting my eyes to face a tall doctor who bursts through the doors.

"Tucker!" he says, all exasperation. "Should have known it was your antics. What's this about? I'm busy."

I can't hear the rest of the conversation. Nurse Robinson delivers me to an underling in a pink and white striped uniform and sails back out to join what looks like a heated argument between Tucker and this Dr. Carr.

I try to put their strife out of my mind and concentrate on holding Suyai as I've been shown, my heart twisting with the knowledge that this may be the only time I will ever have with my son. I have put my faith in Tucker, but I already know faith is a very fragile shield.

Before long, the argument moves into the nursery.

"I won't falsify documents, Haven, not even for you," the doctor says, looking sheepishly at Nurse Robinson who waves away his discomfort as if it were a gnat.

"Stephen, I'm not asking you to falsify anything, just get the birth certificate drawn up before Barnes does and they take this man's son away from him for no good reason other than his politics."

"Politics!" the doctor spits. "Is that what you're calling it now?"

"Dr. Carr, I'll thank you not to raise your voice in here. Don't think I won't deputize you to put twenty-three crying babies back to sleep." Nurse Robinson's voice brooks no argument, even from the elegant doctor.

"Come on, Stephen," Tucker says. "It's a small thing, not illegal, totally within your mandate. It costs you nothing."

Carr looks from Haven to me and back again. "Somehow, Haven, I think it costs me a very great deal."

I have no idea what he means, until Tucker replies. "You know we're going nowhere, Stephen," he says softly.

"You'll lose your place in the practitioner program once Barnes finds out. I won't lift a finger."

"No one's asking you to," Tucker says mulishly, and I find myself wishing he wouldn't antagonize the savior he found for me.

Tucker and Carr stare each other down for a few, breathless moments before Carr drops his eyes. "Damn," he says. "Whose address should I put on the paperwork?"

"Mine," says Haven.

"Don't be stupid, baby," Nurse Robinson says. "You'll lose your job." She turns to the doctor. "You put my apartment building as the address, and I'll take it from there."

"Might as well lose the death certificate on the mother, give you a bit of a head start. Good luck, Haven. I hope you know what you're doing." Carr nods stiffly to me and exits without saying anything else.

"Whoo." Tucker exhales and says, "That's settled, then."

"No, it ain't baby," Nurse Robinson says. "You done burned another bridge with your Love Doctor, and now how do you propose you fix it so Mr. Neyen here can stay in Boston? His boss, and yours, will both know what you did."

"They'll deport me," I say from my seat with Suyai. I wish I could stand and face them both.

Instead, Tucker drags up a chair and sits beside me. "Can I hold him?" he asks. "I love babies."

His plaintive question and frank admission surprises a laugh out of me, the first since this nightmare began. I'm awkward passing Suyai over, but Tucker helps, and he cuddles the little bundle and croons while Nurse Robinson and I look on.

"Well, Hay?" Nurse Robinson asks.

He looks up from the baby, his eyes almost dreamy. "I'm thinking, all right, Alberta?"

He looks at me. "He's gorgeous. Just like his daddy." Before I can form anything like a response to that, he asks a question I can answer. "Where's the nearest Argentine

Consulate?"

"New York, I believe." Then the meaning of his question sinks in. "But there must be another way. I won't find any more sympathy there than I did in that room with Juan Carlos and Mr. Barnes."

"Figures it'd be New York," he says under his breath. "Tadeo, you're going to have to trust me, okay? Just for a little while? I know some people in New York, and I have an idea. The Consul won't be an issue if my idea works."

He may be rash, but I do trust him more than I trust the men in the conference room. I nod reluctantly. Then he turns back to Nurse Robinson. "Listen, you go off shift in thirty minutes, right?"

The big woman nods.

"Get Suyai discharged as soon as you have his paperwork, and take him and Tadeo to your place. I'll meet you there in a couple of hours. I gotta take care of a couple things if we're going to New York tomorrow."

I feel I should say something, but I'm speechless in the face of two strangers helping me, in the face of my exhaustion, and in the face of the deep feeling of helplessness taking root in my gut.

My brain and my voice may be paralyzed, but my heart beats double time when Haven Tucker looks at me. Between my predicament with Suyai and my attraction to Haven Tucker, the helpless feeling compounds, and I can't bring myself to mind.

Chapter 7
In which Haven attends the ballet

With everything in place, I finally leave St. Sebastian's about three hours after my shift officially ended. It would be better for all involved, including me, if my part in busting Suyai out of the maternity ward isn't known. Oh, I'm sure it'll come to light eventually, but I imagine I'll be long gone by then. Someone has to help Tadeo get to New York and deal with the Argentine Consulate. Daddy would sneer and called me a self-sacrificing romantic, and he'd be right, I guess.

Something about Tadeo makes me want to help him. It's not just that he's the most beautiful man I've ever seen, or that he revs my motor like no one since, well, ever. It isn't just that he's an embattled underdog and I have skills and contacts that could help him. It's the way he looks at me, like I'm his last, best hope. It's the way he spoke to Alberta like she's a queen, the royal kind, I mean. It's the way he has this fatalistic outlook on everything that's going down and he just squares his shoulders to take the next hit. It's the way he looks at his son.

But he isn't with me now, and I'd be risking us both if he were. I want him so badly I can taste it in my mouth and smell it on my body, but I can't have him. Not right now, maybe not ever. His vibe gives me hope, but knowing he swings my way and knowing he wants me in particular are two very different things. Yes, I'm a romantic idiot.

As I hit the T station I'm forced to admit I'm a horny idiot, too. I turn away from my usual route home—I can grab Amtrak tickets and make my New York calls later—and jog down to the Green Line and head for the Ramrod. I've got no intention of going to the bar; I haven't been in a leather bar since I broke off my kinky relationship with my leather daddy. But there's a bathhouse nearby, and that's where I need to be, if I can't be with Tadeo.

The cat who takes my money and gives me a towel makes some crack about taking my costume over to Playland. I give him the finger and head downstairs. As near as I can figure, bathhouses vary only in scuzziness, and this one's the better of the two I've found since moving to Boston.

The smell of the place is disinfectant with a dash of sweaty feet. I couldn't say if the smell covers the poppers or vice versa, but ampules are everywhere, including the meaty fist of the first dude who cruises me. I shake my head, but give him a smile anyway. Maybe later. Right now, I need the steam room.

It's early yet, so the population in the steam room is that weird mix of guys who don't have anywhere else to be at suppertime. I wish for a sec I'd been here a couple hours earlier, when the construction workers and utility guys tend to be around. I saunter over to a free bench— I'm in the mood to fish a little and not make a move on anyone yet—and sit on my towel. I've got a tattoo on my right tit from Bangkok and another on my biceps from New York, and I know they harden my image. Doesn't stop a gangly kid from approaching. His vibe screams "hustler", and I shake my head. No smile this time.

I close my eyes and picture Tadeo, which is a stupid thing to do 'cause it means I'm not paying attention. This is not what you'd call a safe place, and I am, after all, naked. It takes effort not to jump when I feel a foot press mine and a hand lands on my bare thigh.

I look over, going for lazy half-interest, and blink at the dude next to me. He's about twice as wide as me. It's not all muscle, but the hard, bearish belly looks good on him. If Daddy Sid from New York was about fifteen years older and black, he'd be this cat. I ignore the particular sickness of that thought and summon up a smile.

"See something you like, friend?" I say, letting my hill

country notes out in a way I never do at St. Seb's. It'll either piss him off or make him laugh.

He laughs, a low rumble without a smile to go with it. "Your white-boy mouth, for starters." His voice is sexy as hell. He may look like a drill sergeant out of central casting, but he talks like a teacher.

"Got a room?" I say, just to let him know my white-boy mouth is his, but that I'm not putting on a show no matter how few dudes are in here.

He makes an affirmative sort of grunt and stands slowly, taking my hand as he does. It's a weirdly sweet gesture, and I'm suddenly more interested. He's hung, but not enough to make you think of stereotypes or anything, and his back is a solid landscape of muscle from his shoulders to his calves. Plenty to hold on to.

I let myself be towed into one of the dingy little cubicles and wait to see if he'll sit or stand. He stays standing, and I cock my eyebrows at him, challenging a little.

He grins, halfway between feral and amused, and lays both hands on my shoulders to push me down. Unbidden, I remember Tadeo's hands on my shoulders not an hour before, when he thanked me for helping him. The force of both the push and the memory gets me going, and I make sure he can see my woody before I settle in. I take it slow, 'cause that's what I'm in the mood for, grateful that slow is an option. Sucking off the Love Doctor is always a hurried affair, partly 'cause he's a quick shot and partly 'cause he made it clear he wants it "efficient." That's the word he used, I swear.

My black bear doesn't seem to be in any hurry, though he leaves one big hand on the side of my head, like a promise for a nice hard face fuck in a few minutes. He smells good, like cocoa butter and musk. Goes straight to my prick, which I reach for only to have Sarge bat it away with his foot.

Toppy, I think to myself, glad I know the score.

I turn on my best technique, lots of tongue and fingers and nice hard suction. When I've got him pumping for all he's worth, holding me by the hair and keeping up a low rumble that's halfway between a chuckle and a growl, I use my neatest trick, learned from a painted boy in a Saigon brothel.

Sarge's balls draw up and his cock is twitching. I dive forward and take him into my throat, which makes him grunt with surprise. But the real surprise is what comes next. I set three fingers against what little Lien called the jen-mo point. All I'm doing is pressing on Sarge's prostate from the outside, which if you do it right can stop ejaculation. I make sure to do it almost right, which slows things down like you wouldn't believe. Sarge hollers like he's shooting through the top of his head, and it goes on forever. I grin at him when he's done, looking up into astonished eyes.

"Fuck, boy," he rumbles.

"If you insist," I shoot back, bright as you please.

He toddles over to sit on the cot. It creaks, but holds his bulk.

"What was that?"

"Secret of the Golden Flower," I say, remembering Lien's adorable accent when he said it in English.

"Nam?" Sarge asks, and I confirm with a nod.

"You were serious about the fuck?" he asks. He gives his still-hard prick a puzzled look.

"I guess," I say. But really, now our moment's passed, Tadeo's back in my head and I don't feel as keen.

Sarge looks into my face. I'm still kneeling, and I'm still hard, but somehow he knows it's not for him.

"I don't think so." He pulls me forward by my shoulder and holds me against that hard, round belly. I nuzzle. "I think I gotta ride this high for a bit. Maybe have my second round with someone new."

I nod against his skin and palm his tits.

He laughs out loud and gives me a squeeze. "I ain't a saint, boy. My mind could change real easy."

I shrug and grin and let go.

"You want to save that for someone?" he asks, nodding

at my prick, "or you want me to jerk you?"

"Save it," I say, wondering what Tadeo would think of that. Sarge wraps his towel around his hips, open over his hard on, and gives me a kiss before leaving. It's about the sweetest visit to a bathhouse I ever had, and I tell him so.

Whatever I told Sarge about saving it, I can't show up at Alberta's sporting wood, and besides, we all have other things we need to be concentrating on.

It's not romantic at all, but I plan our trip to New York while I jerk off in a toilet stall in the locker room.

I skip the showers and head out. It's dark now, but no one will mess with me, not even by the Back Bay Fens. I grab the Red Line out to Somerville, Alberta's duplex, and Tadeo.

Chapter 8
In which Tadeo removes his shirt

Haven arrives at Nurse Alberta's home just as supper is served. He tears in, as I'm discovering is his wont, to shouts of greeting and reprimand. I'm also discovering he's not a man who arouses milder emotions in others.

I realize instantly that even in my thoughts, the word "arouses" comes too readily in association with my new friend.

"We needed you for the hush puppies, Hay," says a young woman I've worked out is either a niece or a young cousin to Nurse Alberta. Most of the many people who have entered or left since my arrival seem related in some way to that impressive lady.

"Shoot, any fool can make hush puppies, darlin'," Haven replies with a cheeky look in Alberta's direction.

Alberta scowls at her colleague, causing his grin to widen. "This northern cornmeal don't act like it should. I ain't made a decent hush puppy since coming here."

Ah. My shred of worry over the constitution of "hush puppies" dissipates even as I notice an unexpected relaxation in their speech. They were easy to understand in the hospital, their words crisp and standard. Here, in the warm, noisy, bustling confines of Alberta's second-floor apartment, they are almost slurred, and I have to strain to make them out. I listen hard to be ready in case anyone addresses me directly.

The big square kitchen reminds me a bit of a theater's back stage, and that comparison eases me. Being among so large and confusing a family has unnerved me, and I've been anxious for Haven's return. I understood that we couldn't be seen leaving the hospital together, but his absence, like so much about this day, has unsettled me, and I am impatient for time with him to ask questions.

Ever since Lena went into labor, my life has taken turns beyond my control.

"Come on and eat, Tadeo," Haven says, interrupting my thoughts. I glance into the next room where Suyai sleeps in an improvised cradle. Haven must have followed my eyes, for he assures me, "He'll be fine. You'll need your strength for the night feedings, and we have an early day."

I acquiesce and pull my chair up to a plate of unfamiliar food.

"Soul food," is what Haven calls it, with a reverence in his voice that makes me smile.

"So," I venture while he shovels bitter, buttered greens into his mouth, "you and Nurse Alberta are from the American South?"

He laughs at my question. "Miss Alberta's from the South," he confirms.

Alberta interrupts to add, "Our Haven's just a hillbilly."

To which Haven's reply is an indignant look that makes the children at the table laugh out loud.

My metaphor of a theater, flimsy to begin with, crumbles in the face of this warm camaraderie and teasing. No ballet company was ever so…easy.

The balance of the meal is taken up with gossip about people I don't know, and I relax into the chatter gratefully, hardly aware that my eyelids are drooping until Haven elbows me and says quietly, "You can sleep as soon as everyone clears out."

"Not all these people live here?" I'm surprised—they all seem so at home.

"Nah, only Alberta and her daughter, when she's home from college. Some live upstairs and some live down, and most of the kids just come by after school."

I nod as if I understand and finish the unfamiliar, heavy food in silence.

"Will you see Robbie in New York, baby?" Alberta asks as she stands and directs the children to clear the table and wash the dishes.

"If we can," Haven says. "I have to make some calls."

"Better hurry, baby. Party line's gonna get busy before long." Alberta uses her bare fingers to pluck a glass bottle for Suyai from a saucepan and passes it to Haven, who tests the temperature nonchalantly against the inside of his wrist. I fight an unseemly urge to lick the warm milk away.

Haven nods and tows me into the living room, where Suyai is just waking, wriggling and mewling in a way that brings something like panic to my chest.

"You sit and feed him while I make calls," Haven says. "Take your shirt off."

"Why?" I don't understand.

"Babies need skin to skin contact, and Suyai needs to know you and your smell so he can bond with you a little before we leave tomorrow."

It doesn't make much sense, but it's said with such authority that I move to comply, unbuttoning my shirt. I have no vest underneath, as my rush to the hospital with Lena barely allowed dressing at all. I feel my face heat when the smells of the past day's fear and exertion rise from my body.

Haven sets Suyai in my arms, opening the blankets so the baby's warm-silk skin is pressed against my belly.

"Don't worry," he says. I don't know what he's referring to, and I don't ask. I just let his words soothe me. I'm surprised that they do.

Haven drags an old black telephone onto his lap, and moves between a tattered, leather booklet from his pocket and a fat telephone directory from Alberta's side table. Evidently it's still early enough to reach government offices in New York, though I would have sworn it was the middle of the night, I'm so tired. I'm afraid to fall asleep and drop the baby, so I stare into

Suyai's scrunched little face and listen intently to Haven's one-sided conversations. Perhaps if I do, I will have fewer questions and won't feel so alien, so adrift.

My eavesdropping doesn't help much. By the time Suyai empties the bottle and settles to sleep against me, I've learned only that Alberta's son, Robbie, will put us up and that we'll need a lawyer to accompany us to the Consulate. That last bit of information brings a series of vehement curses from Haven, who pauses a moment before calling another number with angry pulls of his finger around the black metal dial.

"Hey, Justin...yeah, it's me...just lemme talk to Daddy, will ya?" There's a pause in which Haven hisses, "Little bitch."

Haven's voice changes for the third time that day as he speaks to whomever picks up the line—his father? There's some small talk, but it's terse and defensive on Haven's part. By the time Haven gets to the meat of the matter and is explaining my situation, Alberta has entered the room and taken Suyai from me to bundle back into his little bed. She raises an eyebrow at me, and I move to cover my bare torso.

"Haven and his newfangled ideas," she says fondly with a dismissive wave at me that tells me she's seen it all before and wasn't impressed then, either.

"He's talking to his father," I offer in a whisper. "Is he a lawyer?"

"Haven's Pa, a lawyer?" Alberta makes a sucking sound through her teeth. "Not in this lifetime. He's talking to Daddy."

I must look confused. Alberta continues, her voice heavy with disapproval. "That man ain't no one's father. Better let Haven tell you."

Haven rings off with a meek "See you tomorrow, then, Daddy," and stands without looking at me or Alberta. "I'm gonna shower before all the hot water's gone." He stalks from the room.

"Wash your shirts and particulars," Alberta says to

his back. "You'll need clean for the trip if you ain't going home before catching the train." She turns to me. "Don't mind him. I'll dry your clothes over the stove." She tucks Suyai in more snugly and leaves the room.

Haven tells me nothing of this "Daddy" of his, though there's ample opportunity through the long night. Suyai wakes often and I feed him while Haven takes care of bottles and changing him. "You'll have to learn how to do all this," he says as he rolls up another soiled diaper to wash in the bathroom sink. My nod must look bewildered and shell-shocked for he laughs and lays a hand on my bare shoulder. Its weight should rattle me—it's been so long since I felt a man's touch as anything but casual or accidental—but it doesn't. It settles me in my skin in a way I'd forgotten. "You'll be okay, Tadeo. Ain't rocket science, after all."

Blame a fevered imagination, but as I drift in and out of sleep, I'd swear Haven brushes my cheek with a kiss.

Morning comes in a weak, gray glow around the drapes, and I find I'm more reluctant than I would have thought to leave Suyai behind.

"What will happen to him while Alberta's at work?" I ask as Haven rummages in a closet to find an old pea coat for me to wear.

"It's her weekend," Haven says. "We'll be back before she has another shift. And don't let her fool you. She's tickled as hell to have a baby to look after that isn't a patient."

"Language, baby," Alberta says from the doorway, her broad body wrapped in the pinkest bathrobe I've ever seen, her hair hidden under a voluminous headscarf in colors even the dim dawn light can't tone down.

"Thank you for your kindness, Miss Alberta," I say in my best English.

She waves my words away. "Just plain wrong, what them fools tried to do to you. You go set it right, now, hear?"

Loud and clear, I think to myself as I lay a soft kiss on Suyai's brow and follow Haven out the door.

The new Amtrak service to New York is modest by comparison to some accommodations I've had with the touring company, but I don't say so as Haven leads me to a first class compartment I'm quite sure we didn't pay for and orders us coffees and rolls from the passing hostess. He settles across from me and tells me what to expect when we arrive in New York.

I only half listen until I hear the words, "...never go back."

"Beg pardon?" I say, hating the prissiness of my voice.

Haven looks chagrined. "You didn't really think you could go back to Argentina once you defy your company? I mean, isn't your father-in-law some honcho in the government?"

I groan and nod while it all sinks in, what I've done. "Army, actually, though that's pretty much the same thing since the coup."

What will I do, alone with an infant in an alien land? All of a sudden I realize this stranger, this enigmatic nurse with the drawling voice and avid eyes, is my only friend here. The enormity of my actions swamp me, and I sag in my seat.

In a trice, Haven is beside me. "Hey, hey, I know." He croons meaninglessly in my ear as I tremble and gasp and altogether make a fool of myself.

I can't meet his eyes, even after I settle down.

"I'm sorry," I begin. "I've dragged you into this mess, and now you must feel burdened."

To my utter surprise, the man blushes. "I may have an ulterior motive," he says with an exaggerated note of confession.

Then he kisses me. It's quick, and dry, but somehow freighted with intent. I'm too surprised to kiss back, a failure I regret all the remaining hours of our trip.

Haven is a distracting companion. He doesn't sit but rather sprawls. His speech is like a song, and his eyes spend nearly as much time on my body as my face. He listens more than he talks, which I don't expect, and by the time we reach Grand Central Station, he's heard my whole life story and even knows about Josue, though I leave out some of the more intimate details.

"You're an adept interrogator, Nurse Tucker," I say, feeling close enough to tease a little. I never even teased Lena, for all that we were close friends. Our relationship was so serious, such a political statement, that lightheartedness never seemed appropriate.

"Better than you," he teases back. "You don't even know where we're going. I'll fill you in once we're on the subway. Look for signs for the uptown Independent, okay ?" He presses two quarters into my hand.

We take the Sixth Avenue Local to Fifty-seventh Street, and I admit I'm agog as familiar street names pass. This metro is much older than Buenos Aires', and more storied. In all my travels, I've never been to New York. It was to be the next stop on the company's tour, and I suppress a pang of regret that I won't accompany them by calling to mind the sweet weight of Suyai as he slept against my chest the night before. Still, I long to see Central Park and Rockefeller Center. I'm curious about the nightlife I've read about in Greenwich Village and the daytime shadow life of Times Square. I'm embarrassed to be so distracted from a task on which, I realize, my life and my son's life rely, but Haven doesn't seem to notice.

That's when I remember that this "Daddy" Alberta so disapproves of will be meeting us outside the Consulate.

We exit the subway station, and as we cover the short distance to the consulate I finally ask about "Daddy."

Haven watches his feet. His fair curls hide most of his face, but I feel sure he's blushing when he answers.

"Daddy is a …nickname, I guess you could say. He was my…teacher. Met him after I came back from Vietnam. I left him when I finished nursing school and moved to Boston." He pauses. "Tadeo, you know anything about leather?"

I must have missed something and am about to ask what he means when Haven stops walking. We have arrived in front of a gracious brick edifice flying Argentina's blue and white flag emblazoned with the Sun of May. I'm surprised by the lump that blocks my throat when I see it. I blink and swallow, and in an instant Haven's arm steals around my shoulders.

"'S okay, man. They stole it from you, yeah? But it's still your flag."

I nod shakily and let myself lean just a little closer to his warm embrace. How on earth does he understand?

"Haven!"

A man approaches from the opposite direction we did and stops with his arms open before us. He's easily forty, maybe older, with the slightly dissipated look I've seen in hard-drinking men. He's handsome with it, though, and his blue eyes smile though his mouth is stern.

Haven leaves my side and the man bears him into a fierce hug. I wish for a moment someone felt strongly enough about me to enfold me so. Even Josue, whose love I never doubted, held me lightly and with a circumspect shame.

"Sir," Haven says, "Meet Tadeo Neyen. Tadeo, Sid McGrath."

"Sir," I echo Haven. "I cannot thank you enough."

We shake, and the man fixes startling blue eyes on me. By the eyes alone, I'd have believed he and Haven shared blood. "Don't mention it, kid. Let's do this."

Then he leads us under my sad, stolen flag and into my uncertain future.

Chapter 9
In which Haven acts as tour guide

What Daddy told us should be a "perfunctory" visit to the Argentine Consulate on 56th Street turns into a long slog through U.S. government offices when we discover nothing but uniforms inside, just as Tadeo predicted. They're willing to recognize Tadeo's paternity and Suyai's U.S. citizenship, thanks to a flurry of Telexes to Buenos Aires that they make us pay for. Thank God for Daddy's deep pockets, though the look he shoots me say he'd love to take it out of my ass. We hightail it out of there and head down to Federal Plaza when the uniform in charge of us also makes it pretty damn clear Tadeo's expected to return to Argentina with his troupe.

"And that," Tadeo says with a defeated slump I have a hard time not correcting with an arm around his shoulder, "is when the Colonel will find a way to take Suyai from me, or me from him, more likely."

Daddy gets that grim set to his mouth that I remember from our early days and just leads us to his waiting car. He's no dummy, knows more about Argentine politics than I do, which isn't saying much, and plainly believes Tadeo will disappear within days of returning.

Daddy hems and haws for a minute about what to do, not sure how deep into this he wants to get, and I feel the need to hurry along his thought process by saying, "You know what's going on down there, don't you? That coup and all? Well, Tadeo here's on the wrong side of it. He's on the side of democracy and freedom, and it's our duty to help him."

I know Daddy's thinking of 'Nam when I finish my little speech, and he gives me a curt nod.

"I'm surprised you know so much," he says, fondly enough that I know I've gotten through.

I try my "best boy" smile. "Hey, just 'cause I'm a hillbilly nurse don't mean I ain't educated."

We head downtown.

Daddy's clearly confused about my relationship to Tadeo. It's obvious the dancer isn't my boy, but Daddy's old school and thinks equal partnership is bourgeois and het and probably a few other nasty things. I let him think we're lovers, though, and I'm surprised when Tadeo plays along with some pretty significant looks and a furtive touch here and there.

Federal Plaza is a warren of Immigration and Naturalization offices, and Tadeo's jumpy as a rabbit in a snake den. By the time we leave, though, Daddy's got him temporary asylum papers and a hearing date, and we spend the ride to the Village making a list of everything Tadeo will need to make his stay in the States permanent. I'll be needed as a witness. I know it's stupid of me, but knowing I'll get to see Tadeo again, even if it's just to vouch for what happened at St. Sebastian's, makes me feel hopeful.

Daddy leaves us at the Chambers Street station, and we make plans to meet later at some new club he's joined. I don't relish seeing Justin, but there's no refusing Daddy when he wants to float a night on the town.

"You could come get ready at my place," Daddy says, and it's the closest to a request that I've ever had from him.

I shake my head. "I still got my gear at Robbie's." That's where I left it all when I finally left Daddy. No call for club gear in Boston, I thought at the time.

Daddy nods and claps me on the shoulder. Tadeo shakes his hand and thanks him solemnly, and we're off. This is either going to be a great night or a disaster.

❊ ❊ ❊

"The Mineshaft?" Robbie shakes his head in that way that makes him look just like his mother. We served together, sure, had a few go-rounds while we were in-country even though Robbie swings on the straight side of the fence, and Robbie knows all about me and Daddy, but he's never quite wrapped his head around what he so quaintly calls my "lifestyle."

"You don't wanna take fresh meat to a place like that," Robbie insists. "Come out with me, instead."

I wrinkle my nose and look down my nose at him, which cracks Robbie right up. "To some disco? God save me from another night of Rita Coolidge and Andy Gibb!"

He looks offended; I know he has better taste than that, and I know he'd watch our backs in some way-uptown R&B joint. "I thought your type liked a nice torch song?" Robbie has the good sense to dart away from the slap I aim at his beefy ass. He may be big, but he's quick.

"How about you?" I ask Tadeo. "Has Buenos Aires been tainted by disco yet?"

"Nah," Robbie interjects. "Bet it's all tangos and shit, right, man?"

Tadeo shrugs eloquently. I can't wait to get him on the dance floor.

"Perhaps I should not come out," he says. "I feel I should get back to Suyai."

I nod. It's not that I'm unsympathetic, but he and I both need to let off a little steam after the past few days and to man up for whatever's going to come next. "Our return tickets are for tomorrow morning," I remind him.

While Tadeo's showering, Robbie hands me a letter. "Someone looking for you, man, came by just yesterday." Fuck me sideways, I think, worrying it's something about Tadeo. But it isn't. Fuck me twice, it's from my cousins Rupe and Hollis, wanting to get shown a good time in the big city.

"Said you'd moved, but they were here just yesterday. I mighta told 'em you were coming." Robbie says with an apologetic dip of his monster Afro. "Weird coincidence."

"Understatement of the year," I say. Those two crackers must not have talked to Granny before leaving Coal Ridge. Dumbasses. There's a hotel address, and I make a quick call to say I'm in town but will be out with old friends. I even tell them where, to make sure they won't track me down. No way they'd ever be seen at a fag bar, even a rough one.

I shower after Tadeo, and we spend the next hour going through my gear. Most of it's still in style; heck, I've only been gone a year. I skip the leather 'cause I don't want to give Daddy ideas, and go for tight bell bottoms and a snug, polyester shirt with groovy brown and orange paisley over the chest. Then I turn my attention to Tadeo, regretting that I can't take him out in just the ratty towel from Robbie's bathroom.

Tadeo balks at all my choices, but even Robbie puts his foot down. "You look like a poor exchange student in that dress shirt and those pants do nothing for your ass."

I snicker. Robbie scowls at me. "Hey, dude," he says, "I may like pussy, but even I know if you want to get some, you gotta look fine."

I think, but don't say, that Tadeo would look fine in a flour sack.

We settle on a black silk shirt and tight white sailor pants. Robbie rides as far as Fourteenth Street with us and tells us to be careful. "I know you can't believe everything you hear, but the 'Shaft has a rep, bro. See you at home later." He gives me a sharp look. "And if there's a coat hanger on the bedroom door…"

I finish with him: "Sleep on the couch!"

I'm laughing as we make our way to Little West 12th Street, but I sober up as we reach the door. "Listen," I say, stopping and taking Tadeo by the shoulders. "I don't know what you have in the way of gay clubs back home, but this one's liable to be a bit rough. Stay close, okay, and only talk to guys if I've talked to them first."

He nods and gives me big brown eyes. I wonder if I should have tricked us out as Daddy and Boy after all. Sexy as he is, looking so young and vulnerable, he'll have every chicken hawk in the place on his ass if I'm not careful.

"Haven," Tadeo says. "I'm used to underground clubs, and to being wary of my life almost everywhere I go. And there's no place as barbed as a ballet company. I will be fine, and I will follow your lead."

I want to tell him it's not his life but his sweet ass I'm worried about, but instead I nod, determined to be satisfied with that.

I keep hold of his hand as we enter the 'Shaft and use Daddy's name to get in.

It's pretty much like any other members-only club Daddy used to take me to, maybe a little grittier, maybe a few more new-school guys sporting leathers you know they never earned, but I'm on familiar ground at least. I tow Tadeo to the bar, say hey to Daddy, who earned his leathers and made sure I earned mine. I grudgingly introduce Justin, the little blond asshole who took my place, and exchange catty remarks for a few minutes before the lure of the dance floor makes its way into my booty.

Daddy watches us, and so do a hundred other hard guys, whether they have boys or not.

"Boys on leashes?" Tadeo shouts in my ear as we boogie to some pounding shit or other.

I grin and lean close. "What do you think?"

"I think los gays of New York are more creative than in Argentina." There are no slow numbers, but I dance as close as I can, and my prick gets stiff just feeling the sweat fly off his face and splash mine.

There's a pause in the music and the DJ announces "a little something for a foreign guest." I look over at the booth and sure enough, there's Justin smirking at us as some freaky accordion music starts up. Justin used to use his pull with the DJs—and Daddy's ready cash—to get them to play country shit just to get my goat. Now he's using it on Tadeo, and it pisses me off.

"Justin's being cute," I say in answer to Tadeo's quizzical look. "Let's split and get a drink."

Tadeo smiles and stands his ground. "I think not," he says. "I think I should show him how cute we Argentinos can be."

I hesitate.

"Go, sit with Mr. McGrath, and watch." Tadeo gives me a little push and starts marking time with his hips.

The floor's pretty empty on account of no one but Tadeo knowing how to tango, so I have a clear view as I take the stool next to Daddy.

"Your new boy's a bitch," I say.

Daddy grins, and says, "He's just jealous, Hay. You know that."

"Still hope you're gonna beat his ass," I grumble.

I ignore Daddy's answering chuckle 'cause now Tadeo's into it deep, kicking up his feet and circling his arms and bending his back like there was someone holding him up, only there isn't. Damn, he's beautiful.

I must have said that out loud, 'cause Daddy laughs again and tells me I'm solid gone. I know he's right. Justin looks smug when he sits down, but when he sees Tadeo dancing, not being all embarrassed and shit like he wanted, he gets this sour look on his face that Daddy puts a stop to by pushing the little shit to his knees and freeing his prick for Justin to suck. Nope, no regrets, I'm thinking as I watch Tadeo twist and dip.

The accordion and trumpet and guitar trail off, and the guys ringing the dance floor rush back cheering and clapping and more than ready to take up whatever driving beat the DJ spins next.

I'm more than ready to check out one of the Mineshaft's back rooms. Doesn't matter that this place opened since

I left. It'll have back rooms, and I'm going to take Tadeo into one and show him just what his dancing does to me.

"Later, Daddy," I call over my shoulder and dive into the crowd.

Tadeo's waiting for me, just standing still in the middle of all those bodies, and his hand curls around mine, just right, when I reach him.

The back rooms aren't hard to find, and before you can say "raging hard on" I've got Tadeo against a wall, kissing him like I've wanted to do ever since that first night I saw him through my opera glasses.

"Haven, Haven, wait!" he says, all breathless.

I pull back and look into those dark eyes of his.

"Huh?" I'll admit I'm less than articulate.

"You want me? Me?"

I know what he means. I'm not looking to get my rocks off with just anybody. It's him, and I tell him so.

He takes my breath away with a series of tender kisses that really have no place in this grungy, dark place, but I don't care. I kiss back, and before I know it he's spun around, facing the wall, his bare ass presented for me.

I'd have spun for him, easy as pie, but I figure there'll be time to prove that to him later. There's his ass, high and round and hard with muscle, and as I palm it his back muscles ripple under the black silk of his shirt like some jungle cat.

"Oh, man," I gasp, and spit into my hand. He shoves back onto me before I can even get ready, and we're fucking like the world is ending.

I come way sooner than I want to, so fast and hard it hurts, and spin him around again to face me. I drop, don't take even one second to appreciate his cock—it's too fucking dark in here anyway. I just go down on him, right to his short, stiff pubes, and keep him deep in my throat like I won't need another breath of air, ever.

It shatters him even quicker than me, no time for my Golden Flower trick, and when I stand I'm wobbly, but not too wobbly to share a mouthful of him.

"C'mon," I say, between fast, sloppy kisses. "If we get back to Robbie's place first we get the bed."

He grins and takes my hand, and we head into the comparative brightness of the main floor.

I'm heading over to Daddy to say bye and thanks when I hear someone yell, "Hey, Tango Boy!" A hulk of a guy comes between us and breaks my grip, and before I know it we're separated, dragged in different directions by the crowd.

"Haven!" Tadeo sounds scared, and I wave and try to get to him. It's no use. The big guy has a friend, and they're barreling fast through the crowd. That's when I notice what they're wearing. Uniforms. They don't belong here.

Fuck!

"Daddy!" I holler in my hog-calling voice, and he's beside me in an instant, Justin in his shadow.

"Two goons," I pant. "Got Tadeo."

"Bike," Daddy says simply, and puts car fare in Justin's hand. "Straight home," he shouts, and Justin just nods.

I'm ahead of Daddy out the door, trying to keep Tadeo in sight. The two goons bundle him into a dark sedan and peel away just as Daddy revs his Hog. I'm in the bitch seat like I never left, and we're in hot pursuit through the midnight streets of the West Village.

Chapter 10
In which Tadeo wishes dancing were more like fighting

The men in the car hold me between them and speak Spanish. They're congratulating each other on following me, catching me; they're speculating about their rewards from superiors.

I'm terrified, trying not to cry or piss myself.

The drive is short, ending on the wrong side of a tall, metal gate that rattles shut behind us.

I'm dragged into a huge warehouse, into a side room with no windows to the outside, and one window facing the cavernous interior. Through it, Juan Carlos Gutierrez and a man in the field uniform of the Junta peer while my dark-suited captors tie me to a chair.

"Why are you doing this?" I demand and earn a slap across the face that leaves my tongue bloody.

"Juan Carlos! For God's sake, what do you want?" I slur. He can't hear me through the window. With a cold, squirming nausea, I fear I will give him whatever he wants.

I wonder if this is how it was for Josue.

The door opens, and Juan Carlos steps into the little office trailing the other two uniformed men. "You do work fast," Juan Carlos says to the men. "We only called the Consulate a few hours ago." He turns to me. "I want to know where the baby is."

I don't answer. How can this be happening, in a free country, even if it is a capitalist one?

Crack! "You heard the man," the smaller goon says while I catch my breath and spit more blood.

"Come now, Tadeo," Juan Carlos purrs unctuously.

"You got off easy before, when your maricon boyfriend caused us so much trouble. You won't get off easy this time unless you cooperate."

I try to steel myself against cooperation of any kind. "Hijo de puta," I whisper, hating the tremor in my voice.

The bigger goon grabs my hair and pulls my head up. Juan Carlos gets very close, close enough that I can smell days' worth of coffee and cigars on his breath. I gag. "He's a dancer," he says to the men, but he looks right into my eyes. They snicker. "Break his toes."

The pain is unbearable. I'm screaming and begging, but I haven't told them anything. I can't, really—I never did know Miss Alberta's address.

Unfortunately, having thought it, I speak her name as soon as I'm finished screaming from the second break. They've started with my littlest toe, and are working their way in. If they reach my big toe, I know I'll never dance again.

That's when I realize it doesn't matter. They can't let me go. I'm going to die here, without ever seeing Suyai again. Without seeing Haven.

Haven! He'll come for me. The heroic idiot, he will, and they'll kill him too. Then Suyai will have no one.

I realize my thoughts are irrational, that I'm being driven insane by pain and fear, and that I'm drowning in them. Weak, just like the Brothers at the English school always said I was.

Juan Carlos has stepped away to use the phone, probably to find Miss Alberta's address from that hospital boss. They'll set bad men on Miss Alberta's family, I realize with a soul-sucking regret. The leader directs the other uniforms to burn me. He's not going to wait for Juan Carlos to finish his phone call. "Some men can take a bone break," he says, smoothly. "But those tend to crumble over burns. The address, you faggot piece of shit."

Cigarettes extinguishing in my skin are a new

experience, and after two I pass out. Slaps to my face bring me around over and over again, and I'm no longer sure what I've told them, or in what language.

I slip into a place where the pain is distant. No less great, but enacted on some other poor sod. The sooner I can die, the sooner it will be over, but it doesn't happen.

Suyai needs me. And I need Haven. Haven. He's a soldier, a man of science. He wouldn't let these penny-ante goons cow him.

"Fucking pricks," I mumble, imitating my new friend. My lover. Not a very romantic beginning, but who needs romance?

"What the fuck is he saying now?"

"Some bullshit about romance, fucking faggot."

"He's pissed himself. Get his pants down."

That gets through. I start to struggle, and when they loosen the cords around my ankles to get my pants off, I kick out fast. Powerful.

"Aaaah!" I hear two screams, and one has to be mine, for the pain in my foot is excruciating. How had I forgotten my broken toes?

I'm losing it, I know, but still I struggle. I use my strength to twist the chair and come upright, nearly vomiting when I put weight on my bad foot.

I spin as best I can, which is to say clumsily, but I manage to knock the smaller goon and Juan Carlos with the wooden legs. My arms are still tied to the slats, and I fear harder hits will break them, too, but the bigger goon is having trouble recapturing me, so I soldier on, blind with tears and deaf with the ringing of my ears from the blows to my face and the pain in my feet. I feel myself going down.

"Get him, get him!" the Junta man yells, and I collapse under the weight of both camouflaged thugs.

I'm bare from the waist down, and wonder which one will rape me. Maybe all of them. I won't get away again.

"Porca miseria," someone mutters, and I feel my arms untied and my body stretched out on the wooden desk.

Hard hands hold me down. They don't even clear the record books and invoices off it first. Messy. My thoughts are spinning, and I'm spiraling into some place where consciousness is a memory, but still I kick.

I call up Haven's face and let it flash through every aspect I've seen it in so far, from the chilly fluorescence of the hospital, to the changeable light of the train, to the dark club where he took me, where I gave myself to him. In those moments, I stop wishing he were here. I want him safe, and this is no safe place. "Stay away, Haven, away."

My chant distracts me a little, but before long I realize no one's penetrating me. They're beating me, burning the soles of my feet. "More, you bastards, more!" I scream, and they laugh and do their worst. So I think.

"He's babbling, the fucking sissy. Let him rest. Pain's always worse when you give 'em a break," one goon says; the other laughs. Juan Carlos is shouting into the phone, relaying Alberta's address to someone. Maybe they'll stop hurting me now, I think, but the Junta dogs are pacing, watching me, and I fear they will not listen to Juan Carlos. I tell myself not to fall asleep, to stay alert, but I can't obey even my own orders. I'm out with my very next breath.

Chapter 11
In which Haven musters an unlikely cavalry

Our hot pursuit barely takes us out of the neighborhood. Without even time to wonder at the turns of events that perch me behind Daddy once more, we're skidding to a stop on the wrong side of a huge chain-link fence. Before the men who roll it shut behind the sedan can see our faces, Daddy spins and tears off the way we'd come.

"Fuck!" I scream.

"Cool your jets, boy," Daddy shouts over the unmuffled roar of the Harley's engine. "We'll fix this."

We head back to the 'Shaft, it being the nearest place with a phone this far west. Warehouse districts don't have a lot of phone booths.

Guys are streaming out, fearing a raid after the uniforms that took Tadeo rolled through. Makes for chaos, I tell you. Daddy hollers at the bouncer until he leads us to the empty manager's office.

We take turns on the phone, and Daddy uses my turns to round up friends of his who haven't hightailed it away yet. I let Alberta know what's happened, and tell her to get Suyai and everybody else far away from her place. My thinking is that if the Junta bastards have him and this isn't just a kidnapping, Tadeo may already have told them where the baby is. He won't have had a choice. She grumps some, but she's been through this shit before when Robbie was a Panther, before two tours in 'Nam straightened him out. She knows what to do, and she takes care not to tell me where she's going.

My second call is to Robbie on the off chance he's home early. "You got company, man," he says when he answers. My guts freeze. How could the goons chasing Tadeo have traced us to Robbie so fast? Even Daddy hadn't known we were heading there.

But before I get too far with my thoughts, there's fumbling on the other end of the line and a voice full of Coal Ridge and cheap whiskey hoots at me. "Cuz!! Y'all in a fix?"

"Yeah, Hollis," I say. "You got wheels?"

He does, and I tell him where to meet us, a few blocks north of the 'Shaft. By the way Rupe yee-haws in the background when Hollis tells him what's up, I figure they're just spoiling for a fight, not keen to help their queer cousin in particular.

"Hay?" Robbie's voice comes back. "I'll bring your medic kit."

"Hate to involve you, man," I reply, and it's true. Robbie's seen enough combat for five lifetimes.

"Shut up, asshole," he grumbles, and I know I'm forgiven. "This is a street brawl, not the Mekong Delta."

Daddy checks in with Justin, tells him to call a few more of his cronies, and we set off again for the rendezvous, flanked by a handful of growling bikes. Daddy figured it was better not to freak out everybody at the 'Shaft any more than we already had.

I'm trying to keep my cool, to find my battle focus, but I'm too close to this particular situation. We'll meet our backup and get there in time, I tell myself over and over, matching my mental chant to the growl of Daddy's bike.

I wish I was surer about that.

We only wait about ten minutes for Daddy's reinforcements and the battered pickup bearing Robbie and my cousins. "Regular love-in you got there, boy," Daddy says when my redneck cousins tumble out of the cab followed by Robbie's Afro.

Say what you want about Daddy, but the man has a sense of humor. "More like a down-home shivaree," I shoot back. "Ain't we waited long enough?"

Daddy gives me the look that says he's dying to correct my grammar, but lets it go with a sharp nod of his head.

I strap my field kit onto my back and clamber back onto Daddy's Hog. "Bring the truck," he says. "Hope we won't need it."

I know what he means. If Tadeo isn't in shape to ride a bike when we find him, we're in deep shit.

Daddy hollers some directions to the warehouse and warns everybody: "No weapons, strictly fisticuffs," which raises some objections but more laughter. "The fellas we're taking on aren't legit, either, so I don't fancy the legal mess if any of us end up in a city hospital."

"Don't need nothing but five knuckles," some leather dude yells, and right there the walls between cracker and queer come tumbling down. With much back clapping and testosterone-fueled bravado, we're off. The delay may have been necessary, but I shudder to think what those goons, and probably Gutierrez, have been doing to my Tadeo while we got organized.

In the end, it ain't much of a fight. The two guys on the gate scatter when we roll up, two dozen fuming choppers strong. Hollis and Rupe crash the gate. Truck don't look any different afterward, either. Coupla Daddy's guys make sure the gate keepers are out of commission, but not before finding out where in the vast riverside warehouse my man is.

I can't believe that there are only four guys in there with him, where we got close to thirty. I point out Gutierrez to Daddy, and he takes charge of the weasel. The Junta goons take the sedan and squeal out of the warehouse, knocking over a couple of bikes. The one dude in a uniform is the only holdout. Takes both my cousins and Robbie to pound him into submission, but he subsides pretty quick when it's his own pistol in his face.

Tadeo's another story. He's passed out on a battered

old desk, mostly naked, bruises everywhere. When I get up close I see the burns on his legs. "'S okay, buddy," I'm crooning, just like in the field with a shot-up grunt, and checking him over.

"Haven."

He comes around quickly enough to reassure me he's not too badly damaged and says my name before he sees me.

Damn near breaks my heart. "Here, baby. Right here." I keep up the crooning and get him covered as best I can. If those bastards raped him I'll fucking hunt them down and choke them with their own balls.

"Miss 'Berta," Tadeo's muttering in between winces and little squeaks of pain. "I told them about her. They know…Suyai…Juan Carlos made calls."

I try to help him stand, but he screams and passes out again for a few seconds.

That's when I notice his busted toes. Fuckers.

"I already warned Alberta to get the baby out. She'll be okay." I hook Tadeo over my shoulders and keep his feet up while I get help wrestling him into the bed of Hollis' truck.

I need to get my man someplace clean where I can fix him up.

I look for Daddy, and see him talking real low and menacing into Gutierrez' face. I watch as—no doubt—the McGrath credentials as one of the most effective and best connected trial lawyers in Manhattan register with Tadeo's boss. He'll still be trouble, maybe, but not tonight.

"Take him away, boys," Daddy calls to a few of the bikers. I don't want to know what they have planned for him. They came with us hoping for a fight, and I figure they'll get one no matter what.

Robbie ambles up to tell me a few of the fellas need basic first aid, and promises to sit with Tadeo while I see to them. It's easier to go into battle mode now, fixing everybody up, and we're ready to ride in minutes.

The party heads east toward Daddy's loft, though most of the guys peel off before we get there. The night's still young, after all.

Ice and splints and an ampule of morphine let me take care of Tadeo, who's loopy enough by the end of things to tell me he loves me.

I should know better than to take it to heart, but maybe fear makes me stupid. I almost ask him to say it again.

Robbie takes Hollis and Rupe back to his place. Beginning of a beautiful friendship, I shouldn't wonder. Robbie doesn't ask what my plans are—he'll keep up with me through Alberta.

Justin's a decent enough host, though I can tell he's green as a gator over having missed the excitement.

Daddy makes a few more phone calls—I swear, it's a wonder he doesn't have cauliflower ear—and comes in to sit with me near dawn.

"Who you calling so late?" I ask.

"Calling in a few favors," he says cryptically.

I wait.

"Gutierrez and the rest of the troupe will have their visas revoked by morning. They won't be a problem."

"What about those uniformed guys?" We'd pieced together that the uniformed assholes must have been attached to the Consulate and followed us from there. I'm losing my touch if I can't spot a tail anymore.

"Less I can do about them." Daddy pauses and then smiles this feral smile that reminds me why I found him so irresistible when we first met. "But a visit from the Mayor's Office Consular Commission may encourage his bosses to rotate him back overseas."

"And if they're involved?" Tadeo says, his voice all blurry.

Daddy shrugs. "They'll be on notice. Diplomatic immunity isn't what it used to be, you know." He waves my worry away. "What about you two?"

I look at Tadeo, who's drifted off again. "I don't know." I say. "But I'll figure it out. You've done enough."

I do my best not to sound surly. I really am grateful, and I know without Daddy Tadeo wouldn't be free right now. Might not even be alive.

But I can't help wishing I could have saved him all by myself.

Chapter 12
In which Tadeo capitulates, with pleasure

P lease, come with me."

Haven is deploying that come-hither look that I know by now conceals the mind of a soldier and the heart of a healer. It's been, to say the least, difficult to resist until now. Not impossible, as his continued attempts to sway me prove, but difficult, without a doubt.

Today, though, mere weeks after my rescue from a riverside warehouse in Manhattan, two things changed.

My doctor at the free clinic in Somerville has cleared both Suyai and me to travel. I will go on crutches, but I can go. Go where, is the greater question.

The other change is that Haven suddenly has a destination to offer. He's come to the clinic to deliver the news.

"Sister City?" I've never heard of it. "Where is it?"

"South," Haven says with a grin. "But not too far south. On the coast. Big enough to have a hospital that needs an outreach clinic nurse. They don't care that I have a ...'reputation for independent thinking'," he quotes. Then he plays his trump card. "It's big enough to have a ballet."

I pause in my practice with the crutches. The pain in my toes is less than the itching that's begun inside my cast, and my burns are scabbed over nicely. Some may not even leave scars. We stare into each other's eyes. I look away first.

"The doctors haven't said whether I will be able to dance again," I mumble.

"What do they know?" Haven scoffs. "Your physical

therapist thinks you will, and I agree."

"Alberta has said Suyai and I can stay with her," I counter.

"Aw, man." Haven shakes his head. "What's she got that I don't?" He precedes me up the hallway, shaking a very fine example of one asset he offers.

"She wants to help take care of Suyai." I smile at the thought of my son, resting now among the nurses in the clinic's break room. He's a very popular patient.

Haven sobers and walks back to where I stand. It seems once again a momentous decision of my life must be made in some public hallway. Haven fixes me with those gas-flame eyes of his, and this time there's nothing of the coquette in them. "So do I."

I nod. "I must think."

"I start in a week," he says. I know him well enough now to know that, having stated his case, he'll let the matter drop. He respects me.

He also expects me to be his lover. Openly, or at least as openly as one can be here, which is very much so by comparison to what I'm used to. He wants us to raise Suyai together. Make a home. Even he admits it's not a ready option for most men like us.

"But," as he's said more than once, "I ain't your garden-variety faggot."

He certainly isn't. There, in that anonymous, sterile hallway, I decide one thing: neither am I.

"Make him sweat," Alberta advises when I tell her I've decided to follow Haven to Sister City. "That boy thinks he can charm the paint off a church wall."

"And he's right," I finish for her.

I've been staying with Alberta and her family while Haven wraps up his life. His apartment is sublet, his job finished (though that was true before we returned from New York, thanks to Mr. Barnes). He and I have visited

Alberta's church to thank the pastor and his flock who sheltered Suyai without thought to their own safety. Haven has even reconciled with his former lover, the doctor who helped us, though he assures me they were never more than fuck-buddies—a term I despise and have forbidden him to use for me.

Alberta and her brood lay a lavish spread the night of Haven's departure. He arrives with two duffels, surprisingly little, and I realize he's as much a refugee as I am. Suyai has more possessions than I do.

"I must speak with you," I tell Haven as he finishes a second helping of something called chess pie.

"Use my room," Alberta calls over her shoulder. "I'll watch the baby."

"What is it, Tadeo?" Haven always calls me by my given name, though I have a hazy memory of him wrapping me in endearments while he tended to me in New York.

"Your offer is still good? For Suyai and me to come to your new post with you?"

"You mean it?" he says, and the smile on his face makes him look about twelve years old.

I nod, and before I take my next breath, he's in my arms.

"You won't regret it, I swear you won't."

I switch on the little radio beside Alberta's bed. "Perhaps we'd better seal the bargain." And I lean in to kiss him, confident the radio muffles any escaping sounds.

Our kisses grow teeth, and are in danger of leading to other things, when Haven pushes me away, mindful of my cast, which unbalances me still.

"Alberta will kill us if she catches us."

"I have no doubt she would," I agree, but steal another kiss or two before we leave the room, hand in hand. I leave the radio playing softly.

We're hand in hand, or the nearest thing to it, while we ride the train to Sister City. Between us on the seat, Suyai dozes in the soft-sided bassinet Alberta's church friends found for us. My hand and Haven's touch lightly where we each grip the handles.

When I start to move as the conductor reaches us to take our tickets, Haven hisses, "Don't you dare."

He won't let me hide.

I smile at him. Thank you, I mouth for his eyes only.

Haven manhandles all of our baggage onto the Sister City platform near dawn the next day while I wait, swaying on my crutches beside a squalling Suyai. We splurge on a taxicab, and Haven gives an address. "It's near the clinic. I told the director what I wanted, and she assured me it'll suit."

"I have never had a home," I say. "The very idea suits."

Haven beams at me and pays the driver extra to carry our baggage up an uneven, overgrown brick walk. My impression in the predawn gloom is of a small, dingy bungalow. The porch steps creak, and the screen door is patched with tape.

The electricity works, and the place is furnished, albeit shabbily. There's no hot water yet, but I don't care. We settle Suyai beside the bed, wave farewell to the cabbie, and look around a bit.

"I have never seen a more beautiful house," I say, my voice shaking with embarrassing honesty.

Haven simply nods and draws me down onto the dusty coverlet. Our kisses have nothing to stop them this time, and it's only the awkwardness of my cast that prevents me from offering Haven what I gave him in the back room of the New York leather bar.

Instead, he treats me to another of the magnificent blowjobs I remember so well, finishing with a very sloppy kiss to the head of my pinga. It's fast, and I vow to take our time next time. "Love you," Haven says to my thigh as he rests there.

"Come here," I say. "I want to do for you, too."

"No need, sugar. I came when you did."

I'm amazed, but the stain at the front of his dungarees tells the tale. Even so, I tug him up to lie beside me. "I'm so glad you're here," he whispers, kissing my face. "All I've ever wanted." He's drifting to sleep.

Two weeks ago, I lost my wife, events ensured I'd never see my home again, and I grieved. Now, I can turn my head to one side and see my healthy, American son, and to the other to see a lover like I never imagined, and I rejoice. My home is where they are. I joggle Haven's head where it rests on my shoulder. I want him to hear me when I say, "Me, too."

Bedside Manner

House Call
by Jane Davitt

Dedicated to Amy, who came up with the title.

Paul picked up his medical bag and felt the familiar weight tug at his arm. He kept meaning to go through it and see if there was something in there he could leave behind, but the certainty that if he did he'd need it within the week aided and abetted his procrastination. He walked out of his consulting room and headed for the shimmering heat waiting for him once he left the air-conditioned coolness of the clinic. A dry cough halted him before he could pull the main door open.

"I've got an addition to your rounds."

Paul sighed and turned to face Dr. Raines. Nemesis, mentor, boss—the man loomed large in his life for a slight, elderly man, with hands that shook when Raines was tired. He stared into Raines' calm, faded eyes, cleared his throat, and made sure his voice was confident, even chiding, not hopeful. "I'm very busy today."

"I'm sure you are, Dr. Jackson, I'm sure you are." Andrew Raines nodded agreeably, a half smile on his face. "And now you'll be a little busier, which is better than being bored." A file, thick enough to be worrying, was in his hand. He held it out, giving Paul no choice but to walk over and take it.

The name on the file—Matthew Parker—meant nothing to Paul. Three months wasn't long enough for him to have learned who lived next door, let alone acquire the encyclopedic level of detail about Branchton that Raines had built up over the decades. The address was for a house some six miles out of town, in the farmland that surrounded it, and Paul frowned as he tried to slot it into the route he'd planned and failed.

"You can go there last," Raines said, as if reading his thoughts. "Matt isn't in any hurry to see you. You'd think he would be, given he won't be alive by the end of the month, but he isn't. In fact, he isn't expecting you; I've made this appointment, not him."

There was something in his voice, some regret that went beyond a doctor's natural concern for a patient, that softened Paul's impatience at the extension of his already busy day. "You know him well, then?"

"We sat next to each other all through school," Raines said, his expression distant, his eyes squinted half-shut as if he was staring down a long tunnel. "He dated my sister Ruby in high school, and got drunk and threw up in my car when she found someone else to take her to the prom. We've fished Salmon Creek every summer except this one, and we've both buried our wives and outlived at least one of our children. Yes, you could say I know him well."

"I'm sorry," Paul said, the words awkward in his mouth, spiked and edged with guilt that he'd been petty enough to try and get out of visiting the man. "What's wrong with him?"

Raines grimaced in thought, deepening the wrinkles around his eyes. "He's had angina for years," he said slowly. "And a bypass four years ago. He was a carpenter; could turn a piece of wood into just about anything, but he decided to retire last year and take it easy. Old fool still kept smoking and eating food that might as well have been laced with arsenic, though. He had a stroke around Christmas, and though he's come back from that, when I saw him last, well, I didn't need the result of the blood work to tell me that his heart's just about worn out. Not the most scientific diagnosis, but it was what I told him, and he nodded, told me he wasn't going to get cut up again, and that's the last time I saw him."

Raines didn't drive anymore, not trusting his vision, which was the main reason he'd hired Paul, with the carrot of a partnership dangling enticingly if it worked out. "I could come back and get you when I've finished my rounds and take you over there," Paul offered.

"Oh, I'd go in a heartbeat, if he'd let me in the door, but he won't." Raines smiled, a brief twitch of his mouth. "Says he's in too much pain to suffer the sight of my ugly face, and I can wait for the funeral to sob over him."

"He sounds like a real character."

"He's a stubborn bastard and he knows better," Raines snapped, a flush rising in his thin cheeks. "There's nothing I can do for him when he won't let himself be treated, but I could keep him company now and then, at least. His grandson's staying with him at the moment, but it's not the same."

"He's doing it to spare you," Paul said without really believing it. People on their deathbeds tended to make the most of their chance to be selfish, rather than turning into angels.

Raines sniffed. "The Lord never did, so I don't see why Matt thinks he should. Never mind. You go and see him, young man, and let me know how he is."

"Will he even see me?" Paul asked doubtfully. "I don't want to get him agitated or worked up, and if he's not expecting me..."

"Make him see you," Raines told him, emphasizing the words with a poke aimed unerringly at a tender spot on Paul's ribs. "I want to know how he is."

"Yes, Dr. Raines."

Raines gave him a suspicious look and then nodded as if satisfied by Paul's rare meekness. "Off you go then. Patients waiting."

They could be waiting here, like all the others, Paul thought, giving the moderately crowded waiting room to the left a quick glance. Raines, with the assistance of Nurse Gibson, would see to the people who'd come to the clinic for the afternoon session; the bulk of the appointments were made in the morning when Paul could help out.

And in the afternoons, most afternoons, Paul, a map on the seat beside him and a supply of snacks and water just in case he got lost, made house calls.

"But nobody does that these days!" he'd protested on his first morning. "It simply isn't cost-effective for me to—"

"'Cost-effective'?" Raines looked as if he'd bitten into a wormy apple. "Do I look like a man working on his first million, son? This practice is a rural one at heart. I've made it so. Most of the people in town go to Riverview Surgery, and I hope they enjoy being treated by children barely old enough to shave—"

"There are two women doctors over there," Paul pointed out.

"You don't think women shave?" Raines asked tartly. "In this clinic, we deal mainly with the people beyond the town limits. We're not covering a city neighborhood with buses and trains and cabs; some of our patients live way out—"

"And because of that, they all have cars and trucks," Paul interrupted. "The time I spend going to them, I could be helping other people."

"What you mean," Raines said dryly, amusement flickering in his eyes, "is that you're too important to go to them and they should come to you. That 'doctor' in front of your name makes you important, is that it? Well, you're right. To many of these people, you're someone to look up to, like the sheriff, or the mayor. You're the one who keeps them breathing, who saves their children and loved ones, who takes away their pain. And because they respect that, most of them will do all they can to get into town by themselves. But some can't. Too sick to drive, or they've got a houseful of children they'd have to ask someone to mind." He tapped his fingers on the desk that lay between them and nodded sharply. "There're always exceptions, and I hired you to help them, because I'm getting too old to haul ass around back roads when they're flooded or deep in snow."

He pursed his lips. "Mind, there's some too bone-idle to come into town, I'll give you that. But not many. I won't tell you who; guess you'll figure that out for yourself in time."

Which he had, Paul would be the first to admit. Just as he'd freely admit that it would have been no kindness to anyone to insist on Jim Grieves, laid low by food poisoning, coming into the clinic. Not when the man was too weak to walk and Paul had found him slumped on the bathroom floor, a blanket around him, the toilet and a bucket his two best friends. The look of relief and gratitude in Jim's eyes as Paul had handed him two tablets that, within the hour, had improved his condition to the point of being able to keep down a small dish of apple sauce, had stuck with Paul for some time.

He made his rounds, greeted with a wary courtesy that was gradually warming to acceptance with every day that passed without him killing a patient or committing the greater faux pas of admitting that no, he didn't really care about football, and then drove out to the Parker house, west of town. The heat was intense, as it had been for weeks, but there was a promise of rain in the massing clouds overhead. When he stepped out of the car, braced for an assault by the inevitable dogs country people seemed to keep around, he felt a marginally cooler breeze on his face.

He'd thought about keeping some dog biscuits in the car as bribes, but reconsidered when he'd seen the way the farm dogs ate, looking more like ravenous wolves. Doctors needed all their fingers. He glanced around, caution keeping him beside his car, even though there was a welcome lack of barking, and then began to walk toward the porch. Like the house itself, it needed fresh paint, but the structure looked sound. It was a small, neat box of a house with the remains of flowerbeds around it, scuffed over with weeds now, grass reclaiming the once-cultivated earth. A dusty, green pickup truck was parked at the side of the house—dusty, but not rusty, new enough to look incongruous against the faded boards of the house.

Sun-dazzled, Paul only saw the man sitting in the shadows of the porch when he stood and the creak of a wicker chair gave him away. Paul shaded his eyes, squinted, and gave the man a brief nod, too much on his dignity to smile. This was probably the grandson Dr. Raines had mentioned. "Hello. I'm here to see Mr. Parker?"

"You're looking at him." The man walked to the top of the short flight of steps leading up to the porch and braced his hands on the support beams on either side, effectively blocking the way and showcasing an impressive physique; wide shoulders, long legs, and a deep tan that made the blue of his eyes look brighter than they probably were. His hair was black, lusterless and straight, sweat-damped and falling so that it framed his angular face, long enough to brush his shoulders. Paul automatically took in the view with an appreciation he took care to keep hidden, from head to bare toes, and then frowned, recognition stirring along with muted arousal and a warning bell. Tall. He didn't do tall. Didn't like craning his neck back, didn't like being looked down on. He'd never gone for someone three or four inches taller than him, as this man was. Just that one time, that one night....

The man whistled, long and low. "Holy shit. Dr. Feelgood. What the hell are you doing out here, city boy?"

Paul bit down hard on his lip as the memories flooded back, disjointed and chaotic for the most part, but only too clear when it came to the most lurid moments of his night with the man currently looming over him and grinning widely.

He cleared his throat. "It's Steve, right? I don't think you ever told me more than that."

And he hadn't been sure "Steve" was the man's real name, but it hadn't mattered at the time.

"Yeah. I'm touched you remember even that much,

Doc."

"You're...memorable," Paul said. He tried for a lightness of tone he didn't feel, refusing to let his panic show. Two years, and he could still remember the way Steve's mouth had felt on his skin, kissing his neck hard enough to mark it, light as a snowflake on his cock until he'd begged the man to—He raised his hand and let it fall back when he realized he'd been about to touch his neck. "Well, shall we agree this is awkward and move on?"

"Just like that." Steve shook his head slowly. "I don't think so, Doc. You owe me more than that."

"I'm here to see your grandfather," Paul said sharply. "Yes, it's a small world; no, I didn't expect to meet a one-night stand from the city way out here two years later; yes, I suppose you want to discuss...things, but that can wait. I have a patient to see."

Steve considered that and then nodded. "Okay. I won't deny I'm glad you're here—as a doctor, I mean—but, no offense, I'd sooner Uncle Andy had come out."

"Who? Oh, Dr. Raines." Paul shrugged. "I wish he had, too, but Mr. Parker won't see him."

"I know. Stubborn old fool." There was no rancor in his voice, just rueful affection. "I wondered why Uncle Andy hadn't been by, so I called him, and he told me Matt wouldn't let him onto his land. Said he'd send out his new assistant, but the way he talked about you I thought you were thirteen, not thirty."

"He keeps calling me "sonny"," Paul said with a sigh. "It's not filling my patients with confidence."

"'Sonny'? Huh. Guess he just doesn't know you as well as I do, or he'd know you were all grown up." Steve's gaze flicked down, and Paul felt the heat in his face migrate south. "Ask him to make it 'big boy' instead."

Paul took a deep breath. Aggravating, annoying jerk. He'd put this man on, well, not a pedestal given what they'd done together, but when he'd thought about Steve he'd felt pleasantly nostalgic because Steve had seemed like a nice guy.

Alcohol and lust had a lot to answer for.

"Mr. Parker is my last patient of the day," he said evenly. "If you insist, we can talk about—we can talk—when I've seen him. Until then, let it drop, or I'm leaving as soon as I've finished my examination."

Steve studied him for a moment and then gave Paul what might have been meant to be an apologetic smile and a nod. He moved to the side and gestured with a sweep of his arm. "Come on in."

Paul walked up the steps, with a creak of old wood accompanying each footstep, and brushed past Steve, who hadn't moved far enough to give Paul clear passage. The man smelled of clean water and soap, and Paul realized that Steve's hair was damp, not from sweat, but a recent shower. It made him conscious of his own less than pristine state. Hours spent in farmhouses where the only relief from the heat came from a slowly whirring fan, or a window opened to catch a breeze, had left his shirt sticking to him, and the cool air in his car had only served to make the next dip into sweltering heat that much more unbearable.

"You look hot," Steve said thoughtfully without showing any hint that he wanted his words to be taken at anything but face value. "Can I get you a drink? There's some iced tea or fresh lemonade."

The offer of refreshments was one Paul got at most of the houses he visited. Whether it was prompted by custom or genuine hospitality, he rarely had time to accept, but this time he shook his head with more regret than usual. An icy-cold beer was waiting for him at home, but that was at least an hour in the future and the inside of his mouth felt as sticky as his shirt. Lemonade, cool, watery, tart, ice clinking against the side of the jug as it was poured, sounded as inviting as a patch of shade. Reminding himself that the last time he'd drunk with Steve it had ended badly, he followed Steve into the house.

"How is your grandfather today?" he asked, less out of the belief that Steve could tell him anything useful than a need to get the conversation under his control.

Steve paused at the foot of the stairs, and Paul stood beside him, waiting, his attention half on the man, half on his surroundings. The small entrance hall was cluttered with the kind of debris a man would leave, knowing he'd need it the next day, and a woman would tidy away; keys and a newspaper on a table, a jacket over the newel post, and boots on a mat near the door. Or maybe that was just true of his parents. Paul himself was neat enough; he could afford a cleaner, but preferred not to let a stranger into his home to poke around, so he made an effort to keep things orderly. The Parker house smelled of heat and dust, but there was no lingering reminder of past meals cooked or the subtle but unmistakable odor of a home untended where it mattered.

"He's weaker than when I got here," Steve said finally, after giving the question some thought instead of returning a pro forma reply. Paul relaxed, relieved that Steve was behaving now. "That was ten days ago, and he was able to sit up for a few hours a day; now, it's just when I give him his meals, and then he has to lie down again. He looks...old."

"I looked through his file," Paul said. "That's inevitable, I'm afraid. His body is just—"

"Worn out." Steve shook his head. "Yeah, I know. It's just...he shouldn't look this way. He's sixty-eight, and he looks like you should be swapping those numbers around. It isn't right."

It had been a long time since Paul had felt helpless indignation at the unfairness of a disease or disability. With his own thirtieth birthday approaching, he liked to think he was mature, and mature men didn't rail against indifferent facts or drown in pity and sympathy for dying patients and the people who cared about them.

He'd learned his lesson after pouring everything he had into treating a child whose death had, looking back, been inevitable. He'd assured the parents, blank-eyed with grief, that he could do something, had kindled hope where there shouldn't have been any, had exhausted himself to the point of using drugs to stay awake, had come close to getting his ass fired, in fact, and all for nothing. Katy-Anne had died. Her parents, stunned, disbelieving, cheated of their miracle, had been bitter, and Paul had redrawn the lines between himself and his patients and stepped back, kept his distance.

"If you could just show me to his room?"

Steve stared at him for a moment, as if waiting for more, but when Paul kept his face studiously blank, Steve nodded at the stairs. "This way. I wanted to bring his bed down here; there's a TV in the family room, and he always liked to watch the sports channel, but he says he was born in that bedroom, and he wants to die in it."

"He should be in a hospital room, monitored around the clock," Paul said. "But I can see from his notes he turned that down, even though his insurance covered it."

"If it hadn't, I'd have paid for it myself," Steve said. "But you'd need dynamite to get him off his land, and I can't say as I blame him."

It went against the grain not to argue forcefully for Mr. Parker's removal to the nearest hospital, but if the penmanship on the letter in the files had been shaky, the ink a faint tracery on the lined notepaper, the words had been clear and definite. In terse, concise sentences, Mr. Parker had stated his intention of shooting anyone who tried to take him away from his farm, followed by the promise to shoot himself if that wasn't deterrent enough. He'd finished with six underscored words: Tell them I mean it, Andy.

Paul was fairly certain that Matt didn't, but beyond the hyperbole was a statement of intent that was genuine enough. He quieted his conscience with the thought that psychologically speaking a move would be damaging, even fatal, and followed Steve up the stairs to the baked-stale air of the bedroom.

"It's very warm in here," he said to Steve, keeping

his voice low as his patient, a tall man with steel-gray hair cropped close to his skull, was asleep, a thin sheet draped over him. An oxygen tank was beside the bed, out of place next to the dark, heavy furniture in the room. "Could you bring in the fan on the landing, please?"

"I did, but Granddad said the noise bothered him and he couldn't sleep. That's as close as he'll let me put it. I angled it as best I could."

Paul chewed his lip. "Could you bring it in while he's asleep?"

"No, he couldn't, because then it'd wake me up." Matt Parker opened his eyes, a paler version of his grandson's, and eased himself over to his back with a grunt. "Thought you had to have brains to be a doctor?"

"It's helpful," Paul said dryly. "Hello, Mr. Parker. I'm Dr. Jackson and I'm here to—"

"Tell me I'm dying?" Matt coughed, his face twisting in a pained grimace. "Could have saved you the trip, sonny. I already know. Got old Andy to admit to that much, anyhow."

"I'm here to examine you."

"What's the point?"

"Humor me," Paul said, setting his bag down on a chair by the door and opening it.

"And why in God's name should I do that?" Matt's voice was weak, and the bare arm outside the covers showed wasted muscles on stick-thin bones, but he retained a strength of personality that Paul found appealing, though he imagined full-force it might be overwhelming. In fact, he knew it was, because Matt Parker's grandson had inherited that particular trait, and Steve had certainly left Paul feeling overwhelmed.

"Because Dr. Raines sent me, and you and he are friends."

"Andy never did learn that 'no' doesn't mean 'maybe'." Matt closed his eyes. "Oh, do what you have to, sonny. Just don't shove any needles in me. I'm damned if I'll die looking like a pincushion, and I don't have any blood to spare."

Paul flinched at the "sonny", sure that Steve was going to comment, but he stayed silent, his attention focused on straightening a picture on the wall, his back turned to the bed. "I do need to take a blood sample, but I promise that it won't hurt."

"Hurt?" Matt glared at him. "Do I look like I care about it hurting? I just don't want you poking at me." His breathing was labored now, his hand clutching spasmodically at the sheet, long fingers contracting, knuckles showing white. "No needles, you hear me? No goddamned—"

Steve turned at that and took a step forward. "Granddad, he won't, okay? I won't let him."

Paul opened his mouth and then closed it again, because now he had two of them glaring at him, and Steve seemed more than willing to remove him bodily if he even looked like pulling out a syringe. A blood sample wouldn't tell him anything new, he supposed, and the grim irony of getting it and killing his patient in the process by provoking a cardiac arrest wasn't lost on him. Matt grabbed at the oxygen mask on the bed beside him and took some slow, deep breaths, his gaze fixed accusingly on Paul.

Paul took out a blood pressure cuff. "No needles," he agreed with a sigh, and walked over to the bed. Dr. Raines wasn't going to be pleased, but Matt Parker was Paul's patient now.

Not that it would make a difference to Raines when he found out how sketchy Paul's examination had been.

"So, how is he?"

Paul gave the condensation-beaded bottle of beer in Steve's hand a yearning look and then glanced away before Steve caught him staring. The porch was fully in the shade now, but there was no relief from the heat yet, though a storm was definitely coming. The air was still, as if it was holding its breath, and it felt charged with electricity. If there had been a cat around to stroke its fur would have given off sparks, tiny zaps of static. Over to the west, where the sun was heading, dark clouds were massing, waiting to rain down water onto the thirsty soil. Above them, the deep, pristine blue sky was beginning to look hazy, and the birds had stopped singing. Paul rubbed at his head, aching from tension and the drop in pressure, and tried to frame his words tactfully.

"It's the first time I've seen him, so I can't comment on how, or if, his condition has changed—"

"Spit it out."

"Are you always this impatient?" Paul demanded.

Steve shrugged. "You're the one who drove up looking as if you were in a hurry to turn around and leave, even before you realized who I was. I thought you'd appreciate the chance to speed things up."

"I—" Paul paused. He had felt that way, usually did on these house calls, but it didn't mean that he'd wanted the patients he saw, or their families, to pick up on it. "I didn't mean to give that impression," he said finally. "I'm sorry."

"So sit down and tell me how he is." There wasn't much to tell. Matt Parker was dying, his body betrayed by his own lifestyle in part. Steve must have read that on Paul's face, because he sighed. "Let me put it another way: how much time does he have?"

"Days," Paul said flatly. He sat down on one of the porch chairs, the wood polished shiny on the seat from years of being sat upon. It was surprisingly comfortable, but more than that, the act of sitting, of choosing to stay however briefly in one spot, was relaxing. He felt as he did when he returned to the small house he rented a few blocks from the clinic, a tiny patch of yard in front of it, a tangle of weeds at the back that he meant to tackle one free weekend. It was like living in a dollhouse after years in his parents' home, glossy, huge, forever changing as his mother redecorated. Even the over-priced modern apartment with thin walls and a view of the lake if you had binoculars handy that he'd moved into after college had been larger. This house, quiet and old enough to have acquired a certain dignity, suited him perfectly, though, despite its size.

Apart from the dripping tap in the kitchen, which was driving him nuts, but he never seemed to have time to fix the damn washer.

"I didn't realize—days?" Steve looked stunned, his empty hand closing, contracting sharply, as if he was trying to hold on either to the passing minutes or his grandfather's life. Paul remembered Matt's hand on the sheet and shivered, but Steve's hand was strong and tanned, not pale and wasted. "Are you sure?"

"I'm sorry."

"I guess that means 'yes'?"

Paul nodded. It never got easier to tell someone that they were about to lose a person they loved. Or to tell a patient that they were about to die. People expected miracles, reprieves, last-second saves like the ones they saw on TV or read about in the papers. They didn't want to hear that they weren't one of the lucky ones.

"He really should have someone here around the clock—a nurse, I mean, not just family like you. Someone who can monitor his situation and do what little can be done in the way of medication. I'm sure you're doing your best, but looking after a patient who's bedridden isn't easy. I checked, and so far he has no bedsores, but they're something to watch out for, and his diet needs to be tailored to his condition. Would you like me to arrange for someone to come out here? We have several suitable people that we can send, and I'm sure—"

"He won't have anyone but me," Steve said. "Before I came the neighbors were calling in on him a few times a day, and he was able to potter around a little." He drank from the bottle, causing Paul to swallow reflexively, tasting nothing but spit and his own thirst. "Then Stella

Grayson—she lives a quarter-mile down the road—found him on the kitchen floor and once she'd gotten him into bed, she called me in Chicago. He was so mad about that he wouldn't let her come back again and now no one will, because Uncle Andy aside, he doesn't have that many friends. Too outspoken to be popular or easy to get along with."

"You live in Chicago now?" Paul allowed his surprise to show. When they'd met in a Chicago club, Steve had told him that he was just visiting for the week. "I moved from there about three months ago. I used to work in the family clinic at Mercy Hospital."

He hadn't told Steve that two years ago. He hadn't told him anything but his first name and that he was a doctor.

"Yeah?" Steve tilted his head and stared at Paul for a moment, as if he was thinking about something. "So, what brings you here?"

"Cutbacks," Paul said succinctly.

"Not a problem I have," Steve said. "I'm self-employed. I restore old cars. Really old ones. We never got around to talking much, or I'd have probably bored you to death telling you about it."

"No, it sounds interesting," Paul said with a mendacious politeness.

"It is," Steve said and grinned, clearly not fooled. "You lie really badly, you know that? You fix bodies; I fix engines; not so different, really."

"No, but if I fail, someone dies; if you put a spark plug in upside down, well, you can always turn it right way up."

Steve shook his head, amusement brightening his eyes. "You really don't know much about cars, do you?"

"I know where to put the key and how to drive one; anything else, I get a mechanic to handle."

"Well, don't come to me," Steve said and flipped his hand dismissively at Paul's two-year old Mazda. "I don't fix anything that's younger than I am."

"Are there really that many people in Chicago with vintage cars?" Paul asked curiously. "I can't imagine you having many customers."

It was proving very easy to forget that Steve could expose him as gay with a single phone call to a friend and that there was an awkward conversation in front of him. Hazy though Paul's memories were, he could remember it being the same at that first meeting; within a few minutes, he'd felt as if he and Steve were old friends.

Steve smiled. "I moved to the city because it was more convenient, but most of my customers work in TV or the movies. People who need an old car for their 1920s mystery show or a mint version of a classic for something set in the fifties. I find what they need, make it run if I can, shine it up and ship it out. Some of my customers are collectors, but not many. Most collectors like to do the restoration work themselves; it's part of the fun."

"Oh." Paul readjusted his ideas. "Okay, that sounds more interesting, but it shouldn't really; you're still up to your elbows in grease, no matter how old the car is."

"Beats blood, shit, and vomit."

Paul grimaced. "True enough." He decided to change the subject. "Why was your grandfather so angry with Mrs. Grayson for calling you? I would have thought he'd want his family with him."

Steve picked at the label on the bottle and separated off a shred of paper that skated through the condensation as he pushed at it with a fingertip. "He didn't mind me coming; he likes me. We get on fine. He just thought I'd bring my dad with me." The look Paul got was bleak. "He needn't have worried. Dad said nearly dead wasn't enough to get him out here, and he wasn't coming for the funeral if he had something better to do, either." He drained the bottle in three long, slow swallows and then set it down on the porch floor. "My family isn't what you'd call close. Dad hasn't spoken to Granddad since Grandma died. She was the only one who could make them act halfway decent to each other."

"I'm not exactly flavor of the month with my family," Paul admitted, deliberately choosing to match Steve's frankness, partly to keep the conversation going, partly because he was so damn tired of keeping everything bottled up and buttoned down tight. It had been his choice to hide that he was gay in this small, rural town, but it didn't mean that he wasn't enjoying the time out, even if he'd pay for it later when Steve started asking him questions.

Steve raised his eyebrows. "You're a doctor; isn't that something they're proud of?"

"Oh, they liked my choice of profession," Paul said. "But they wanted me to be something splashy, something highly paid. They're not hurting for money themselves; Dad's a lawyer, Mom started up this decorating company as a hobby and it took off big-time. My sister and I are expected to match their successes. A clinic attached to a big hospital, well, they put up with that because they thought I'd make contacts, meet the right people... it didn't happen, because I didn't make it happen, and then came the cutbacks, and a lot of us were suddenly all looking for jobs..."

"I get it." Steve nodded. "So you came out here, to a small town, with no prospects, and they're pissed?"

"More or less," Paul said, the evasion tasting bitter on his tongue. There were limits to what he was willing to share. His parents hadn't been pleased, no, but they'd accepted his assurances that it was temporary and could be spun to look good when he returned to the city.

Finding out that he was gay, an impulsive disclosure a decade or more overdue and something he'd given up waiting for them to work out for themselves, had been the main reason they hadn't fought harder to get him to stay nearby. He'd never realized just how much they'd been waiting for grandchildren; he and his sister had always seemed like necessary annoyances in their lives, shuffled off to boarding schools and summer camps, so the desire to dangle winsomely smiling tots on their knees seemed odd.

Janet, his sister, might oblige them on that front in the future, but as she was a career-driven executive in New York, too busy to come home for the last three Christmases and two Thanksgivings, he couldn't really see her making time for offspring or visits to Chicago if she did get the urge to reproduce. He didn't even know if she was with someone; relationships were time-consuming, after all.

He loved her, loved all of them, but in a dutiful, distant way that didn't require any effort on his part. No turbulent emotions or dramatic scenes, of course; Paul's parents hadn't even bothered to yell at him when he'd told them he was gay. They'd just looked stunned, then disapproving, and had changed the subject with a cool finality, freezing him out of their conversations for the rest of his visit, made a week before moving to the country. The front door had closed before he'd gotten in his car, and he hadn't heard from them since, not even on his birthday.

Janet had taken the news with an impatient sigh when he'd called her. "Well, I knew that already, Paul, but I was hoping you'd—"

"Grow out of it? Come to my senses? Change my mind?"

"Don't be silly. I just hoped you'd never tell them, but I suppose that was too much to expect. You always were selfish that way. They didn't need to know. You could have kept taking women home as dates—how much did they cost you, by the way?—and kept it quiet."

"Forever? Hardly. I've lied for long enough. With a normal family, it wouldn't have worked for a month, let alone years. You do realize that?"

She'd chuckled at that, a flash of humor showing. "Brother, dear, we define normal; we don't talk, we don't share, we don't show weaknesses. For our parents, that's the perfect set of family dynamics."

"And I never paid any of my dates. They were just friends willing to do me a favor in return for a weekend away with some good food and a concert or party thrown in."

"If you say so." She yawned down the phone. "Okay, I'm dead. Have fun in Sleepy Hollow and call me, oh, whenever you get the chance. No rush."

"Sure thing, sis."

"Just don't call me that."

He'd grinned and mouthed it softly once more, just to annoy her, and heard a sharp click as she hung up. But she'd sent him a birthday card.

"Are you sure you don't want a beer?" Steve asked, breaking Paul's reverie. "I might even let you off the hook about digging up the past, seeing as talking won't change things."

"I have some questions," Paul said, feeling his heartbeat quicken. Two years of waiting to ask this..."Just why didn't you—"

"You know, let's forget it," Steve said firmly. "It's pretty quiet here, and some company would be nice. You're the first person besides Granddad that I've spoken to in days, and if we start talking about that night we'll end up yelling and we can't fuck our way back to being friends. So, I'll ask again: want a beer?"

Paul wanted to say yes. Wanted to take a beer from Steve's hand and sit here drinking it as the storm rolled in, getting to know the man the way he should have done before they'd fucked. Should have—but they hadn't been able to wait. They'd left the club after half an hour, and when Steve had flipped the lock on his hotel room door, they'd been naked in under a minute, slowed down only by the need to touch each other. He remembered whimpering with frustration, trying to get a sock off using his other foot, because his hands were cupping Steve's face, holding it still to be kissed.

And he wanted to make Steve answer his question, by force if needed.

Common sense vetoed either acceptance or starting an argument. The storms here were spectacular to watch but hell to drive in, and he didn't want to get caught on a dark road, rain sheeting down so heavily that he couldn't see through his windshield.

He was also getting worried about how easily Steve had gotten him to talk. Sure, Paul's biggest secret was something that Steve already knew about, but he wasn't sure that he trusted Steve's promise to let things slide, and he really wasn't sure he could keep his hands off Steve. His skin knew what that straight, dark hair felt like against it, cool like water, and he wanted to feel the heavy, dragging caress of Steve's hands again and to writhe under Steve, wanton and willing. God, there was nothing he wouldn't have done or allowed that night. Pure lust.

Everyone should have one night like that, and even though it'd had ended badly, he'd never regretted it—but it had only happened because he'd thought it was a one-off and he'd never see Steve again. He could do anything with a man who was going to walk out of his life forever in a few hours.

And now Steve had walked back in.

"I have to go back to town," Paul said. He stood, desperation forcing him to an ignominious retreat.

"Hot date?"

"No, no date." Paul licked his lips and tasted the salt of his own sweat. "I just want to, uh, take a shower and cool off. It's been a long day."

"Sorry," Steve said, the warmth gone from his voice. "Didn't mean to keep you." He stood and headed for the front door, not looking at Paul again, a rejection that stung more than it should have. "I'll call if Granddad gets worse."

Paul began to answer, but Steve gave a sudden, startled grunt of pain and lifted his right foot off the wide planks of the porch floor. "Goddamn it." He leaned against the wall of the house and, limber as a cat, stood on one leg, examining the sole of his foot. "Picked up a splinter."

"That's what happens when you have bare feet on wood."

Steve rolled his eyes. "Going to tell me not to run with scissors next, Doc?"

Paul ignored the sarcasm. "Sit down and I'll get it out for you."

"I think I can handle it," Steve said and poked at his foot which, Paul noted automatically, was bleeding, scarlet welling up sluggishly from the small rip in the skin. "It'll work its way out."

It was Paul's turn to roll his eyes. "It's an open wound, which means dirt can get in, and you've got a germ-ridden piece of wood embedded in your flesh, which means it already has. Hop over to the chair, sit down, and I'll get it out."

"How much will that set me back?"

"On the house," Paul said. "And don't be so rude."

"You've got a great bedside manner, you know that?" Steve said, managing to make hopping look graceful as he went back to his chair.

"I don't talk to my patients like this," Paul said as he opened his bag in search of gloves, tweezers, and disinfectant.

"If you start poking me, I am a patient."

Paul dragged the chair he'd been using close to Steve's and sat down. "I don't plan on poking you." He knew how it would sound when he said it, but he didn't care. Tiredness, the resurgence of memories, the prickling on his sweat-damp skin as the storm approached—they were combining to make him feel reckless.

Or maybe it was just the way Steve watched him, intent, appraising.

"So, is getting poked something I can make an appointment for?"

Time to close this down. Time to freeze up, hide behind a metaphoric white coat instead of sitting here, his expression naked, listening to the hurt and hope that lay behind Steve's clumsy flirting.

Paul pulled on a pair of gloves, the thin latex clinging to his skin, picked up Steve's foot without answering, and brought it up onto his knee, the weight of it reassuringly solid in the curve of his palm. The heel was roughened, but the nails were cut neatly. Paul tilted Steve's foot back and got a look at the sole, the residual buzz of arousal dying away as he saw the dark gray intruder that had been driven deep. Nothing of it protruded from the wound, so he was going to have to dig a little before he could use his tweezers.

"I always suck 'em out when they're in my fingers," Steve said. "Spit's antiseptic, right? A little bit of sucking does a body good, I say."

"It can be," Paul said evenly as he wiped the blood and dirt away from around the small wound, refusing to let his mind go where Steve's words were pointing. He took refuge in lecturing. "Saliva is mostly water, but it also contains proteins that can kill certain bacteria, which is why animals lick their wounds. I think you'd have trouble reaching your foot with your tongue, though, and although I might have to poke you, I don't plan on licking you."

Steve gave him a thoughtful look, his forehead furrowed. "Shame. I seem to remember I liked it when you—God, that hurt!"

"Don't be a baby," Paul said, and pressed his thumbnail against the buried end of the splinter again, trying to push it toward its point of entry. "I think there's enough showing for me to grab now. Hold still."

"You're enjoying this, aren't you?" Steve scowled and yelped at the first touch of the tweezers against his skin. "It would have come out by itself."

"Leaving you with a possible infection." Paul glanced up at him. "I had a patient once, a sweet old lady who loved gardening. She fell and got a rose thorn—just one—in her arm and didn't realize it was there. Blood poisoning. Arm swollen to twice its size. Nasty."

"Sounds like it. Was she okay?"

Paul tugged with infinite care at the splinter. He could have yanked it out, but if it broke...and part of him wanted to impress Steve, which, given that he was doing something any parent could do equally well, possibly with a screaming, hysterical child to deal with, was probably a lost cause.

"What? Oh, yes. Fine. But if I hadn't caught it in time...."

"Looks like I've had a narrow escape."

Paul finished extracting the splinter and held it up. Steve grinned. "Hey. Monster splinter. So was I brave, Doc?"

"I've had worse." He smiled. "If you were twenty years younger, this is when I'd offer you a sucker. I keep a few in my bag."

"How about we just make plans to meet up some time? I can persuade Granddad to let Stella back for a few hours or so. We could go for a drink, maybe...oh, you know what I want." Steve's hand covered Paul's for a moment, the brief touch enough to make Paul shiver. "Don't you?"

The air felt syrup-thick and sticky, hard to breathe when a storm was approaching, Paul thought, desperately holding onto that reason for the tightness in his chest. "I—I can't."

He stuck a Band-Aid on the sole of Steve's foot, working on autopilot and grateful for the excuse to look away from Steve's questioning gaze. "There."

"Why can't you?"

"I really have to go." Paul stood and tidied the supplies he'd used back into his bag with hands that were clumsy not through nerves, but need.

"No date. Okay. I get it." Steve thrust his hand through his hair, a gesture Paul remembered, and nodded, his mouth tight. "Will you come back to see Granddad? Or have I scared you off?"

A flash of anger that Steve would think him capable of deserting a patient steadied Paul's nerves. "If I'm needed, yes, of course I'll be back, and I'll make sure that I come by in the next few days. Here's my card; you'll be able to get in contact with me using those numbers. If he changes his mind about a nurse, let the clinic know and one will be sent out immediately."

Steve stared at him in silence and then nodded again. "Sure. See you."

He'd vanished back inside the house before Paul had opened the car door.

Driving away from the Parker home, Paul found himself gripping the steering wheel tightly enough to hurt his fingers in an attempt to stop that shaking in his hands. He was hard, sweating, hurting, desperately turned on by nothing more than the weight of Steve's foot in the cup of his hand and the heat and hunger in Steve's deep blue eyes.

Steve still wasn't his type.

It didn't matter; Paul knew that if he'd stayed there much longer and Steve had touched him again, even a prosaic handshake, he'd have signaled his availability loud and fucking clear. It'd be just as if they were back in that club, the lights low, the music loud, the room full of shadows to swallow them up.

"Stupid, stupid," he muttered aloud and struck the wheel sharply with the flat of his hand just as the thunder rolled overhead and the rain began.

Steve walked up the stairs, Paul's card tucked away in his pocket. He knew Paul's last name and phone number at least, which was more than he'd had before. He stood in the hallway and checked in on his grandfather. Matt was sleeping, a grayish pallor adding years to him, lying so still that Steve held his breath until he could be sure that his grandfather's chest was still rising and falling with the effort of breathing.

Everything was an effort for Matt now, the strong, vital man Steve idolized reduced to skin and bone, held together with an iron will that pain and weakness were rusting away.

Days. They only had days left together in this life, and Steve didn't much believe in another one. Hard to know how to deal with filling that short a span of time, and even harder to accept its brevity. Matt had, on one level at least. He spoke of his death as imminent and certain, and each time he did, it sounded more convincing.

Steve turned away and walked back downstairs to his chair on the porch, restless and more disturbed by the doctor's visit than he'd thought he would be. He'd been expecting bad news, and Paul had delivered that, flatly, coolly, with apparently only mild sympathy. Well, why should there be more than that? He didn't know Matt.

Bad news, yes, he'd been prepared for that, but meeting up with Paul again had been a shock. As had the instant renewal of an attraction strong enough to leave his skin feeling starved for a touch. When Paul's hand had closed around his foot, Steve had gotten a hard on that hadn't settled down until long after the dust Paul's car had stirred up had stopped drifting across the yard. Arousal had driven him to tease and push, something he wouldn't normally have done with someone as hostile and skittish as Paul. He knew that the attraction was still mutual, though. The look in Paul's eyes as he'd stood at the bottom of the porch steps staring up had given that secret away. You could hide a lot of things, but not that flash of heat when your gaze fell on something you wanted. Steve had felt warmed by it, his depression lifting for a short while.

He should have been happy just to have met Paul again, a meeting that he'd given up expecting to happen a long time ago, but he wasn't a man who was used to taking a pinch when he could fill his hands to overflowing with very little more effort. Something about Paul riled him up, spiced things up, and that wasn't just based on the memories of a one-night stand a couple of years ago. He wanted to muss the man's neatly combed hair, bite the severe line of Paul's lips swollen and soft, wanted to make the unconscious air of superiority melt away as his hands and mouth taught Paul how to forget he was a doctor and remember he was a man.

He recalled Paul's reaction to his job and snorted. He didn't know how much doctors made, but his business was doing just fine, thank you. In the last eight years, he'd built up both a reputation for being the best man to go to in his field and a nationwide network of spotters to locate spare parts. The Internet was a godsend, but sometimes you needed someone to dive into the mountain of metal at a scrap yard and mine it for gold in person. Steve paid well and got results and still did plenty of mining himself. There was nothing like the thrill of satisfaction when you found a heap of rust and saw it for what it could be, or spotted a small, obscure, original part to replace a modern stopgap. Steve wasn't rich, but he hadn't wasted his earnings on a big, empty house full of fancy furniture or any other status symbols, and he wasn't hurting for cash. He'd intended to use his savings to get his grandfather the best care possible, and there'd been a bed waiting for Matt at, ironically, Paul's former hospital.

Matt had heard him out as Steve outlined the plans for getting him to that bed, and then he'd shaken his head and said, "No," and kept on saying it until Steve had been forced to accept it.

Stubborn old man, but Steve loved his grandfather, and when he loved, he did it wholeheartedly. His father was the same when it came to hating, which was why Steve wasn't looking down the long driveway leading up to the house and expecting to see his old man's truck bumping along it.

He wouldn't mind seeing Paul's car, though, or more of Paul. More of him in every sense; more time spent with him; more to see than the little a suit and shirt revealed, which wasn't much. Steve wanted to peel the stiff, hot clothes off Paul in a dimly lit room with a fan stirring the humid air to a fleeting coolness, watch Paul's nipples harden, cinnamon brown smudges darkening as he bit them and shaped them to points with his tongue. He had plans for Paul's body and a head full of memories to match against an imperfectly recalled reality. His hand could curve as if it was wrapped around the solid thrust of Paul's dick, but after all this time, Steve wasn't sure if he was remembering it as thicker than it really was. He'd like to check his facts.

He sat until the first raindrops pattered down and then went to stand in the open and tilt his face up to catch them. He'd been read a poem at school once that had called rain "God's tears", which had to be the stupidest idea ever. Tears were hot salt and sadness; rain, clean, cool rain like this, was pure joy.

He started to shiver as his clothes got wet and heavy and the thunder announced the true arrival of the storm. It felt good to have his skin prickle up into goose bumps, and if he hadn't been in his grandfather's yard, if he'd been deep in the woods, alone, he might have stripped down and felt the rain drive into his skin and wash over him.

Wash all his sadness away. Grief at the imminent loss of his grandfather and a different sorrow that he'd met Paul again and it hadn't gone the way he'd planned it in a score of imagined scenarios. They'd all ended with Paul fervent and apologetic, explaining exactly what had happened with a perfectly reasonable excuse for not calling and Steve cutting Paul off with a kiss, his hands busy.

Paul had turned him into a fucking romantic and broken his heart in the process. Good going considering he'd only had a night to do it in and Steve was generally a fuck 'em and walk away kind of man. Simpler that way, he'd always thought, and by God, he'd been right.

Nothing about his sex life had been simple after Paul. It wasn't that he'd been obsessed with Paul; truthfully, he'd doubted that they'd ever meet again, resigned himself to that probability. It was just that the sex with every man he'd been with since had been held up against the way

Steve had felt fucking Paul and none of the encounters had measured up to that night.

None.

Some had come close, maybe; he'd met a few great guys, hot, amusing, one of them into racing cars, which had given them something in common. He'd seen Jake off and on for a couple of months before realizing that neither of them was getting as much out of it as they had at the start.

Maybe that would have happened with Paul, too, but he'd have liked to have had the chance to find out, damn it. Resentment, thick and bitter, rose to choke him. Paul had left him wanting, spoiled him for anyone else, and then walked up to him a score of months later and treated him like a stranger.

And Steve still wanted the man.

It looked like stubborn and stupid ran in his family.

Paul sank down deeper in the bathtub and let the hot water scald his skin scarlet and tingling. He'd taken a quick shower when he'd gotten back from the clinic to cool down, his ears still burning from Raines' less than complimentary assessment of his actions at the Parker farm. The shower cleaned away the sweat and grime, but he couldn't think with water pounding and hissing around him. He ate, drank the beer he'd promised himself, and watched TV for an hour, letting the images and voices flow past him.

Then he'd lain on his bed and listened to the water pour into the bathtub, waiting for the sound it made to change, warning him that it was close to full. The silence when he twisted the faucet closed, the air empty of sound, was like a blow, as intense as the heat when he slid into the water. His skin prickled as if he was in a winter wind, and his breath had been taken for an instant. It hurt and he loved it.

Another beer was in his hand, ice-cold and so damn easy to swallow, and he sipped it and thought about Steve in disjointed flashes, unable to organize his thoughts into anything resembling a logical progression. Steve and he seemed doomed to be ships passing in the night. When Matt died, Steve would return to Chicago, just as after the night they'd spent together; Steve had come back here, to Branchton, and left Paul in the city.

Looked at one way, that was good; Steve had more to think about than outing Paul to the town and, really, Paul didn't think that Steve would be that petty.

Except—fuck, Steve didn't know that Paul wasn't out. Why would he? They'd met at the Oasis, and that wasn't a club that made any secret about its preferred clientele. Paul had been there with two colleagues from work, and he'd all but crawled into Steve's lap in front of them.

In and out of the closet; Paul was used to flipping back and forth. Out at work; straight for his parents for all those years; it hadn't been too difficult a decision to pose as straight for his time in Branchton. There was always the city, a ninety-minute drive away, if he needed to stop pretending for a while.

It occurred to him that maybe Steve was the same; maybe he'd gone to Oasis to blow off steam in a way he couldn't in this small town where everyone knew everything about everyone—or thought they did.

He set the bottle down on the tiled ledge that ran around the deep corner bath and sank under the water. The world turned distant, muted, water sloshing in his ears, lub-dubbing like a heartbeat. Too many what-ifs, too much worrying. All that he had to do was tell Steve— ask Steve—

"Beg me."

"What?" Paul had laughed and heard it shred to a whimper as Steve's hand slid down lower until it caged Paul's cock and balls without touching them. His head had been against the wall but his hips had arched futilely, hopefully. "Oh, fuck, you tease, you fucking tease—"

"Won't tease if you beg me not to." Steve licked a line across Paul's lips, a flick of soft, wet warmth. "I'll do anything you want me to if you just—"

"Beg?" Paul said, his hands clutching at Steve's ass.

"Say 'please' for me," Steve murmured. "Say it and tell me what you want, and I'll do it. I'll do it for you. I'll do anything."

Drunk enough to be reckless, to be seeing the world with a deceptive clarity, Paul caught his breath. "God, you sound like you mean that."

Steve's other hand stroked the back of Paul's neck before clasping it, thumb moving in slow circles behind Paul's ear, each completed circle sending shocks of pleasure through his body. "You know I do."

"I don't do this."

"Be specific. You're doing lots of things right now, Doc. Breathing—panting, really—squirming, oh, yeah, lots of that, but it's not getting you very far, is it? What 'this' are we talking about?"

"The 'this' when I pick up a stranger and go to his room. The 'this' when—shit, that's hard to say." Paul's lips felt numb from vodka and kisses. "The' this'," he said again experimentally and snickered at how it sounded.

Steve kissed him with a mouth that curved in a smile after a moment, which ended the kiss, both of them laughing quietly.

"I don't do it often, either," Steve said. "Too risky. Too...cold. But I do it when I need it and God, I need you."

"Why me?"

"Because you're different, because—" Steve shook his head, and strands of his long, dark hair struck Paul's face, soft whips driving him onward toward...something, somewhere. "Damned if I know. No, wait. Because if I didn't bring you back here, I'd have gone on my knees right there in the club and sucked you, and somehow I don't think they'd have let me do that."

"The Oasis?" Paul considered it, but regretfully

decided that Steve was right. "Maybe not."

"But I can do it here," Steve said and slid down to his knees, his hands planted against the wall, on either side of Paul's hips. Paul looked down as Steve shook the fall of hair back from his face and stared up, blue eyes shining. "All you have to do is…"

"Please," Paul whispered, his hands light as snow on that dark, silk hair, his fingers brushing over Steve's parted lips. "Please suck me."

Paul hadn't known at the time who'd been giving the orders and who was obeying them, and he wasn't sure he knew now.

Now, he jerked off in the bath, his eyes open, seeing not the steam-filled bathroom but that cheap hotel room, until his come spilled out, white on his red skin, clouding the clear water. It didn't take long. He'd been hard, off and on, since he'd seen Steve; holding off until now had been the challenge, but he'd wanted to make himself wait.

Steve had made him wait hours to come, until he'd been sobbing, his fists striking the bed in an agony of frustration, tears squeezing out from tightly shut eyes. He could have made it all stop with just that word, got Steve to finish him off any way Paul chose, but Steve was doing so much to him, everything Paul told him—asked him—to and it had all felt so good…

Paul never wanted it to end, even as his heart hammered in his chest as if he'd run for miles, his skin tender, awake, alive, raw and new because no one had ever touched him or kissed him the way Steve had.

It would end when he came; he knew that. Steve had told him so in a lull as they caught their breath, lying beside him on the wide bed, his hand locked in Paul's. "It's a pain in the ass, but I've got to see someone tomorrow; it's why I'm here in Chicago. The room's mine until eleven, so use it until then, but I've got to meet him at seven, because he's got a flight to catch."

"Seven?" Paul squinted at the bedside clock. "'S'already

three…"

"I can sleep any time. I can only fuck you tonight."

"No." Paul shook his head. "You can fuck me any time. Any time. Any, any, any time you like. Please."

"How can you be getting drunker and not sobering up?" Steve smiled at him and rolled over, one leg heavy across Paul's. "God, you're so fucking hot, you know that? Want you so fucking much, want to take you or bend over for you, again and again—"

"But we only have time to do it once."

Steve nodded. "You'll crash when you come," he said regretfully. "Out like a light. I'm making you feel good now, though, aren't I, Doc?"

"Doctor Feelgood," Paul said and chuckled. "But I don't do drugs. I just hand them out. Make other people feel good."

"You make me feel good." Steve's hand was touching Paul's cock, firm, strong strokes now. "Fuck me? Please?"

"I thought I was the one who had to say 'please'…" The room was turning fuzzy around the edges, but Steve's hand—oh, he could feel that—

"Then say it." Steve's voice was as urgent as the movement of his hand, as if somewhere the final grains of sand were falling out of an hourglass. "Ask if you can fuck me and let me tell you yes—"

And he'd asked, and Steve had answered, and he'd pushed slowly into that tight space, watching Steve's eyes for a flinch of pain or rejection that never came, and felt it accept him; listened to Steve's breath turn ragged and understood why Steve had made them both wait, because this was worth waiting for. Each thrust, each withdrawal, had left him shaking with an arousal that sober he might have shied away from, but drunk he was brave enough to submit to.

He'd come and felt every muscle lock, heard the sounds they were both making, inarticulate, incoherent, involuntary. Words weren't needed. There was nothing he had to say to Steve with Steve's come wet on his belly and their mouths on each other, biting, not to hurt, but to mark, to claim, that Steve didn't already know.

And then, as Steve had told him he would, Paul had fallen asleep. He'd been barely aware of a fumbled clean-up and the room being plunged into darkness, his awareness fading fast, Steve's arm draped across him, warm and heavy.

The next morning, he'd woken alone, with a hangover that had lingered all day. He showered and dressed and left Steve his phone number on the table in the room, but no name, discretion returning with sobriety.

Steve hadn't called him. Paul was too old to wait by the phone like a teenager, lovelorn and desperate, or check his cell obsessively to make sure it was turned on, too proud to go back to Oasis week after week, or bribe the hotel for Steve's last name or address. He gave it a week, two weeks, and then found someone to fuck him, slam-bam, no waiting, no kissing, no connection but skin on skin.

It had felt like dragging his hand over a still-wet painting and smearing it irrevocably, but what the fuck was he supposed to do? Stay faithful to a memory of a man he'd picked up for a single night? Stay celibate?

Hed convinced himself that the alcohol had fuzzed his brain and the impression he'd had of something, oh, hell, something special between them, had been both maudlin and mistaken. After a while, he'd even forgiven Steve, or thought he had until he'd seen the man again today.

It had been really difficult to remember that he was a doctor on duty when all he wanted to do was pin Steve against the nearest wall. To make him admit that the night they'd spent together had been pretty fucking fantastic, and that walking away from it had been the biggest mistake Steve had ever made.

He got out of the lukewarm bath and toweled off, then went to lie on his bed, the overhead fan cooling his damp skin and making him shiver with pleasure.

Maybe Steve had had a good reason for not calling. Maybe they could sort things out, meet up somewhere safe. Paul stared down at his cock, hardening again, hopeful, blindly optimistic. He slapped at it moodily and winced, not at the fleeting sting, but at the jolt of arousal that flashed through him. He had the feeling that he was going to be jerking off a lot in the next few days.

The phone rang, the insistent clamor of the bedside phone echoed faintly by the one downstairs.

"Doctor Jackson speaking."

"Paul? It's Steve." There was a tremor in Steve's voice as if he was holding back panic. "Can you come back here? Please? Granddad's—he's—shit, Paul. He's dying."

Paul stood and began to dress one-handed, a skill he'd learned over the years. "Call 911 and get an ambulance out there. I'll go directly to the hospital. I'll be waiting there and I'll make sure—"

"He won't go."

"What? No! He has to, Steve, I know he wanted to stay at home, but—"

"He'll never forgive me if I do that."

"Well, if he's dead, it won't matter," Paul snapped. He took a deep breath. "I'm sorry. It's just that he needs to go there or his chances aren't good."

"He's dying," Steve said flatly. "And I promised him he'd do it here, on his land, in his home. I gave him my word. I called you because you gave me your number and you seemed to understand what he wanted."

"I want to see you again, I really do, but I don't want— no pressure, okay? Just…call me."

"Don't know your name. Don't know your number."

Steve chuckled, and Paul felt something scratch at his back, lines drawn on skin. "There. Now you do."

Paul clutched at the phone, Steve's voice distant in his ear, the memory too vague for him to be sure it was real and not a dream. It didn't matter; his patient did. "I'm coming over."

"Thank you." Steve swallowed, the sound audible.

"I've got to go."

Paul hung up and began to dial 911 himself and then changed his mind and dialed Andrew Raines instead. Paul finished getting dressed as Raines' sister went to wake him from a post-supper nap, the rain drumming insistently against the windows.

"Get over there," Raines told him. "I'll join you as soon as I can. Matt's not going to keep me away from him now. No, don't call by for me; there isn't time. I'll get Susan to take me. Ambulance? Son, are you deaf? He doesn't want to die in a hospital bed, and you and I both know that's what will happen. It's his time and his decision. Now, go."

Driving was a nightmare of poor visibility and rain-slick roads, high winds buffeting the car. Paul found himself hunched over the wheel, straining to see past the frantically whipping wiper blades. Once he was outside the town, the unlit, flooded roads reduced him to a crawl, and he couldn't help wondering how Susan Raines would cope. He crossed the bridge over the river that wound past the town and felt it shudder under his tires. The sky lit up from time to time with bolts of lightning and the thunder was a near constant background noise.

If ever there was a night to be home with a drink and a few candles lit, snuggled up to someone on the couch, this was it. Not that Paul had ever done that, but it was a pleasant image to hold in his head as he skidded in the mud and fought to keep his car on the road and out of the ditch.

The power hadn't gone out at the Parker place, which was something. Steve had every light in the house blazing out a welcome, and Paul felt something tight in his gut relax as he pulled up in front of the porch, as if he'd reached a refuge.

He didn't knock; Steve wouldn't have heard him over the wailing howl of the storm, anyway. He took the stairs quickly, his bag in his hand, water dripping from his hair, because even the short sprint from car to porch had gotten him wet.

Steve was kneeling beside the bed, Matt's hand in his, his face contorted with grief. Paul walked over to him and put a comforting hand on his shoulder, attention focused mostly on his patient. Matt was unconscious, not asleep, his labored breathing the loudest sound in the room.

Steve turned his head, his eyes dull. "He was fine. After you went, he woke up and we talked. He wasn't hungry, but he had some juice. I went to make myself a sandwich and when I came back he was just slumped over the bed and he wouldn't—I couldn't make him hear me—"

"I'm sorry," Paul said gently. "Dr. Raines is on his way over, too, and we'll do all we can."

Steve nodded, his expression still dazed. "Okay. Sure. Is there—what do you need?"

"Space to work," Paul said. He ran his hand over his head. "And a towel?"

Steve nodded again and got to his feet. As he left the room, his hand caught at Paul's arm. "Thanks."

Paul put his hand over Steve's for a moment and felt its warmth seep into him. "I'll do everything I can," he said.

It wasn't enough. Raines called an hour after Paul arrived, his voice tight with the same grief that had reduced Steve's voice to a husky murmur, to tell Paul that the road was washed out and their car had slid inexorably into a tree, luckily within a quarter-mile of a friend's house where they were staying the night. He listened in silence as Paul told him that Matt was slipping away and not likely to regain consciousness. Paul had waited for a response and finally Raines had said quietly, "I see," and hung up after trying and failing to control his voice long enough to finish passing a message on to Steve.

Matt's time was drawing to a close. Paul worked to save him, by candlelight after the power went out, the uncertain light flickering as the wind found its way into the house. In the end, there was nothing he could do. Stimulants failed to have an effect, and the once-strong body felt frail and light under his hands.

Steve made him stop trying in the early hours of the morning, when the storm had blown out.

"Let him go."

"He's my patient. I can't just—"

"Let him go," Steve said with finality lending his tired voice power. "Please, Paul."

Paul wiped his hand across his mouth and noticed that it was shaking. He was exhausted, his head buzzing, his eyes gritty. He was conscious of being overwhelmingly thirsty, though Steve had brought him coffee at some point. He stared at the mug on the bedside table, still full.

"There's nothing I can do anyway," he said and went to lean against a wall, the plaster cool and smooth against his back through the thin shirt he wore.

Matt moved, then turned his head slightly, the smallest of movements, and Paul, through the haze of tiredness dimming his vision, saw Matt die. Unmistakable, that final breath, that exhale as the body went limp and still. Training and instinct made him spring forward, a febrile energy surging through him, but Steve warded him off with an upraised hand and then sank to his knees by the bed, his head bowed, not in prayer, but grief.

Paul had barely spoken to Steve in the hours they'd spent in this small room. Brief words of reassurance or instruction that Steve had accepted with a passivity even their short acquaintance told Paul wasn't like him. Paul didn't know what to say now. In the face of a grief and personal loss he'd never had to endure himself, he was tongue-tied.

"I'm so sorry," he whispered into the quietness that filled the room. "Steve—"

Steve stood without looking at Paul and stumbled from the room, his hands outstretched as if he was blind. The power had come back on an hour earlier, but the candles still burned, golden patches of light against the dark walls. Paul blew them out and automatically noted the time of death.

Then he did what was needed to the shell of Matt's body and drew the sheet up over the still, empty face.

Paul came out onto the porch, but didn't speak. Steve supposed he should feel grateful for that, but every emotion felt trapped behind glass, unreachable. Grief, guilt, loss: he wanted to feel them tear apart the numbness, turn the world colored again, instead of the sepia vagueness swimming in front of his eyes.

Nothing.

"He only had me there," he said and felt tears, hot and stinging, well up. "No friends, no children...just me."

"He had you," Paul said, and the words splintered the glass. "He wasn't alone."

"I wasn't enough!" He turned and saw Paul standing framed in the doorway, brown hair, brown eyes, like one of the photographs hanging in the parlor, but unlike them, not washed-out and faded, but warmly vital. All that Steve had to do was walk over to the man and Paul would hug him, hold him. Even with all that lay between them, Steve knew that Paul would give him that comfort. He'd seen the decency in Paul during the long night. It was an old-fashioned word, and it felt odd to use it with regard to a man who'd featured solely in his fantasies before today, but it fit. Paul had fought to save Matt without once blaming Steve for not overriding Matt's wishes and having him admitted to a hospital or complaining that he was tired and working under difficult conditions. Steve guessed if he'd thanked Paul, he would have gotten a surprised look and been told that it was Paul's job, and maybe it was, but it didn't change how grateful Steve felt.

"He deserved more than that. They'll all be at his funeral, yeah, even Dad; he cares too much about what people think to stay away, but he won't know that they're there; it won't help."

"He wouldn't have known that they were there last night," Paul said bluntly. "Does that help?"

"No!" Steve felt his heart hammering so hard it scared him, anger and adrenaline rushing through him as the sky began to lighten, pale and gray, a few clouds scudding across it, wisps of white. "And it won't make Uncle Andy feel better either. God, I can't believe Granddad wouldn't let him come out here so that they could tell each other goodbye."

"I wish Dr. Raines had come anyway."

"So do I."

They stared at each other, and then Paul took a tentative step forward. "Steve?"

"Oh, God," Steve choked out and felt himself start to cry, helpless, pointless tears. He closed his eyes and listened to Paul close the short distance between them, Paul's footsteps soft and fast like rain.

Being hugged felt better than he deserved. He rested his forehead on Paul's shoulder, Paul's hair tickling his ear, and was embraced, gentle hands stroking his back. He waited for words, but they didn't come; just an endearingly clumsy series of kisses at intervals, placed on his cheek and in his hair.

Crying didn't really help. He sniffed wetly, raised his hand to swipe at his eyes, and then eased back. Paul produced a handful of tissues and tactfully looked away as Steve used them.

"Fuck," Steve said tiredly.

"I should—I need to make calls."

"What? Oh, yeah. Sure." Steve nodded, the effort of lifting his head back up immense. He'd pulled plenty of all-nighters in the past, but he'd never done it sober; weariness was making him feel physically sick, but he knew that if he lay down he'd just keep seeing Matt's face as the light left it. "Granddad had it all arranged and paid for. Funeral home, service…"

"Is there anyone you'd like me to call?" Paul took out

his cell and then glanced at his watch and shook his head. "Damn. I hadn't realized—it's too early, but later I could notify the funeral home for you if you need to speak to your family."

"My dad's the last person I want to talk to," Steve said and felt a savage anger rise. Good. He wanted someone to feel mad at, someone to attack. "He left his own father to die like that because of a hundred stupid arguments over the years they've had, and as far as I'm concerned, he's blown it. He's had his chance. If he wants to come to the funeral and pretend to be sad, let him, but today, no, he's not coming here today, not to Granddad's home."

"Okay," Paul said entirely too reasonably. "Then why don't you go and rest and I'll—"

"No!"

Paul sighed. "You're stubborn, you know that? Fine. Stay awake until you pass out; I'll catch you when you do." He glanced over Steve's shoulder and his eyes widened. "Holy shit, the storm did some damage."

Steve gave the flooded fields and branch-scattered road an indifferent look. "Yeah."

"I hope that the road's clear."

Something about that rubbed Steve raw, and he lashed out without thinking, clinging to the chance to argue as an alternative to retreating back into that awful grayness. "Why? So that you can go back to town and tell everyone how dumb Matt Parker was for choosing to stay in his home when a hospital could have saved him? Or are you glad he died, because it means you're spared having to see me again?"

Paul pursed his lips. "You know, you're being an asshole. I'm going to let you get away with it, because I'm too tired to fight and because you're hurting, but, for the record? Asshole."

"You left me waiting!" Steve stabbed his finger into Paul's chest. "I didn't even rate a call to tell me thanks, but you weren't interested in a repeat? Easier, cleaner, to just pretend I didn't exist? And that lie about not doing it before; the hell you didn't! I can't believe I fell for that one."

Paul's face was frowning, irritation and bewilderment fighting for first place. "What? I was telling the truth! You were the first man I ever picked up in a bar—a complete fucking stranger, for God's sake—and went home with. Everyone else I'd slept with, I knew, or we'd been on a few dates. And how could I call you? You didn't leave me a number, you stupid son of a bitch."

"Yes, I—"

"But I left you mine," Paul said, ignoring Steve's protest. "I left a note, right on the bed, my number, and, yeah, just my first name, but, still, it was all you needed to get in touch with me, all you needed to know that I was interested in seeing more of you."

"You left me your number," Steve said flatly. "On a bed in a room I'd checked out of and wasn't going back to? That bed? That room?"

"What? No, wait, you said you had a meeting..." Paul gave Steve a pleading look. "You didn't say you weren't coming back."

Steve exhaled. "God, you were so fucking out of it, I'm surprised you even remember that much," he muttered. "I left, yes, paid my bill and asked them to let you sleep. Cost me a twenty-dollar tip, but it was worth it."

"Sex with me was worth—" Paul flushed red. "You arrogant—"

"No," Steve told him tersely. "It was worth it to let you sleep it off. You looked as if you were going to wake up with a hangover, and I—I tried to wake you to say goodbye and you just grunted, and, man, you were talking, but your brain wasn't connected."

"Oh." Paul had the grace to look apologetic. "Sorry." His mouth tightened. "So why didn't you leave me your number?"

Steve closed his eyes for a moment. "You have a romantic impulse and it's about the only one ever, and you'd think that would be a hint that you suck at them, wouldn't you?"

"You're not making any sense."

"I wrote it on your back. In pen. Backward writing, so you could see it in a mirror." Steve took a deep breath. "I even added a fucking X for a kiss at the end, that's how goddamned mellow I was feeling, okay?"

"You wrote on my back?" Paul said incredulously. "You wrote your phone number on my—"

"Yes! On your back! And you grinned into the pillow and wriggled your ass as I was doing it, and I spent the next month worrying that you thought the three in the middle was an eight or something because you made me smudge it doing that."

"That has to be the single most stupid thing I have ever heard." Paul shook his head. "I got—no, I crawled—out of bed, peed sitting down because the room was spinning, and threw up in the sink. Then I showered, oddly enough without studying my body for cryptic messages, though I had one hell of a hickey on my neck, and I imagine you can work out the rest." He eyed Steve, his head tilted to the side, a mannerism Steve found himself remembering. "Thanks for the glass of water by the bed, though; that helped. Well, I threw it up five minutes after drinking it, but still."

"You're welcome." Steve felt his world tilt and shift with the new information he'd had thrown at him. "So, you would have called me?"

Paul nodded. "Sure. I'd have maybe left it a day or two in case you thought I was being pushy, and to recover from the hangover, but I wanted to see you again. Really wanted to."

"Me, too." Steve sighed. "A month ago, I'd have been ecstatic to find out you weren't the bastard I thought you were, even if it did mean discovering I'm an idiot, but right now..."

"If you mean you want to pick up where we left off, I can't," Paul said and sounded regretful. "Not here. In fact, as we're discussing it, I'd, well, I'd appreciate it if you'd keep it to yourself that I'm gay."

"What?"

"I'm not out here," Paul clarified. "No one in town knows, apart from you."

"Well, I'm out and no one's tarred and feathered me." Steve grimaced. "My dad wanted to when he found out, but Granddad stopped him. That was one of their more spectacular arguments. I ended up living here for six months until Dad got over himself."

"God, how old were you?"

"Sixteen. Old enough to have a crush and to know it was on the cheerleader's boyfriend, not Sally, cute though she was."

"And people didn't care?" Paul sounded skeptical, and Steve felt a flash of irritation.

"Living in the city doesn't automatically make you broadminded and tolerant, any more than living in a small town makes you conservative and prejudiced. Stop generalizing. Sure, Branchton's never going to have a Pride Parade, but it's got two openly gay teachers at the high school, and I can point you at a few couples living together who might keep up the appearances of separate bedrooms, but everyone knows…and mostly, nobody cares. They're part of the town. Like me. I grew up around here, people know me, and when I came out, sure, I got hassled, but no more than I could handle."

"You're saying I'd have got the job even if I'd been up-front about it?"

"I'm saying exactly that," Steve told him. "But telling people now, months later…that's not going to go down well. Young, good-looking, single? You're probably on a lot of 'hunt down and seduce' lists."

Paul smiled, amusement reshaping the lines that exhaustion had drawn on his face. "I am. You have no idea how many."

"I wouldn't count on that. I could probably guess the names. And for what it's worth?" Steve stepped closer and ran a single finger down the side of Paul's face, tracing the line of his jaw, rough-edged with stubble. "You're still on mine."

He was going to kiss Paul, and Paul was going to let him. Two years of wanting that mouth under his, two years of fighting to hold onto every single fucking memory, and now he could start to make new memories. The hell with Paul's fears about people finding out he was gay here and the lies he'd told to fool them, because they didn't matter when Paul's eyes were telling Steve all he needed to know about what Paul really wanted.

Steve brought the palm of his hand up to cradle Paul's face, a light caress, as undemanding as he could make it, because he didn't want this to be rough and hot the way it had been the first time, not with the sun rising on a world empty of a man who'd been more of a father than a grandfather to him.

Steve wanted sweet, wanted gentle. He hoped to God it didn't start him leaking tears again, but it would be worth it. He got a moment when Paul's lips were kind against his, Paul's hand threaded through his hair, tugging him closer, and then Steve heard the muted sound of a car engine and Paul jumped back like a startled rabbit, wiping his mouth guiltily.

"Relax," Steve said and couldn't keep the sarcasm out of his voice. "We're not in sight of the road until they come around the corner; your reputation's safe."

He walked off the porch and toward the approaching car and left Paul waiting, irresolute, behind him at the house. Uncle Andy deserved to be told that he was too late to say goodbye without his junior partner watching him fight for composure.

In the three weeks since Matt Parker had died, Paul had seen Steve just twice. Once at the funeral, standing beside a man who looked enough like him that discovering he was Steve's father, Michael, was no surprise. Once on the sidewalk, talking to a redhead with long legs and a sweetly predatory smile, as Paul drove by. Paul knew her. Teresa had come onto him hot and strong at a fundraiser for the local theater and had pouted at him when he'd turned her down, her eyes cool and appraising. He'd exchanged some polite, meaningless words with Steve at the funeral, conscious of the many watching eyes—and slowed to a crawl in the street, his eyes on Steve's back, until the impatient honk of a horn brought him to his senses.

He'd learned, without needing to ask a single question—people in town liked to talk and this was prime news—that Matt had left Steve his house, and that Steve was living out there and planning to build some garages for "those old cars of his" and renovate the house in his spare time. Opinion was divided on whether he'd stick around long after living in the city with all that it had to offer, and united in condemnation of Steve's father for holding onto his grudge for so long.

Paul was chagrined to discover that Steve had been more or less accurate when he said the town didn't care if Steve was gay. He overheard some pursed-lip tutting, and at least one person trotted out some dog-eared Biblical references to back up his belief that Steve was going to burn in hell. Mostly, though, the people who mentioned the subject appeared less interested in the gender of Steve's dates, which for them was a given, than the identity of the next one.

The gossip got more oblique at that point, laden with references to people Paul didn't know, voices lowered, but he heard enough to recognize that at least one of Steve's exes—not counting him—was still in town and available.

The redhead's brother, in fact; Cal Trent, which had come as a surprise to Paul, who hadn't realized that Cal was gay. Cal owned a restaurant on Sallis Street, diner food with a modern twist. It was generally busy, and Paul had eaten there a few times without ever seeing Cal, who was involved in the managerial side rather than doing any of the cooking. They'd exchanged a few words at the Fourth of July picnic, but that was all. Cal had been with a party of good-looking, well-off people, male and female, and hadn't spent long making nice before driving off in a car that Paul guessed Steve wouldn't be impressed by, all flash and red paint.

If Paul was surprised that Cal was gay, he was even more surprised that Steve had fallen for the guy. Even if he'd been out, Paul would have turned Cal down. Cal was good-looking, but there was a lemon-twist of arrogance souring his smile that grated on Paul. To be fair to the man, if Cal had his suspicions about the way Paul leaned following Paul's rejection of his sister's offer, he'd kept them to himself. Or maybe Paul just wasn't on his radar.

Twice in three weeks. Paul felt Steve's proximity like an itch he couldn't scratch. Blindfolded and spun around, he felt he could have still pointed unerringly to the Parker farm—assuming Steve was there and not with Cal, that was.

He'd had the vague idea that they could be friends, could meet and chat casually, maybe even go out for a meal sometimes, or travel into the city together—but that was starting to seem as unrealistic as an open relationship had been. It just wouldn't work. The stab of longing he felt when he saw Steve told him that.

All or nothing, and for now, it had to be nothing.

"Matt was like a father to Steve." Andrew was talking about his friend, not Steve, the stoic silence of the last few weeks crumbling as he came to terms with the fact that he would never see Matt again, but Paul was still guiltily hungry for any mention of Steve's name.

"He—Steve, I mean—said that he'd lived with Matt for a while."

Andrew's eyes narrowed. "He told you that? When?"

"We were there all night, remember," Paul said, the evasion plain to his ears at least. "I find that people open up in times of—"

"Did he tell you why?"

Paul licked his lips nervously. "He came out. To his family. Matt was the only one who was supportive."

"Ah." Andrew leaned back in his chair. "So you know he's gay."

Paul nodded and felt the need to unburden himself. "Dr. Raines—"

"You can call me by my name." Andrew gestured around the small room the clinic provided for its staff. It was shabby, furnished with couches that had seen years of use and tables decorated with rings, but the coffeepot was always kept full of fresh coffee and a tin beside it was kept filled with homemade cookies. There was a coffee fund, but Paul had bypassed the hassle of weekly donations and silently handed over fifty dollars to the receptionist, Sue, which he figured covered him for the rest of the year. "No one here to get shocked by your lack of respect for an elder and better."

It would have been easy to smile, but Paul wasn't entirely sure that Andrew was joking. "There's something I want to tell you."

"Not that you want to leave, I hope? I've just gotten it into your head that you're not God, and I'm enjoying the new, more humble you."

"Leaving? No. Unless…" Paul swallowed. "Unless you want me to after I tell you."

Apprehension gleamed in Andrew's eyes. "I'm a doctor, not a priest or a policeman; save your confessions for them."

"I haven't done anything wrong," Paul told him. "And I haven't lied to you, well, not exactly."

"A sin of omission?"

"Something like that."

"Let me save you stammering and trying not to shock

me; you're gay, too?"

Paul felt that he should have guessed that Andrew would know already. It was hard to get anything past him. "Yes. I thought that you wouldn't approve and wouldn't hire me if you knew and I, well, I wanted to work here."

"Young man, you're an idiot," Andrew said with a certain satisfaction plain in his voice. In the few months that Paul had know the man, he'd discovered that there was little Andrew liked as much as being able to point that fact out to a fellow human being. "If I rejected you on those grounds, you could have sued me for discrimination."

"I wouldn't have done that," Paul said flatly.

Andrew patted the table with his hand; his version of an apology. "I know, sonny, I know. Well, now that you're gotten that off your chest, I'll stop telling women who ask that you're available, hmm?"

"You've been doing that?"

"From time to time when you were particularly annoying, yes."

"Please stop," Paul said, and couldn't hold back a glare. "I can get my own dates, thanks."

"Be careful," Andrew cautioned him. "I wouldn't want you to run away with the idea that everyone's as broad-minded as I am." He rubbed his chin. "If it comes to that, I'm not really, either; I just like Steve too much to care who puts a twinkle in his eye, and it doesn't seem fair to treat anyone else differently just because I don't know them."

"I knew Steve before I came here," Paul blurted out.

Andrew blinked at him in silence, which was all the encouragement Paul needed to continue.

"We met in a club two years ago, spent the night together, and then we—we lost touch. Seeing him that day at the farm was...I never expected to see him again, and there he was. It was like—"

"Spare me the details of your heart going pitter-pat," Andrew interrupted. "You? You're that Paul? My God."

"Steve told you about me?" Paul felt the top of his ears

go hot. "You? What did he say?"

"He didn't tell me the lurid details—I'm assuming it did get lurid? Yes?—just that he'd met someone he got on well with and he couldn't find you. He asked me because you'd told him you were a doctor, and he seemed to think that we all know each other." Andrew snorted. "Not likely, with the little he had to give me. Just how drunk were you both?"

"We, ah, we..." Paul shook his head. "Never mind."

"So, are you still attracted to my godson when you're sober?" Andrew inquired. "You could do worse, you know."

"I told him that I didn't think it was a good idea. That I wasn't out here in the town," Paul said baldly, gloom filling him like dirty water. "I think he's moved on."

"Back to Cal Trent, you mean." Andrew pursed his lips in consideration. "I don't like him," he pronounced finally. "Conceited. And his sister's no better."

Paul laughed, his misery at hearing his suspicions confirmed slipping away in the face of Andrew's distaste. "He's got plenty to be big-headed about, I suppose; he's rich, good-looking—and he's known Steve longer than I have." Depression returned. "Damn." He glanced at Andrew, an unlikely Cupid, but still, it couldn't hurt to pump him for information as his boss seemed to be in a remarkably forthcoming mood. "I don't suppose you've heard if they are seeing each other again?"

Andrew pushed back his chair and stood. "If you want to know so badly, I suggest you ask Steve. Now, if you'll excuse me, I've got patients to see to, and listening to Mila Harper describe her bowel movements in detail is more appealing than listening to you imitate a teenager with a crush."

He eyed Paul for a moment and then sniffed. "To be frank, from what Steve said, I expected someone taller."

"If you don't want to date me again, how about skipping the hearts and flowers and just blowing me?" Cal said. "Right here in this kitchen if you don't want me in your bed. For old time's sake."

Steve gave him a half-hearted grimace. It would have been a grin if he hadn't been sure that Cal was serious. Had Cal always been this blatant and pushy? Looking back at the short time they'd been together, Steve remembered the sex first, and, yeah, it'd been good, but now that he had Cal here in his face again, all wide, practiced smile and engagingly twinkling eyes, the manipulative side of the man's personality was coming back to him.

Cal was the one who'd wanted them to fuck in public places, where getting caught was a certainty, not a risk, get kinky, try a threesome…and had gotten pissy as hell when Steve, younger than him by three years, dazzled by Cal's veneer of sophistication, had still shaken his head and said no.

"Come on, baby," Cal persisted. "You're not seeing anyone or I'd know about it, and I'm at a loose end… You're stuck out here on this dump of a farm; you can't tell me you don't have an itch I can scratch."

"By giving you a blowjob? Were you planning to return the favor?" Steve asked pointedly. Cal was a taker, always had been. Steve had been left high and dry more than once in the past, dick aching, hard, as Cal murmured excuses and left, his own needs taken care of.

"In these pants?" Cal chuckled, and glanced down at the floor. "Maybe not."

"I didn't think so." Steve nodded at the door. "It's been nice catching up, Cal, but I've got work to do. Going to be a busy morning and I got a car delivered earlier in the week that I have to work on."

"Oh, yeah; the mechanic job, right?" Cal didn't sound interested. What Steve did for a living didn't have anything to do with Cal getting off, so it didn't matter. Steve had run into that wall of self-centeredness around Cal before.

Steve didn't bother to explain what he did. Cal would have liked to hear the stories of the stars Steve had met when he'd delivered the restored vehicles, some of them as interested in vintage cars as Steve was, and some who'd done more than buy him a drink on top of his fee, but Steve didn't want to share. Besides, he was a mechanic and he wasn't ashamed of it. Oil on his hands washed off; from the gossip he'd heard about Cal's business deals, sleaze was a little harder to scrub away.

"That's right."

"Well, if you're sure." Cal gave him a lazy appraisal that left Steve feeling grubby, his gaze lingering at Steve's groin. "Change your mind, and you call me."

"Not going to happen," Steve said, and watched Cal leave with a feeling of profound relief. Jesus, the guy was pathetic.

Cal was one reason Steve hadn't pushed Paul to change his mind. He'd wanted to go and see Paul, to talk to him about the decision to hide what he was, but with Cal at his side most days since the funeral, as annoying as a buzzing fly, he'd given Paul the space he'd been craving for himself instead.

Paul knew where he was, and Steve wasn't planning on going anywhere any time soon. Which didn't mean that he wasn't hoping for a visitor, tired eyes lighting up when they saw him. It was killing him to know that Paul was so close and still out of reach. He lulled himself to sleep promising himself that tomorrow he'd do something, his hand flat against the cool, empty sheets beside him; every morning, he forced himself to wait another day.

He was busy, which helped to distract him. Matt had told him bluntly not to hang onto anything out of sentiment.

"I lived with my grandfather's couch all my life, and the damn thing wasn't comfortable new and the years haven't changed that. You've got money; sell what you can, give away the rest, or burn it, and start fresh. This place needs it." And when Steve had protested that he didn't know shit about decorating and furniture, Matt had poked him in the arm, scowled, and told him to pretend it was one of his cars.

So the place had been gutted, more or less, and he'd ignored the sidelong glances and whispers about disrespect and how Matt wasn't even cold in his grave, and started to make plans to renovate it, slowly, room by room. Structurally, the place was sound, but the plumbing was ancient and four small bedrooms made no sense; he'd had a local builder over to discuss knocking two of the rooms into one and expanding the bathroom.

For now, he had a new bed standing in an empty room on a bare floor and his clothes in boxes all around. He had paint, not oil, spattered over him, and his shoulders and back ached in different places. When he got bored with painting, he went out to the barn he'd turned into a temporary workshop and worked on the '53 Corvette housed in there.

He was happy enough, unless he thought about Matt, which was often, and Paul, which was too often.

And he was scared shitless that one night Cal would come calling when he was buzzed from a six-pack and he'd let the man in.

He'd hate himself in the morning if he did.

It wasn't weird to eat here, even if they did share an ex-lover, Paul told himself as he walked into Cal's diner. Cal probably wouldn't even be here, and Paul had to eat somewhere. The lunchtime crowd got a simpler, cheaper menu than the evening customers, with an emphasis on soup, salads, and sandwiches—but the bread came in a dozen varieties and several of the soups offered, in the summer at least, were chilled. The avocado bisque was one of Paul's favorites.

He sat, ordered walnut and apple salad with the tangy house dressing, and promised himself a slice of carrot cake to follow, deliciously moist with frosting a sinful inch thick.

As he waited for his salad to arrive, he exchanged nods and smiles with a few people he recognized, breaking eye contact as soon as he could. He really didn't want to eat lunch with someone telling him about their symptoms, and that was something people seemed prone to doing. Off-duty didn't really exist in anything but theory when you were a doctor.

He studied the framed photographs on the wall beside him. Cal had taken photographs of the town itself in all seasons and of the people who lived there and used them to decorate the walls. It was a good move; people would come in and ask for the booth next to the picture of their kid, gap-toothed and grinning as he was awarded a prize for biggest pumpkin, or come in just to see the latest addition, and order a meal while they were in there. One above the booth next to his caught Paul's eye, and as the booth was empty, he stood and walked around to give it a closer look.

Cal and Steve, arms around each other's shoulders, heads touching as they walked down the street that the diner was on. The street hadn't changed much in the years since the photograph had been taken, but Steve had. The dark hair was shorter, his body lanky, with just a promise of the muscles he had now.

"That's a good one of me, isn't it?"

Paul turned to see Cal staring at the photograph with unabashed appreciation. As Paul's attention had been given mostly to Steve, he had to sneak a quick peek back over his shoulder to find something polite to say about Cal.

"It's really captured your, uh, style." Flashy and expensive.

"I've always had that," Cal agreed.

The man's ego was astonishing. In a way, Paul was glad of it; there was no way that Steve could be interested in someone this self-absorbed.

Why? Because you're not? Steve liked him once, remember. Look at the way he's smiling.

Ignoring the gibing voice in his head, Paul smiled tightly at Cal and returned to his seat. Uninvited, Cal sat down opposite him and spread both arms across the back of the seat, playing the expansive host to perfection.

"We haven't really had the chance to talk much, Doc."

"I suppose not."

"Or can I call you 'Paul'?"

Before Paul could come up with a tactful alternative to "Hell, no," Cal added, "Like Steve does. Steve Parker, that is. I noticed you two seemed friendly at the funeral."

"I'd just like to say how sorry I am for your loss."

Cal's hand was cold as Paul shook it, the long fingers stiff and unresponsive against his, but he nodded. "Thanks. I appreciate it and all you did for him that night."

"I wish it could have been more." Paul hesitated. "Steve—if there's anything I can do for you—"

Steve met his eyes with a dull apathy that hurt to see. "I don't see how you can. Not now."

"If you ever want to talk—" God, listen to him trot out each banal cliché in the book. "Steve, please, I just want you to know—"

"That you're there for me as a friend. Got it." A not unwelcome flash of anger replaced the apathy for a moment. "It's not enough. Now, if you'll excuse me, my Aunt Rosa's about to start crying again and she likes to have a literal shoulder to cry on."

"It was a sad occasion," Paul replied carefully. "I'm sorry I never got to know Mr. Parker."

"Old Matt?" Cal twitched his face. "He could be sweet as pie if he liked you—he loved Steve—but if he didn't—whoo-hoo, watch out!"

"I'm guessing he didn't like you?" Paul said, unable to resist the opening.

Cal flushed. "He liked me just fine," he said shortly. "Everyone does."

Really? Because I don't.

With a visible effort, Cal pasted a smile back on his face. "You know Steve and I used to be an item, right?"

"No," Paul lied without compunction. "I'm new to town, remember. I have a hard job keeping up with the current gossip, let alone ancient history."

"Oh, it's not all that ancient," Cal said, his eyes watchful. "I was out at the Parker place just this morning, as a matter of fact. Steve looks good sweaty and stripped down to the waist, don't you agree?"

Heat washed through him, jealousy and lust burning a hole in his gut. "I wouldn't know."

"Wrong answer, Doc," Cal said softly. "You're supposed to tell me that as a straight and narrow kind of guy, the very thought of it turns your stomach."

"I'm not that narrow-minded," Paul managed to say.

"Glad to hear it." Cal pursed his lips. "Well, if you ever want to…expand your horizons, I'd be happy to lend you a helping hand."

"What?" The offer was made so bluntly that Paul found himself floundering for a response. "Look, I'm not interested, okay?"

"In men, or just in me?" Cal inquired, his eyebrows raised.

He'd told Dr. Raines, and he knew that word would spread fast even if Raines kept it to himself—it just did—but it was way too early for Cal to have found out that Paul was gay, and Cal obviously knew.

It didn't take much to work out who had to have told him.

"Let's just say I'm picky about who I sleep with," Paul said and stood, his appetite lost. "And where I eat." He put a twenty-dollar bill on the table and left Cal sitting in the booth, a knowing smirk on his face.

By mid-afternoon Steve was sweating and tired, but

he'd torn up the kitchen floor and loaded the debris into the back of his truck, ready for a trip to the dump. Underneath the worn, scuffed linoleum was hardwood, wide boards in oak. Not very practical for a kitchen, maybe, but he was tempted to sand off the adhesive, get the boards down to clean, bare wood, and refinish them. If he could get oak cabinets to replace the ones that had been installed in the seventies, it might look good.

He drank a glass of water straight from the tap, well water, cold enough to make his teeth numb in the winter months, pleasantly chilled even now, and decided that floors and carpentry were one thing, but if he found himself fussing over drapes and cushions he was going to need therapy. Slippery slope, he told himself sternly. Just paint it all white and it'll match.

He heard a car approaching and sighed. If it was another curious neighbor with a casserole, he was going to have to find a polite way to refuse the gift; his freezer was full of foil-wrapped food, none of which looked appetizing.

It wasn't a neighbor; it was Paul, driving too fast and parking with a cloud of dust rising around his car. Steve stood on the porch and watched Paul stalk toward him, wondering if he looked as baffled as he felt. Paul's expression defined furious, and Steve couldn't think of a damn thing he'd done to put that look there.

"Where's the fire?" he asked when Paul reached the bottom of the porch steps.

"If I was your fucking boyfriend, I'd say something cheesy like 'in my pants', but I'm not, so I won't." Paul smiled thinly, there, then gone again. "I'm in a hurry because I'm supposed to be headed back to the clinic to finish off some urgent paperwork, but—"

"But you decided to take a detour to yell at me?" Steve breathed in sharply, his happiness at seeing Paul completely gone, like water poured onto dry, thirsty sand. "Thanks. Just what I needed. And before you made even more of a fool of yourself than you just did, I don't have a boyfriend. I just have a one-night stand with a weird double standard. Sucks to be me, I know."

"Speaking of sucking, your boyfriend came onto me a few hours ago in that overpriced sandwich shop of his," Paul said, his voice icy. "You told him about me, didn't you?"

"What?" Steve held up his hand in a futile attempt at placation. "No, of course I didn't. Cal's been around a lot recently trying to get me to, uh, well, pick up where we left off a long time ago—really long—but I haven't mentioned you at all. What was I going to tell him? That I made such a good impression you're not interested in a second night with me?"

Paul shrugged impatiently. "Don't be stupid. You know damn well I'm interested. I just—I asked you not to tell anyone I was gay, and even if—"

"And I haven't," Steve interrupted, "but I'm not the only person Cal could get his information from. He goes clubbing in the city often enough, and if he got suspicious and asked around about you…well, maybe an ex of yours knows a friend of his… And if you're going to ask why he'd be suspicious, I hear you turned down his sister; for Cal that's enough of a hint. She's pretty fucking hot if you're into women."

The anger was fading from Paul's face. "I did as it happens, but…" He bit his lip and looked up at Steve. "You really didn't tell him?"

"Really fucking didn't."

"Is this the part where I apologize?"

"Depends how you plan to do it."

"Want me on my knees?" Paul asked without the slick of innuendo Cal would have larded onto the words, his gaze direct, even warm. Or maybe the heat spreading through Steve like melted butter was down to the image Paul had just placed in his head.

"God, yes," Steve said, "but not to apologize."

"If I was down there, I'd probably find myself getting distracted," Paul said thoughtfully.

"You just—you change on me, you know that?" Steve said helplessly as his body reacted predictably to the thought of Paul's mouth and hands on it. "First, you were furious; now you're flirting—and you haven't been near me for weeks, damn it. What comes next, Paul? Give me a fucking clue here, won't you?"

Paul's feet were still on the baked soil of the driveway, not the wood of the steps. Steve stepped, not forward, but back, and gave Paul the space to join him, if that was what Paul wanted to do; an invitation, not a command.

Paul eyed the increased distance between them, and Steve felt a moment of doubt that he'd sent the wrong message, but then Paul smiled and walked up the steps. He didn't stop, just moved into Steve's arms. Steve opened them instinctively and kissed Paul. A hungry sound spilled from Paul's mouth through Steve's lips.

Kissing. In the heavy drowse of the late afternoon sunlight, in the open; not that there was anyone around to see, but still... Steve wasn't sure what had prompted Paul's change of heart, apart from the certain fact that once rebuffed Cal would spread the word that the new city doctor was gay with a malicious glee, but he wasn't interested in asking questions right then.

Not with Paul's tongue in his mouth, a warm, wet flicker against his. Steve made a stifled, strangled sound without meaning to do it, and kissed Paul back fiercely, one hand slipping down to cup Paul's ass. His fingers dug in, maybe too hard, but he'd lost the ability to be gentle somewhere around the time that Paul bit down on his lip and licked away the sting.

Paul crowded in closer and slid his leg between Steve's, rocking up against him urgently, his hands moving in short, restless passes over Steve's back and ass, as if he couldn't decide where he wanted to touch next. Steve didn't care where Paul's hands were as long as they were on him. His only regret was that they weren't naked, but that was something that they needed to be inside for no matter how much he felt like stripping Paul down right here where they stood. Paul's skin, warm in the sunlight... he'd like to see that, feel that, find out how it changed the taste of it against his lips.

He walked backward, taking Paul with him, and reached behind him to fumble the screen door open.

Inside the hall, cool and dim once Paul had kicked the door closed and Steve had locked it, they broke for air, staring at each other, panting. Paul's mouth was already lush and damp, kissed that way, and his hair was tousled. Steve flexed his fingers and remembered pushing them through wind-tangled strands to find the shape of Paul's skull, as if nothing was more important, his teeth sharp on the sweet, soft skin on Paul's earlobe.

Paul was still wearing a white shirt and pants smart enough that Steve bet a matching jacket was in Paul's car, waiting to be slid on as needed, but with an extra two buttons undone on the shirt and an erection straining against the thin, summer-weight wool of the pants, he looked nothing like the doctor who'd started his rounds earlier that day. Steve wanted to keep taking off those clothes, until nothing was left but the man.

"Upstairs?" he asked, trying to remember which of the boxes upstairs held condoms and lube—if he even had any around. Shit. Why hadn't he been optimistic enough to buy some?

"Takes too long," Paul said briefly, before he put his hands on Steve's shoulders and guided him back a few feet, until Steve's shoulders hit the wall. "Here. Let me do it here..."

"Don't want you kneeling down," Steve said and let his hand find the hot, smooth skin of Paul's nape and grip it lightly, getting the yielding shiver of arousal he'd been hoping for. "I want to see your face when you come, and I can't do that if you're on your knees."

Paul's breath caught, his eyes darkening. Steve brought his free hand up, brushing the back of his knuckles over Paul's cheek and then turning his hand to stroke his fingertips over Paul's parted lips. He closed his eyes for a moment and, blind, felt Paul start to smile and then the push of a kiss against his fingers.

"Just to warn you," Paul said, "the way I feel right now, you're going to see me coming about three seconds after you touch me. Hell, you can just keep looking at me like that and it might be enough."

"Like what?" Steve asked and undid another button on Paul's shirt and then, because Paul swayed toward him, another. Steve hooked his fingers in the fabric and pulled the shirt open enough that one of Paul's nipples was visible, and then dragged his thumbnail over the back of Paul's neck before tightening his grip on it. The nipple hardened, inviting, enticing, and Steve bent to mouth it roughly until Paul moaned, and then delicately, teasing at it with his tongue. "Like I want to eat you? Like I want to get you in my bed and fucking tie you to it, if I have to, until I've gotten everything I've dreamed about the last two years?" He caught the nipple in his teeth and tugged at it until Paul's clutching, desperate hands on his shoulders started to hurt. "Is that what I look like?"

"Yes." Paul's voice was thick, husky. "Steve—oh, God, I'm going to come, I—"

"God, yes," Steve said, and filled his hand with Paul's hair, holding Paul in place as his other hand slid down to rest over the leap and jerk of Paul's cock. Wetness soaked through the fabric, and he breathed in the familiar tang of come, sharp and evocative.

Paul's cheeks were flushed, hot with blood, his eyes screwed close as his face contorted, a private moment Steve had every intention of sharing. "Like that," Steve said. "Oh, yeah, just like that…"

A moment later, Paul slumped against Steve, resting his forehead on Steve's shoulder, his breathing ragged. "I can't believe I just did that."

Steve smiled past Paul's head at no one and nothing in particular and patted Paul's back with a damp hand. Neither could he, but he was damned if he was going to tell Paul that. "Want to do it again, this time naked and horizontal?"

Paul moaned. "God, you're killing me here."

"Feels more like I'm bringing you back to life," Steve said. "Come upstairs. Please?"

"Yeah. Sure." Paul straightened and rubbed his hand over his mouth, still looking dazed. "I came here to fight with you."

"I think we did," Steve said and led him toward the stairs. "Now we're having the make up sex. Get with the program."

"Dr. Raines knows I'm gay," Paul said.

Steve came to a halt halfway up the stairs, barely repressing a shudder. "Please don't mention Uncle Andy when my head's full of ideas about cleaning you up and then getting you messy again. It's disturbing."

"I'm trying to tell you that we can—if you want to, we can—"

"We are," Steve said, and took the last few steps as quickly as he could.

"I don't care about who knows now; I just got mad about Cal knowing because—"

"I get it," Steve said. "God, will you just stop talking? I've got a life-threatening case of blue balls here; you're a doctor; cure me."

"That's cheesier than the line Cal used on me," Paul told him.

"Mentioning Cal's even more of a turn-off than Uncle Andy."

Paul walked past him into the bedroom Steve was using at the back of the house, looking out at the woods, green and cool. "If I strip and you're not hard, I'm getting dressed again. Is that enough of an incentive for you?"

"Yes," Steve said. "But I really didn't need one. I'm hard. Trust me, I'm hard."

They undressed standing on opposite sides of the bed Steve had neglected to make that morning. He didn't think Paul would care, though. The space between them made the task easier, but Steve found his fingers slowing as he fumbled with his belt, his attention captured by the way Paul's shoulders moved as Paul shrugged out of his shirt, the spatter of come on Paul's belly as he pushed down his pants and shorts. Paul's cock was still half-erect, pale against the cloud of wiry, dark hair around it.

Naked, even in the sultry heat of the room, with the air heavy and languid, Steve found himself trembling as if he was cold. The bed between them was a gulf that he wasn't sure how to cross, the mattress pressing into the front of his legs. Paul solved the problem by getting onto the bed and knee-walking across it, his gaze fixed on Steve's cock, intent, avid.

Steve took a breath he seemed to need more than usual and bit down on his lip to keep himself from crying out as Paul's hands cupped his ass and Paul's mouth began to kiss its way down his stomach. Low, lower…a detour to nuzzle into the hollow of his hipbone, then Steve hissed out the breath he'd been holding as Paul sprawled sideways across the bed, that mouth closing over the head of Steve's cock.

Paul made a soft, appreciative murmur that turned into a caress. He swirled his tongue in what felt like a dizzyingly complex pattern to Steve's overloaded brain. He hadn't been celibate since that night with Paul, far from it, but each encounter had been mundane enough to make jerking off preferable. No connection. No spice. Water, when he'd wanted wine. Steve had never realized how boring a blowjob could be until he'd found himself staring down the bed at a briskly bobbing head and wishing his cock would get on with it and come already so he could go back to watching the game.

Steve wasn't bored now, and much though he wanted this to continue, he knew that he wasn't going to last for long. He could smell Paul, sweat and come overlaying clean skin, and the combination was doing more for him than any manufactured cologne could. Each breath brought him another lungful, and if part of him wanted to grin at the idea of sniffing his way to an orgasm, the rest of him was busy trying not to give into the temptation to hold Paul's head still and fuck that wickedly teasing mouth until Paul was tasting him with every swallow for the next hour or so.

He reached out, blindly groping, needing to touch Paul, and stroked the silk-soft hair away from Paul's forehead with a hand that shook slightly. Paul paused to swallow spit and catch his breath, jacking Steve's cock as he waited for his breathing to steady. Steve dragged his fingers over Paul's mouth and then pushed two inside, gritting his teeth as Paul sucked on them, tongue lapping industriously.

"You are so fucking hot," Steve whispered, the words as sincere as any he'd ever spoken. "God, tell me you've got a condom or three with you?"

Paul jerked his head back and blinked at Steve. "I've just finished making house calls," he said. "I don't generally plan on getting lucky when I do those. Are you telling me that you don't have any?"

"If I do, I don't have a clue what box they're in," Steve confessed.

"Then I guess you'll have to settle for coming in my mouth or on me," Paul said, matter-of-factly enough that it took a moment for the words to hit home and make Steve's cock harden a fraction more in a warning that his climax was imminent. His balls were tight and high, and he could feel each stir of air in the room, the scratch of the sheet against his thighs, as if his skin had thinned and every nerve was exposed. Paul's voice, and the images it conjured, were unbearably arousing.

"Stop talking," Steve said. "God, please stop talking."

Paul grinned and opened his mouth for Steve's cock with a prompt obedience Steve didn't entirely trust, but was still profoundly grateful for. He slid inside the waiting, wet warmth and felt Paul's lips form a tight seal around the base of his cock before they parted enough that Steve could move if he wanted to.

For a moment, Steve hesitated. He could come just from this; the flicker of Paul's tongue, the gentle scrape of Paul's teeth, but Paul was making urgent, wordless noises, hands curved around Steve's ass, urging him forward. Paul wanted more and Steve wanted to give it to him, everything Paul wanted, always. The indulgent impulse might wear off once he'd come, but he doubted it. There was something about Paul that called it out of him. In the club, he'd watched Paul glance around, a lost, searching look on that face, and wanted to be what Paul was looking for just to change that expression to a smile.

The angle Paul was lying at didn't look comfortable; his neck was cricked. Steve didn't think it was going to take him long to come, and Paul didn't seem to mind, but still…

"Lie on your back?" he murmured. "Let me do it like that? Is that okay?" So many questions at the start of a relationship, before the shorthand developed and the limits were known and charted; Steve hadn't had many partners that he'd gotten to know well, but he'd played this version of Twenty Questions often enough.

Paul didn't waste time discussing it. He nodded and rubbed his hand over the back of his neck, massaging the muscles there. Steve grabbed two pillows and tossed them at Paul who turned to his back and shoved them under his head.

Steve moved to straddle Paul's chest, but even as close as he was to coming, he had to pause to look, kneeling beside Paul. Paul, spread out, legs wide, his hands restless on his body, stroking over his peaked nipples and then down to cup his hardening cock, was worth looking at.

"Tell me if I'll get to do this again with you," Steve said, and forced his hands to stay at his sides. "If this is another one-off, I want to know."

"Will you stop if it is? Walk away?"

Steve shook his head. "I don't think I could ever walk away from you. But I'd make it last more than it's going to if I thought that it was all I'd ever have."

"I can't promise this is going to work," Paul said, and propped himself up on his elbows to meet Steve's eyes. "We don't know each other all that well, after all. But if it helps, I want more, too." His gaze went to Steve's cock. "And right now, I want more of that." He bit down on his lip, his teeth pressing against it, small dents in the red. "Want to get to know you, wine and dine you, show you off at parties, get jealous when you flirt. Want to make up for two years just fucking wasted, but right now, I want that in my mouth, and I'm going to keep talking until you shut me up—"

Steve put his hand over Paul's mouth and kept it there as he positioned himself over the man, then shifted it to cup Paul's cheek, his thumb brushing over the corner of Paul's mouth.

"Close your mouth," he said, and when Paul, after a pause where he almost visibly decided not to ask why, did as he'd been told, Steve drew the head of his cock across the tight seam of Paul's lips, painting them shiny. "Now lick them clean," he said and felt lust rip through him, tearing at him, when Paul did just that, eyes half-closed, breath quickening. "You just—God, what you do to me," he said in a whisper, not sure he wanted Paul to know, but needing to say it anyway.

Paul raised his head and kissed the underside of Steve's cock with a murmured sigh of pleasure. "You're doing plenty for me, too, you know." He laid back and smiled up at Steve. "We had fun that night, didn't we?"

Steve smiled back. "Yeah, we did," he agreed. It was one of the reasons he'd kept looking for Paul; the sex had been good, but the way they'd clicked had been better. He nudged at Paul's chin with the tip of his cock. "Now, shut up again," he said, and watched Paul's grin widen before Steve made those lips take a different shape.

Paul watched the shadows move across the wall as the evening breeze shook the trees outside the window. Steve lay beside him, drowsing deeply enough that he didn't wake when Paul eased away from the arm that Steve had draped across him as they slept. Its weight felt good, reassuring and intimate, but it was just too hot. His skin was damp with sweat as it was.

He propped himself up on a pillow and studied the man he'd fantasized about off and on for months. Maybe he'd given up hoping he'd find Steve sooner than Steve had given up on him, but it didn't mean that he wasn't equally happy that they'd met up again and that it looked as if they were going to try for something more than the snatched hours of their first encounter.

Odd to be so certain that it would work, but he was, and he could tell that Steve shared his conviction. Optimism wasn't an emotion he normally indulged in, especially when it came to relationships, but with his body still lax with pleasure, suffused with contentment, he couldn't view the future any other way.

Reaction might set in; there could be some less than pleasant encounters in his future—with his parents as well as the town, especially a frustrated, rejected Cal—and Steve could decide that reality didn't measure up to dreams.

Paul grimaced, the bubble of happiness surrounding him quivering, about to burst.

Steve rolled over, muttering something that Paul couldn't decipher. Steve's hand reached out, groping, and found Paul's. The frown puckering his forehead smoothed out and Paul smiled and felt his world solidify again.

In Sickness and Health
by Sean Michael

Dedicated to Jarheads' fans everywhere. Your support inspires me and I thank you.

Rig headed upstairs with a book, a bowl of popcorn, and a beer. The house was empty and quiet, and there wasn't any real work to do. He was going to read about zombies and possibly nap. He so deserved it, too. Flu season had hit hard this year, and the clinic had been full of sick kids and parents for weeks. Now he was having an enforced day off after doctoring runny noses, aches and fevers for nine days straight.

He settled on the sofa, stretched out, opened his book, and boom.

Sound asleep.

Soft, warm lips slid against his own. A hot tongue pushed into his mouth. Mmm. Good dream. Rig moaned, reaching up for his mystery lover. Square jaw, high and tight: Rock.

"Mmm. Blue." Rig shifted, happy as a clam.

"How'd you guess?" Rock chuckled, rubbing their lips together.

"Years of practice... You home for good or just for lunch?"

Beautiful motherfucking man.

"Lunch," Rock said. "Of course, I could be convinced to call in..."

Rig stretched out, body sliding against those amazing muscles. Rock groaned for him, blue eyes like lasers as they looked into Rig's own.

"You're hungry." He slid his hands down over Rock's

shoulders, fingers digging in, rubbing.

"Always." Rock moaned, body pressing him down into the couch.

Rig chuckled and held on tight. Fuck, he loved that smell—sweat and soap and man.

"There anything good in the house for lunch?"

"Uh... There's chicken salad, there's leftover roast. There's me."

"Bingo." Rock grinned, and then they were kissing, Rock giving it to him the way Rig liked it. He knew just how they'd fit together—body-to-body, Rock's fat prick snuggled into the curve of his hip, his cock sliding over those amazing abs.

"Mmm..." Rock's purr rumbled through Rig. "Be even better naked."

"I like naked." He was a fan. Not as big of a fan of nudity as Dick was, but still.

Rock's hands slid over him, knowing where to rub, where to dig in. Just a little, just so he could feel Rock right there with him.

"Blue." Oh, that was a little dizzy-making.

"Mmm..." Rock's mouth closed over his, fingers pushing his T-shirt up.

Their tongues pushed together, sliding over and over, tasting each other. This never got old, the way they tasted together, the way Rock's kisses felt. Rock found his nipple ring, tugged it, and all thoughts of sentimentality disappeared, dissolving in a flash of pleasure.

"Jesus fuck. Blue. Again."

Rock's chuckle was deservedly smug as he twisted and tugged on the nipple ring, knowing how to play it.

"Oh, fuck." Rig rippled, eyes rolling a little, his heart pounding. So fucking hot. So good.

"Yeah, yeah, that's what you always say." His Blue had that pleased cock-of-the-block-look, though. Rock's other hand was busy, working at the button on his old jeans.

"It's what you like to... to hear. That I fucking need

it." He was a slut for this, always had been. God willing, always would be.

"That's because you do. You need this." Rock tweaked his nipple ring. "And this." Rock pushed two fingers behind Rig's balls, rubbing over his hole.

"Fuck yeah." Rig nodded happily, smiling at his own personal stud. "And you."

"You know it."

Rock found the lube under the cushions, and those two fingers playing at Rig's hole got down to business, pushing into him and opening him up. He started rocking, driving himself on those fingers, taking more and more. Rock's mouth covered his again, the kiss deep and hard, just like those fingers. He found Rock's matching nipple ring with his fingers, running them over the tip of that pierced nipple before sliding the ring through its channel in Rock's skin. Rock groaned, filling Rig's mouth with the sound as those big fingers stuttered a moment inside him.

Hell, yeah. He tugged a little, grunting as Rock added another finger, stretching him wider. Those blue eyes were locked onto his, Rock searching with those fingers, finding his gland and pegging it hard.

"Jim." His shoulders curled up off the couch, his entire body singing with pleasure.

"I've got you, Rig." Rock kept hitting that spot, making him light up inside.

"Uh. Uh-huh. Oh, damn. Blue." He was a little stupid with it, the pleasure driving everything out of his mind.

"Uh-huh." Rock grinned, keeping him right there. "Just a couple more..."

"Couple more." Anything. He'd take anything.

Rock nodded, hitting his gland again and then again. "See? Couple more." Then those thick fingers slid away. Rig couldn't fight his whimper as he was emptied.

"Hold your horses. I'm coming in." Grinning down at Rig, Rock pushed into him, fat cock spreading him so good.

"Mmm." Now that was more like it, just what he needed. That heavy prick filled him up, stretched him.

Rock kept pushing into him until that thick cock had sunk all the way in. He nodded, hips starting to move, to take Rock in deeper. Rock grabbed his legs, bringing them up around the solid waist, then rolled him up, sinking in that little bit further.

"Oh, fuck yes." Rig nodded, hands sliding down Rock's amazing, thick-muscled arms.

"Gonna feel me clear into next week."

"Promise?"

"You know it." Rock began to move, thrusting into him.

Rig went with it, his body bucking, riding Rock's amazing fucking heat.

"Nothing like you, Rabbit."

"Yeah, Blue. I hear you." Rig rolled his hips, bucking a little.

Sound rumbled out of Rock, something needy and sexy. His Blue moved faster, harder. When Rock pegged his gland, Rig gasped, shuddering hard.

"Fuck yeah. Right there." Rock knew how to push that button once he'd found it, and he pushed his thick cock into it with every thrust.

"Fuck. Rock. Oh, sweet Christ." He bore down, helping, letting Rock drive him out of his motherfucking mind.

They kept moving together, the couch beginning to move a bit as they fucked. The springs groaned in time with Rock's thrusts. Noises poured out of him, grunts and moans and little gasps, things that he couldn't hold in. Rock's sounds were deeper, vibrating against his chest.

"Harder. Harder, Blue. I'm close."

"Uh-huh." Grunting, Rig grabbed his cock in one hand, tugging quickly as Rock pounded into him.

"Fuck!" Rig bit the word out and shot, calves going tense.

"Yes!" Rock shouted, hips punching that cock into

him through his orgasm.

Rig gasped and let Rock keep taking him and taking him.

"That's it. Almost there, Rabbit."

"Fucking made for this." He moaned as Rock kept working his cock, keeping him hard, keeping him going.

Rock didn't say a word, kept on pumping into him. Rig whimpered, moaned, focused on squeezing and loving on Rock with all he had.

"Fuck! Rig!" He could feel Rock's prick getting that much harder, ready to pop.

"Yeah. Yeah, Blue. So fucking good."

Rock groaned for him, mouth dropping open as Rock thrust one more time and froze, filling Rig with heat. His eyes closed and his body held on, squeezing that pretty prick tight.

Rock's weight came down on top of him, fingers stroking his sides.

"Mmm. Hey, Blue."

Rock gave him a long, slow smile. "Hey."

Rig reached up and stroked Rock's lips. "Glad you came home. If you call in, we could go have huge steaks and drink beer and be bums."

"That sounds fucking perfect. You're on."

He clenched around that amazing cock, still buried in his ass. "No, Rocketman. You're on."

Dick went through the order that had come in, checking items received against the invoice.

They'd started getting healthier choices in everything. They were more expensive, but the stuff sold like crazy. Besides, it was better for their customers. And themselves. Not that he'd mention that to Rock.

He and Rig quietly checked labels these days and replaced Rock's salt with interesting not-salt salts. As long as they didn't make a big deal out of it, Rock usually didn't notice. Occasionally even he and Rig gagged over the "healthy" choice, but most of the time Rock never noticed. Hell, it wasn't like Rock wasn't a simple meat and potatoes man on the whole anyway.

Of course, one of the drawbacks of their system was that Dick had put himself in charge of the ordering for the gym, too, because Rock didn't need to know he was cherry-picking any of the goods they sold.

He finished the last of it, ticking all the right boxes, making sure copies went in the billing tray and giving the rest to Natalie, who ran the little store they'd recently put in. The "a few items behind the reception counter" area had soon outgrown itself.

"You need help stocking the shelves?" He hoped to hell she said no. Rock had left at lunchtime, and Dick had spent the ensuing hours imagining exactly what was going on back home given that Rig was home on a Saturday. It'd left him horny and wanting his men.

"I don't think so, no. Saturday afternoons are dead. I'll be happy with something to do." She grinned at him, hefting a tub of protein powder. "Besides, this is a workout."

"Yeah, it sure is. All right, you know the number if there's any problems. See you on Tuesday." Dick gave her a wave, made sure the office was locked, and headed out for his car, eager to get home.

Traffic was good—most people were heading into town not away from it—and in no time at all he was pulling in behind Rock's truck.

The mutts welcomed him home, and he spared a pat for everyone before looking for Rock and Rig.

Not in the kitchen. Not in the bedroom. He headed upstairs, where he found them at last on the big couch Rig loved. Naked, asleep, Rock holding Rig close. Dick would bet they hadn't even eaten. He was torn, for all of two seconds, as to whether he should go fix some food or wake them up.

Naked men won out over food every time.

He stripped down quickly and went to kneel by the couch, kissing first Rock and then Rig.

Rig woke up and smiled for him, humming softly. "Mmm. Pretty."

"Hi." He grinned and took another kiss, tongue diving in to taste Rig.

Rig's kisses were always eager, focused. Heated.

He knew the minute Rock woke up, the big guy grunting and then sharing in their kiss. Fuck, three-way kisses were one of the best things ever invented.

They both shifted, Rig's skinny ass snuggling into the back of the couch so Dick could climb up on the wide cushions. He fit just right, snuggled in with them, one of Rock's big hands spread across his ass cheek. Groaning, he played with their tongues.

One of Rig's hands worked his cock, moving over his shaft sweet and slow, thumb nudging his slit on every upstroke. Fuck, that was good. Dick started moving between their hands, keeping up a nice, slow rhythm. Things were building easily, the pleasure slowly ratcheting up.

Rig was chuckling, nibbling on his lips, teasing Rock with kisses. Rock rumbled, the sound vibrating between them. Dick started to make noises, letting it all out, letting them hear how good they made him feel.

Rig scooted down, hand working his cock faster, lips on his nipple.

"Fuck!" Dick jerked, not quite sure which way to push now, not really caring, either.

"That what you want?" Rock asked, fingers sliding over his crack.

"Uh-huh."

"Mmm. I'll suck. You fuck. It works for us." Rig kept heading south.

"Oh, fuck yes." Dick nodded eagerly. He was down with that plan. Or up with it. Whatever.

Rock chuckled, fingers disappearing long enough to make Dick fidget. Then they were back, slick, one teasing its way into his hole. Rig licked Dick's belly, chin nudging his cock, teasing him and making him gasp. His hands slid down to stroke through Rig's curls. Rock pushed his leg forward. He slid it over Rig, moaning as Rock's finger went deep.

"Mmm. He's leaking for you, Rock. He wants your cock." Rig's tongue flicked out, slapping his prick.

Dick gasped again, and his hips jerked, pushing him forward and then back. "I do. And your mouth. Fuck." He was the luckiest guy on earth.

Rock's chuckle teased the skin of his neck, and one finger became two, spreading him nicely. Rig took him in, swallowing hard, pulling on his prick.

Dick shouted out, hips already moving, rocking him between Rig's mouth and Rock's fingers. "Oh, fuck. Please."

Rig's fingers joined Rock's, both of them fucking him. A sound ripped out of Dick from deep in his belly, the two of them blowing his mind. And his cock.

Rock hummed low, lips on his shoulder, and he knew - he knew—that Rock was watching Rig's head bob.

"You now." He didn't want to blow before Rock was fucking him.

"Uh-huh." Rock's fingers slid away, leaving Rig's behind.

Rig held him open, spread wide for Rock's fat prick, Rig's hum around his cock sweet. Moaning loudly, Dick closed his eyes, all the breath pushed from him as Rock's cock shoved into him. They worked Dick like he was still a virgin— fucking and sucking and fingers sliding, both of them knowing exactly where to touch.

"Fuck! Oh, fuck! Yes!" Dick sawed between them, seeing stars.

Rig's fingers cupped Dick's ball sac, rolling his nuts. He shouted, his hips snapping his cock deep into Rig's throat as he came, his ass squeezing down on Rock's prick.

Rig hummed happily, cleaning his prick with that hot tongue. Rock kept pushing into him, moving more slowly now, the two of them making him shudder and shake between them.

"Mmm. Pretty." Rig climbed back up his body, licking at his lips.

"Hey." He took a kiss, groaning into Rig's mouth as Rock kept moving.

"You taste good." Rig's eyes were warm, as gray as dove's wings.

"Kid must have eaten something sweet."

He chuckled at Rock's words, rocking back into the next thrust.

"As long as it wasn't asparagus." Rig hated the way asparagus made them taste.

"You know I don't eat that." Dick could live without asparagus. He couldn't live without blowjobs. Hell, Rock didn't like anything green. Not having asparagus was easy for him.

"I know. Y'all are good to me." Rig winked, knowing Rock would take the credit for it.

"You know it." Right on cue.

Before Dick could tease, Rock hit his gland and he groaned, his cock jerking.

"Mmm. You're going to rev him up again." Of course, he wasn't the only one revved up.

"There something wrong with that?" Rock asked.

Dick couldn't think of a single problem, himself. He had a hunch Rig wouldn't be able to either.

"Not a thing." Rig leaned and took Rock's lips.

Dick groaned, watching them kiss, the sounds they made wet and sexy.

Rock hit his gland again and he cried out, cock throbbing. Rig chuckled, lips right under Dick's ear now, fingers sliding down to cup his balls again. He wrapped his leg around the back of Rig's thighs, pulling the man in closer.

Rock's hand reached down between him and Rig, wrapping the big fingers around both their cocks. He drank Rig's groan down, smiling at the sound.

Rock moved faster, thrusting into him with all that strength, hand working his and Rig's prick's like a pro. Rig's hands slipped around him, reaching for Rock, holding on tight. The three of them moved together, rocking and rubbing, the sensations fucking awesome.

Rock's free hand came up, fingers pushing into Rig's mouth. Rig started sucking hard, making Rock shudder behind him. He licked at Rig's lips, Rock's fingers, loving the taste of both of them. Dick could feel Rock—throbbing and pushing inside him, moaning for them both.

He found Rig's nipple ring, tugging on it as he panted, Rock's hand sliding on his cock, squishing it with Rig's.

"Fuck, y'all." Rig looked a little dazed.

"Yeah. Fuck." Dick grinned and took a kiss, tongue pushing into Rig's mouth.

Rig's lips wrapped around his tongue, his lover sucking on him. He moaned, Rock's prick pushing up against his gland. Fuck, they were making him crazy in the best way.

Rig watched him, the look happy, warm, lean body moving faster. His fingers trailed along the scar on Rig's stomach, the proof that his lover was better now, healing.

Dick wished they could do this for hours, but he could already feel Rock swelling inside him, his own balls aching and ready.

"C'mon, Pretty. Gimme." Rig nipped his lip.

"Rig!" Dick cried out, heat splashing against his and Rig's bellies. His ass squeezed tight around Rock's cock, and the big guy grunted, hips snapping, come pouring into him. Rig followed right behind, Rock's huge hand knowing where to touch.

They kept moving a moment or two longer, and then slowed, stopped. Dick made an inarticulate humming noise, going limp.

Rock's stomach rumbled, the feeling vibrating against Dick's spine.

Dick started to giggle. "You guys skipped the actual

'eating' part of lunch, didn't you?"

"There was popcorn... somewhere. And we talked about steak."

"Steak. Want." Rock slipped out of him. The big guy shifted, arranging everyone to his liking.

"Mmmhmm. I could eat steak. Salad. Maybe some pie." Rig stretched.

"We could go out. I bet Anna would give us the good table in the corner." Dick loved the old restaurant on the beach, they all did. Owner Anna Mayra loved them right back—she was good to her regulars.

"Mmm. We should shower first." Rig was always the first to suggest getting wet together.

This time Dick had to go along. "Yeah, we are a bit rank."

Rock snorted. "It's a good smell."

Rig whapped Rock's hip. "You're biased."

"I know what I know."

Dick leaned in and whispered loudly enough Rock could hear him. "Shh, he's trying to be romantic."

That earned him a swat from Rock.

"Come on, y'all. Shower. Soap. Steak."

"Sounds great."

"Yeah," Rock admitted. "It does." He chuckled and stood, holding hands out to them. "Come on, both you lazy asses. Steaks are waiting."

Dick took a moment first to bring them all in for a hug. Rock chuckled, hand patting his back. "You okay, kid?"

Nodding, Dick grinned. "Yeah, I'm good. I'm way good."

"All right, then. Let's get wet."

Sunday mornings were still the best.

Still the only day of the week Rock could be sure he'd get to sleep in, he made sure he took full advantage.

Rig and Dick would usually come in around noon and wake him up his favorite way together, and then he'd make everyone his special pancakes.

He glanced over at the clock—nearly noon. Smiling, he kept his eyes closed, waiting.

It didn't take long before he heard Rig's soft chuckles, floating down the hall. "...lord, that was fun. I really like those little kayak deals, Pretty. Good idea. I tell you what, though. My shoulders are aching. It's a workout."

"The massages after the kayaking is one of the best parts, though."

The both sounded loose and happy. Rock rumbled, pleased, his cock tenting the sheet as he lay on his back.

"Mmm." Rig's drawl was out in force. "Look at that, Pretty... It's like a feast all laid out for us."

"Yeah. The best feast ever." One of them tugged the sheet off him, exposing him to the air.

Rock couldn't help but puff up at that, and he rumbled happily. "Just for you two."

Someone's tongue slid around the bone of his ankle, slick and hot. Someone else's started at his collarbone, teeth nibbling there as well.

Rock stretched, hummed happily.

"Mmm." That was Rig, that happy, satisfied sound against his knee as Rig moved north.

Rock reached down, fingers of one hand sliding through Rig's curls, the fingers of the other finding Dick's longer hair. Dick turned to kiss his arm and then headed for one of his nipples, lips and tongue and teeth working his skin.

Dick found Rock's nipple at the same time as Rig's lips parted around his balls, drawing them in. It was like his nipple and balls were connected by a line of electricity and his whole body bucked, a low, needy moan coming out of him.

Fuck, they were good at that.

The kid's hand joined his on Rig's head, both of them touching now, making Rig moan. The sound vibrated through Rock's balls and made his cock throb. Dick began to continue on down his chest, kissing and licking, heading slowly toward his prick. Rig beat him to it, though, his greedy cockhound.

They kissed over the tip of his cock, tongues flicking and teasing his skin. Rock moaned, hands on their heads, hips pushing, wanting more of that hot and wet on his cock. They gave it to him, too, mouths sharing his prick. Up and down they licked and sucked, teasing him with their teeth.

"Fucking good," Rock rumbled, legs working restlessly against the sheets.

Rig's hand cupped his ass, fingers sliding over his crease, tapping his hole. He jerked, cock going harder as the touch made his balls draw up tight against his body.

They were taking turns now, sucking and moaning, working his prick while Rig kept touching him, over and over.

"Fuck. Gonna. Soon." They made him nearly incoherent.

"Mmhmm." Rig's hum vibrated through his prick.

"Fuck. Yes." Rock grabbed a hold of Rig's head and pushed his cock deep into Rig's hot mouth, coming down Rig's throat.

"Mmm." Rig took him all in, swallowing hard.

Dick kissed up along his belly and chest, giving him a good morning kiss. "Wakey, wakey."

He swatted the kid's ass.

Rig kissed the tip of his cock. Rock rumbled happily, reaching for Rig and tugging him up for a three-way kiss. Rig's lips were swollen, soft, parted, tasting like him. He wrapped an arm around each of them, tugging them in close.

"Morning."

"Morning, big guy. You gonna make us pancakes?"

"You know it. In a bit."

"Mmm. Pancakes." Rig rubbed against him, rolling his shoulders. "I kayaked."

"Yeah?" He slid his hands over Rig's shoulders. "You work hard?"

"I... Uhn. Blue..." Someone was tense, their muscles tight, hurting.

Rock growled. "On your stomach, Rabbit."

Dick grinned, helping Rig roll over on the bed next to him. "Told you there'd be a massage involved."

"Oh, y'all. You don't have to." Still, Rig let him, didn't he?

Dick laughed and slapped Rig gently on the ass. "Since when did Rock do anything he didn't want to?"

Rock snorted as he straddled Rig's ass. "I ate that damn green shit on my plate last week, didn't I?"

"You did. I thought it was sort of nasty, really."

"You made me eat shit even you thought was nasty?" Rock growled, digging into Rig's shoulders.

"Hey, I had to eat it, too!"

"I'm telling you, those things are unnatural." Rock kept working at Rig's shoulders, digging into the sore muscles.

"Oh. Oh, damn." Rig moaned. Dick grinned up at him, sheepish.

"How far did you guys go, anyway?" Rock asked.

"A hundred thousand miles, at least. Maybe two."

Chuckling, Dick shook his head. "Not quite, but we were out there nearly two hours. Hey, at least we remembered to put on sunscreen."

Rock shook his head. "You gotta start slowly, build up to long jaunts."

Dick knew better than to let Rig overdo. Their cowboy never had been the strongest man, muscle-wise.

"We lost track of time. Besides, you've got him covered. He's good, right, Rig?" Dick looked ready to accept any blame if Rig wasn't.

"Right as rain, y'all. Hell, I'm happy as fuck, right now."

Rock growled. "Just be more careful next time."

Dick nodded. "We will."

"Good." Rock let it go, kept working Rig's muscles.

Rig hummed, going all melty for him. Rock fucking loved making Rig melt. He grinned over at the kid, Dick smiling back, leaning in for a kiss. His cock was starting to fill again, to swell as he rubbed against that tight cowboy butt.

Dick's tongue slid with his, their kiss lazy, not interrupting his massage of Rig's shoulders. Rig moaned, stretching and shifting underneath him.

Dick's hand dropped to his cock, rubbing and playing. "You want him again, Rock? You want a piece of Rig's ass?"

Rig chuckled. "Only a piece?"

"Rig's right. I want the whole fucking thing."

Dick laughed at him. "I want his cock. I'll suck while you fuck."

"It's a plan." Rock did like it when a plan came together.

"Are y'all sure I'm in on this plan?" Rig asked. Uh-huh. Right. Like tall, blond and redneck horndog wasn't in on the fucking plan.

Dick pounced, kissing Rig hard. "You've got the cock and the ass in question."

Rig grabbed the kid, tongue pushing into the sweet, swollen lips. Moaning, Dick sank into the kiss, fingers pushing through Rig's curls.

Fucking sweet.

Rock admired the view for... oh... a second or two... then flipped his cowboy over. Dick laughed and got with the program, finding him the lube before going back to kissing Rig silly. Rig's hands tangled in the kid's hair, his long cock starting to fill.

"Now there's a sight." Rock grabbed the lube, slicking up his fingers.

Dick reached down and grabbed Rig's cock, rubbing for him, letting Rock see. He rumbled, pushing two fingers into Rig's ass, spreading that little hole as he watched Dick play with Rig's prick. He heard Rig's little groan, eyes on the place where his fingers disappeared into that tight body. Rock spread them apart, watching his fingers stretch Rig's hole wide.

Rig's toes curled, his lover into it, into them, into Dick's touch and his touch. Dick gave him a grin and leaned up for a kiss from him, and then down for a kiss from Rig. Sluts, the pair of them.

Fuck, he had a good life.

He pushed in deep, hard, listening for Rig's grunt. Dick moaned, the kid knowing what he was doing. Rock pushed in at a different angle. Rig jerked, toes curling up, cock curving over the flat belly.

Dick groaned. "Come on, Rock. He's ready."

"You just want at that cock."

"Yep."

"Marines. Boys. Y'all. Focus." Rig sounded almost— almost—like he was laughing.

"I got your focus right here." Rock nailed Rig's gland as he said it.

"Blue." Oh, hell yeah.

"Yeah, and don't you forget it." He stretched Rig a moment longer, nudging that sweet gland.

"Never."

Rig was staring right at him, eyes dead serious.

Rock grunted, nodded, letting his fingers slide away. "All right, then."

He grabbed Rig's legs and put them over the tops of his thighs, nudging that little hole with his cock. Rig's body knew his, better than anything, better than anyone, and that sweet ass took him right in. Groaning, Rock sank all the way in, his balls slapping up against those sweet cheeks.

Dick moaned as he watched, long fingers still wrapped around Rig's cock.

"Mmm. You are good at that, Rocketman."

"You know it." He took a few strong thrusts before nodding to Dick. "Come on, kid. He's waiting on your mouth."

Dick didn't need to be told twice, the kid taking Rig's cock in, just like that.

Rig grunted softly, eyelids drooping. "Yeah."

"Fuck, yeah." He couldn't agree more.

Dick's mouth worked Rig's cock, head bobbing slowly. Rock picked up the rhythm, taking Rig's ass with long, slow thrusts. Rig looked like he was in fucking heaven, stretched out and relaxed, moaning softly. He and Dick moved together; they knew instinctively when to speed the rhythm up, how long to hold at one speed. They worked together like they'd been doing this forever. It felt fucking good.

Those gray eyes were staring at him, watching Rock like he was the center of the fucking universe. Rig was stroking Dick's hair, loving on the kid as well. Rock could hear Dick humming happily, and he offered a rumble or two, his own sounds of fucking happy. His fingers rubbed Rig's thighs, and he sped up a bit, watching Dick's head bob faster in response.

"Damn. Damn, y'all." Mmmhmm. Exactly.

He grinned down at Rig. "You're still almost coherent. We better work harder at it, kid."

Dick's cheeks hollowed out in response, suction no doubt increasing.

"Fuck!" Rig bucked up, moaning under his breath.

"That's it. More of the good stuff, kid."

Between the two of them, they worked Rig hard, looking to make their cowboy fucking fly. Rig's ass gripped his cock, rippling around it, moving and working his shaft.

"Fuck, yes." Rock moved even harder, grunting as he got close.

"Harder. Harder, y'all. Close."

Dick's head bobbed faster, and Rock pulled Rig into each thrust. "Now, Rabbit."

"N..." Rig jerked, body convulsing around him.

"Yes!" Rock pushed in hard one more time, Rig's body pulling his orgasm from him.

They hung there for a bit, all breathing hard, panting. Then the kid groaned, hips humping the bed, breath panting against Rig's cock, Dick's head resting on their cowboy's belly. Rock leaned over and pushed a hand beneath Dick's chest, finding the kid's nipple ring and twisting it. Dick jerked and cried out, the smell of his spunk filling the air.

"Mmm. Nice move." Rig grinned at him and winked.

"Uh-huh. I know what my men want."

Dick groaned and shifted, curling up next to Rig. "You do."

Rig nodded. "Pancakes."

"You only want me for my pancakes," Rock grumbled.

"No, I like your steaks, too."

Rock laughed, giving Rig a smack on his thigh. "Ass."

"That's my leg, Rocketman." Rig grinned up at him.

"Really? Huh." He winked down at his favorite cowboy.

Dick was giggling madly.

Rock aimed a glare at the kid, but his heart wasn't in it.

Rig grinned. "I'll make the bacon and eggs. Dick has coffee duty."

"You want chocolate chips in your pancakes?"

"Blueberries."

Weirdo.

"How about pecans?" He wasn't ruining perfectly good pancakes.

"Mmm. I love pecans." Rig nodded, kissed him.

"Then I'll put pecans in them."

Dick stretched and grinned. "Blowjobs at noon and pancakes with pecans. It must be Sunday."

"Must be. Either that or we've made it to heaven." Rig slipped from the bed. "Let me shower and I'll be right there."

Rock shook his head. "No. Let's all shower and we'll

be right there." It was Sunday, there was no reason for them to do anything in a hurry.

Grinning, Rock held his hands out to them.

Rig was right. It was Sunday and heaven.

"Doc Rigger? Do you have time to work in Jenny Rappaport? She fell and gashed her arm. Needs stitches, it looks like."

Rig nodded and stood. "Put her in room three and tell Helen to prep. I'll give Harry and Diane their news and be right there."

One no, it's not cancer, one yes, you're pregnant, and one screaming five year old kid. Rig chuckled. He loved his life.

His cell rang, his Pretty's number coming up.

"'Lo?"

"Hey, Rig. How're you doing?" Dick sounded harried.

"Having a busy day. What's up? You okay?"

"I don't know, coming down with something I think." Dick cleared his throat and then lowered his voice. "You coming home soon?"

"I've got patients until six, Dick. Is Rock okay?" He always knew, when Dick had that tone in his voice, that something was up.

"He's fine. Got a cold or something. You know what he's like—running me ragged fetching this and that. We'll be fine—just bring supper home with you, okay?"

"I'll bring soup and meds and tea. No stress." Fuck.

"Thanks, Rig. You're the best."

"Yep. That's me. Doctor Best." Rig sighed and rubbed the back of his neck. He needed to get a prescription for Tamiflu for the boys, just in case.

"Can you bring popsicles, too? My throat's a bit off."

"I can. I'll set y'all up." He made a quick list. "I have to go, Dick. I have patients waiting."

"Sure think. Thanks, Rig." There was a noise that might have been a kiss and then the phone went dead.

Lord have mercy. At least it was Friday and he'd been on call last weekend.

There was a knock on his door, Helen's head popping 'round his door. "You got those patients waiting..."

"I know. The boys are sick. I'm moving." Moving, moving, moving. He grabbed his files. "You get Jenny numbed up."

"Oh, no. Is it serious? Do you want me to see who I can reschedule, or call in someone to take your appointments for you?"

"No. If I have to call in Monday, I will. But we're good."

"Okay. I'll make sure any emergencies are covered by someone else so you can leave as soon as you're done with your last appointment." Helen patted his arm. "And you tell those boys of yours to get better soon."

"I will. Go on, now. Stephanie will be in hysterics over Jenny."

"Yes, Dr. Rigger." She gave his arm a squeeze and hurried off to tend to Jenny.

Rig grabbed his files and headed out. Thank God for Fridays.

Dick managed to get Rock into the shower and standing under a nearly-too-hot spray of water.

He left the big guy there and went out, closing the door and then leaning against it. Rock could be a pain in the ass when he was sick. And the flu was the worst, because Rock felt like shit, but didn't feel like he ought to let something like a cold slow him down all that much.

Still, he'd only been playing nursemaid for about half a day—he shouldn't be this wrung out from it. A sneezing fit suggested that maybe the reason why he was already exhausted was because whatever Rock had, he was coming down with, too. Which also might explain why it felt so damn cold out there in the hallway.

He backtracked to their bedroom, grabbing a sweater and pulling it on as he headed for the kitchen. He was pretty sure there was some orange juice in the fridge.

Rig was there when he returned, unpacking odds and ends, his ball cap still on. "Hey. I brought stuff. Come sit down. Where's Rock?"

"Man, is it good to see you." Dick sat with a thump. "Rock's taking a hot shower."

"Okay. I'm going to give you a pill to help make the duration shorter." Rig popped a thermometer in his mouth, poured juice, and plopped three pills in front of him. "The others are for the fever and the pain. There'll be soup soon. You want the bed or the couch?"

Wow. Whirling Dervish Rig.

"Whith one geth me cuddled?" He asked around the thermometer. He wasn't as sick as Rock, yet. He'd notice if he was being cuddled or not.

"The couch, I suppose. Although you might be more comfortable in bed." Rig took the thermometer, sighed, cleaned it. "Okay, you take those. I'll go check on Jim."

Dick nodded and grabbed the pills with one hand, the cold glass of juice with the other. "Thanks, Rig. I'm really glad you're home. Rock's like, the worst patient ever. Except for you."

Rig kissed the top of his head. "I got your back, Pretty."

He leaned into Rig for a moment. "And I've got yours."

"I know. Let me go rescue our better third."

Dick nodded, watching Rig's ass as it headed out. His cock only twitched half-heartedly. He must be sick.

He downed the pills, enjoying the way the juice felt on his sore throat. He was going to get up and get some covers together or something, but instead he just sat and stared. He wasn't sure how long it was before Rig showed back up, but suddenly there he was, tugging.

161

"Come on, Dick. Rock's in bed. There's a movie playing. I'll bring soup in a minute."

"Oh, soup. Sounds good."

He let Rig help get him up and headed toward the living room, pleased not to be stumbling too badly.

"No, Dick. Bed. You're going to snuggle with Rock. He's cold."

He nodded, and then regretted it. "I'm cold, too."

"Come on. I've got you."

He leaned on Rig. "Be careful you don't get sick."

"I won't. I'm Mr. Healthy."

For some reason that tickled Dick, and he giggled, the sound turning into a cough. "Fuck." Damn it, he hated getting sick almost as much as Rock did.

Rock was already in bed, propped up with pillows, remote in one hand, juice in the other.

"You look cozy." He crawled in beside Rock. "Hey, you are cold."

Rig got him tucked in, too. "Okay. I'll get soup."

"Can you put a different movie in?" Dick asked hopefully. They'd seen Rambo about five thousand and sixty seven times.

Rock growled. "I like this one."

"You've already watched it twice today."

"Stop it. Pretty, I'll get you your iPod and your headphones, hmm?"

"Yeah, okay. If we can watch something different after."

Rock grunted. "Maybe."

"Stop it, Rock." Rig whacked Rock's thigh. "You'll be asleep by the time the movie's over anyway."

Dick stuck his tongue out at Rock.

"Maybe. Maybe not. And you only get to stick that out if you're going to use it, kid."

"No one's using anything. Lie there and be good."

"Bossy," muttered Rock.

Dick giggled.

"Yep. That's me. I'm the best. Boss. Whatever. Y'all

lay quiet for a minute, 'kay?"

"Yeah, yeah. I just want to watch my movie."

Dick smiled over at Rig. "We'll be good, Boss."

Rig patted his foot on the way by, and he leaned into Rock's shoulder.

Rock's arm came around his shoulders, tugging him into the muscled body.

He opened his mouth, and Rock squeezed his arm. "Shh. Watching movie."

He laughed softly, but didn't say anything.

Soon Rig came in with a tray of soup and crackers, more juice, and chocolate pudding. Dick and Rock rearranged themselves, the tray fitting in between their laps.

"Can I skip the soup and just have pudding?" Rock asked.

"Nope. You need both." Rig leaned against the doorframe, sipping a cup of coffee. Their lover was still in his work clothes.

Dick began to eat, pleased to find the soup was from their favorite sandwich shop in town.

Rock picked up his spoon, but his eyes were on Rig. "You planning on joining us?"

"I need to change and feed the dogs. You know, normal stuff."

Rock pouted.

Rig hummed, coming over to the bed. "Eat your soup, turkey."

"It's turkey soup?" Rock frowned and poked at it.

Dick's lips twitched.

"Chicken. Eat." Rig smiled, winked at him.

"A steak would make me better."

Dick watched, eating his own soup.

"A steak would make you queasy, Rock. You don't want that."

"Couldn't really be worse than how I'm feeling now." Rock picked up the bowl and spoon, shoveling the broth in.

"It could be worse." Rig started stripping, work shirt going into the hamper.

"Yeah, check it out—we've got a floorshow that rivals anything you're going to see on that TV."

Rig chuckled under his breath. "I have old, saggy cowboy butt."

Rock snorted. "I'm not so sick I can't see that's not true."

Dick finished his soup and grabbed one of the chocolate pudding cups. "Rock's right. You're looking sexy. We'd have to be dead not to notice."

"Speak for yourself, kid. I'd notice even if I was dead."

"No dying." Rig chuckled, stepping out of his slacks and briefs.

"Nobody's dying," Dick said softly, happily watching Rig get naked.

"Some of us happen to feel like we are," growled Rock.

Dick hoped he got a milder version of whatever it was, because Rock had been miserable all day.

"Eat your soup, Rock. Do you want some more juice?" Rig stepped into some soft, worn jeans and tugged on a sweater that was one of Dick's discards, the thing five sizes too big.

Dick nodded about the juice and held out his glass as Rock worked on his soup.

"Nothing tastes right," complained Rock.

"Yeah. You're all stuffy." Rig took his glass and Rock's. "I'll be back in two shakes."

Rock put down the soup, his bowl still half-full, and grabbed his pudding.

"That's cheating," Dick warned.

Rock seemed unimpressed by his comment.

"It probably has vitamins in it or something," Dick teased.

Rock stopped with the pudding halfway to his mouth, gave Dick a glare, and then shoveled it in. "Doesn't taste like it's been poisoned."

Dick nearly snorted pudding out of his nose. They were both chuckling when Rig came back in, more juice and more pudding in hand.

"Oh, you're the best, Rig." Dick reached happily for his juice and his bowl of pudding, drinking nearly half the juice in one go. It was amazing how much better he felt just being able to relax, knowing Rig was there to take care of them.

"Yep." Rig made things easier, taking trays and adding blankets, turning the lights down.

"Sitting with us?" Dick asked softly. He didn't figure he was going to last much longer than Rock in the staying awake department, but he wanted it to be all three of them for a bit.

"You know it." Rig settled on the bed, touching his cheek, Rock's forehead.

He and Rock made nearly identical grunting noises, and then they finished their pudding and their drinks. The tray was relegated to the floor and they all cuddled in.

Rock was asleep before the movie was half over, and Dick himself was close to dozing. It was a good place to be; he almost didn't feel sick, half asleep and with his lovers like this.

He didn't even notice as he drifted off.

Rock felt like death fucking warmed over. In fact if he was dead, he wouldn't have to keep coughing up a fucking lung. And somebody was fucking snoring to beat the god damned band.

"Shut the fuck up!" he growled, reaching to poke at Dick. Shit, talking made his head pound like someone was taking a sledgehammer to it.

And Dick was still snoring.

"Rock, come on." Rig pulled on his arm, getting him moving, out of bed, and toward the bathroom.

"I don't need to piss," he growled, keeping his eyes half closed. Even the light hurt.

"I know. Shower, it'll loosen the mucus."

"Sounds fucking gross, Rig." The mucus, that was; the shower sounded good.

"Uh-huh. Come on." Rig kept him moving.

He followed along like a kid. The trip to the bathroom had never seemed so long.

"I have the water going already, Blue. All you have to do is breathe."

He snorted—or at least tried to. "Easier said than done."

"Yeah. I know. I know. I've got you."

He let Rig lead him right into the shower, the water almost too hot. Almost, but not quite. He groaned, putting his head beneath the spray. The steam eased his breathing almost immediately, and the hot water on his head loosened the gunk in his sinuses, the horrible pressure scaling back a bit, just enough.

"Better?" Rig petted his stomach, his chest.

He nodded, leaning against the tile. He could stay right there for the rest of the day. Rig's hands kept working him, dragging over his muscles, easing him. "Feels good."

"It's supposed to."

He grunted, turning his face into the hot water, the tightness in his sinuses finally loosening a little.

"My poor Rocketman." Rig's fingers dug into his neck, Rig rubbing, stroking.

"Oh, fuck." That felt amazing.

"Easy. I've got you. Just let me touch."

"I can do that." Just stand here and let Rig make him feel better? Yeah, he was into that.

"You can do that. Who at the gym was sick?"

"Huh?" Sick? "Me an' the kid."

"Yes. Who gave it to you? You both had your flu shots."

"You think someone got us sick on purpose?" Rig wasn't making any sense.

"No, Rock. But if you had your flu shot and it wasn't the right kind, I'd like to be able to track the disease."

"You turning me into a science project?"

Rig's wet hand swatted his ass. "When I start draping you in aluminum foil, then you'll be a project."

"Ow!" He chuckled, wrapping his arms around Rig. "I don't know who was sick. Ask the kid."

"Okay. You want to go sit in your chair for a while or head back to bed? You need some more Tylenol."

He thought about it, but the thinking hurt his head. "Bed."

"Works for me. I'll prop you up to help with the coughing."

"I could probably manage some more chocolate pudding..." Oh, he must be sick. This was his third bowl.

"There's plenty."

"And you'll sit and watch *Predator vs. Alien* with me?"

"I will. All the way to the bitter end."

Now, that was love.

Sick or not, he was a lucky fucking man.

There was a pot of soup on the stove, bubbling away. Rig could hear the symphony of hacking, wheezing coughs coming from the bedroom. Lord.

Rig fed the dogs and made himself another pot of coffee. Man, he wished they'd guessed right on the damn flu shot. At least the dogs couldn't get it. Which was a good thing given that Trouble and Mutt had taken to lying by Rock's side of the bed, whining every time Rock had a coughing fit and otherwise watching Rock with mournful doggie eyes.

He got the good cough syrup, the Tylenol, and a

couple more glasses of juice, along with two big stadium cups filled with Sprite. "Okay, Marines. Time for your drugs."

Dick groaned and rolled away, hiding under the covers.

Rock only grunted and sat himself up, leaning against the pillows. "Movie time, too?"

"Yep. I have Independence Day and The Matrix and Indiana Jones." He poured out Rock's medicine. "Open up."

Rock made a face, but dutifully opened up. Of course the original face had nothing on the one Rock made once the medicine was in his mouth. You'd think he was trying to poison his Marine with the way Rock carried on. Of course, it said something that Rock took it. That cough was a bear.

"Okay, Dick. You're next."

"It tastes bad." Man, Dick didn't usually whine that much when he was sick.

"I know. I brought you Sprite."

"Oh, man. You rule." Dick unburied himself and half sat on the pillows, reaching for his meds. Poor Pretty was looking anything but, with his nose all red and his eyes bloodshot. Not to mention the mouth-breathing.

Rig poured a spoonful and popped it in Dick's mouth, then immediately handed over the Sprite. "There. Painless."

Dick nodded, sucking hard on the straw. "Mostly."

"Wuss," Rock pronounced.

Dick might have answered, but he had a coughing fit instead, Rock joining in a moment later.

Rig propped them up higher on the pillows so they could drain. He was worried about their ribs; his musclemen were strong enough to hurt themselves.

"We're not watching Rambo again," murmured Dick once the fit had passed.

"Don't worry, kid, even I'm sick of that one."

"The Matrix?" He put it in without waiting for an

answer. He needed to stir the soup and bring his paperwork in.

"Oh, I like this one." Dick sipped some more of his Sprite, looking happily settled. Rock was starting to pout, though.

He closed his eyes on the way out the door, counting to thirty as he headed to the kitchen and sucked down a beer.

Okay. Peace and harmony. Motherfucking light and goddamn joy.

"Rig?" Rock's croak from the bedroom interrupted his mantra.

"Yeah, Blue?"

"Are you coming back?"

"I am. I was stirring the soup." Breathing. "I have to grab my portable, too."

Rock's answer was another coughing fit.

"Breathe, man. In and out. I'll grab the humidifier." He ran for the bathroom and got the humidifier out, filling the tub with water and the little diffuser with Vicks.

Dick wandered in while he was busy at it, headed for the toilet. "You taking care of yourself, too?"

"Mmmhmm." Rig got a towel hot, too, and headed into the bedroom, plopping the towel over Rock's chest.

Rock sniffed and sighed. "Feels good."

Dick was back a moment later, stopping to rub his back for a minute before going around to get into bed.

"You shouldn't have to play doctor on your day off."

"Hey, I'm not playing. I'm a professional."

"Even worse. You're working on the weekend."

"Shut up, Pretty." He reached over, patted one foot. "Y'all are worth it."

No matter how gunky or sick his Pretty was, Dick still beamed at him.

"Can I get you anything?"

Dick shook his head and patted the bed between the two Marines. "Watch The Matrix with us?"

He looked at his laptop, then at his Marines. Spoiled

brats. Beautiful spoiled brats. "Okay. I can do that." He crawled up into the bed, settling between them. They curled in on either side of him, heads on his shoulders. Dick's hand slipped into his. "Mmm. Y'all rest. I've got you."

Rock grunted and Dick nodded. Within minutes his Marines were both asleep.

He smiled, patting Rock's thigh, then he slipped from the bed. He had a little work to do.

Dick woke up feeling better than he had in days. He wasn't feeling great by any means, but he thought he might live. He felt well enough to realize their bedroom stunk. Sick Marines and stuffy air. Blah. Rig deserved a reward for putting up with them.

He slipped out of bed and headed for the bathroom, intent on taking a shower and washing away some of the cruddy feeling. He could smell something cooking, something spicy and good. He detoured from the bathroom to the kitchen, following his nose.

Rig was at the kitchen table, papers and computer and sundries spread out around him.

"Hey, Rig. It smells good in here."

"Chili. Thought it might taste good after two days of chicken."

"Yeah. I bet it clears out our sinuses, too." He grabbed a chair and moved it closer to Rig, sitting. "What day is it?"

"Monday afternoon. I called in." He got a warm smile. "Do you want something to drink?"

Wow. He'd lost two whole days. "Yeah. Yeah, I would." He would have gotten up, but Rig was willing, and he had to admit, the walk from the bedroom had zapped most of his energy.

"Orange or apple?" Rig got up, wet a rag, and grabbed a glass.

"Orange, please. I like the way it feels scratchy on my throat." A cool rag was placed on the back of his neck, and then Rig poured the juice. Dick groaned, the cool cloth feeling good. "Thanks."

"Any time, Pretty."

"Yeah, well, I'd actually rather not need it. This flu is nasty." He hadn't felt this bad in ages. Of course, Rig usually made sure they got their shots and had their vitamins and shit. Come to think of it, they had gotten their flu shots this year.

"Yeah. It's going around. Sometimes they miss the strain that's going to hit."

"That sucks." It really did.

"I should be over the worst of it now, though, right?"

"Yeah, but you'll still need to take it easy for a week or so. I called the gym and arranged for y'all to be out until Thursday."

"'Til Thursday? Oh man, Rock isn't going to be happy about that."

"Well, you can go back, but you'll relapse. You have to heal."

Dick nodded. "I'm willing. We might need to tie Rock to the bed, though, if he's feeling lots better."

Rig nodded. "He has enough sense to know when it's time to rest. He knows his body. For all the bitching that I do, I know he listens to his body."

"He listens to you, too, in the end." Rock liked to pretend he was nothing more than a tough guy, but he and Rock knew better.

"Yeah. I am the pro, hmm?" Rig chuckled, kissed his cheek.

"Our very own doctor." He waggled his eyebrows. "All the other kids are jealous."

"They ought to be." Rig gave him a grin. "I give the best head."

"Yeah, you do. Like ever." He reached out and slid his hand along Rig's arm.

"Absolutely." That arm clenched under his hand, Rig

flexing for him.

He squeezed Rig's arm and then stroked some more. Man, he'd missed touching.

"So, I thought I'd go to the video store, rent some movies, resupply."

Dick chuckled and then had to wait for the ensuing coughing fit to stop before he could speak. "We have kind of run our supply into the ground, huh?"

"You know it. We missed our weekly shop."

"We missed our weekly everything."

"We did, but you two were very busy."

"Yeah, I can do without that kind of busy, thank you."

He drank down his juice, moaning softly at how it tasted, how good it felt going down. Rig stood behind him, hands on his shoulder, massaging lightly.

"Mmm..." He tilted his head forward, enjoying the touch, the way it eased his flu-weary muscles.

"That's it." Rig hummed softly, hands working him, over and over.

He was almost falling asleep right there at the kitchen table—Rig's hands were making him feel so good.

"Come on, Pretty. You want the couch? I need to change the sheets on the bed once Rock gets up."

"Yeah, sounds good. Would be even better with a bowl of whatever that is you've got cooking up..." He gave Rig his best winning smile, which he figured had to be at least half the usual wattage, given how he felt.

"You want crackers or Fritos in your chili?"

"Crackers. And a big glass of milk." And he could probably get it himself, but he was feeling tired and it always tasted better when Rig dished it up anyway.

"You got it. I put quilts on the sofa. Go sit."

"Thanks, Rig." He tugged Rig down and kissed him on the cheek, not wanting to share his germs.

"Anytime, Pretty."

He dragged himself out to the living room, curling up in the nest of quilts Rig had prepared on the couch. There was a bottle of water on the coffee table, along with the remote, all within easy reach.

It didn't take long for Rock to come stumbling in, blinking some. Rig was close behind, bowl of chili in hand. "Rock. You want a bowl?"

Rock grunted as he settled in his chair. "Of what?"

"I made chili. There's Fritos."

"Yes." Rock nodded, pulling a quilt up.

"'Kay." Rig gave Dick his chili and milk and headed off again.

"How you doing?" Dick asked, digging in.

Rock shrugged. "Better. Still fucking weak as a kitten."

He nodded. He got that.

Rig came in with another bowl, a glass of juice. "Here you go, Rocketman."

Rock grunted. "Thanks."

"Rig offered to go get us new movies."

"Yeah. And if you want something from the grocery store, holler."

"Oranges," Dick said as Rock grunted and said, "Brownies."

"Orange brownies. Got it." Rig was muttering on the way out.

"Fuck, no!" Rock growled. "No fucking fruit in a perfectly good piece of baked goods."

Rig sighed, rolled his eyes. "I'll be back in two shakes. Any movie requests?"

"Nothing girly."

Dick laughed. "I don't know, girly might make a nice change from what we've been watching."

"Mmhmm. I'll find stuff."

"Hey, Rig. Thanks."

Dick watched Rig go.

"Turn the TV on."

Dick rolled his eyes and started surfing.

Jesus, he was tired.

Rig headed into the house from the truck, hauling a load of groceries. He'd seen something like fifty patients today, twenty of them with the flu. He had another full load tomorrow, too. Damn it.

He knocked on the door. "Y'all? Let me in!"

Rock pulled open the door, the dogs trying to trip him up. Suddenly his grocery load got lighter, Rock hauling them out of his arms. "Is this all of them?"

"There's a couple three bags out in the truck. I brought stuff for supper."

"Oh."

"Just bought some dried spaghetti and sauce and hamburger meat. If y'all want something else, that's fine." He really didn't care.

"The kid kind of did something up. Put a table cloth on and everything." Rock led the way to the kitchen which was, coming to think of it, smelling awful good.

"It smells good. How're y'all?" God, his eyes hurt.

"Better." Rock put down the groceries and hauled him in for a kiss. "I showered. Even helped the kid make the bed."

"Good." He gave Rock a hug, leaning a little. "You look better. Almost back to normal."

"Yeah. You called it right, about not going in, because damn, just being up is an effort, but I feel human again."

Dick came up the hall, wearing a T-shirt and jeans, hair damp. "Rig! You're home. Cool. We made supper."

"Excellent. What is it?"

"Roast chicken, roast potatoes and," Dick covered Rock's ears, "peas and carrots and salad."

"Sounds luscious." The spaghetti fixings would keep. "Absolutely wonderful. I'm going to take off my boots and all. I'll be right back."

"I'll get the rest of the groceries." Rock groped his ass.

"You're a prince among men." He wiggled and

winked.

Rock squeezed a couple times before his hand slid away. "You know it."

It was good to see his boys perking up. Feeling better.

He wandered into his office, plopping his laptop on his desk and sitting down hard.

That's where Dick found him some time later. "Hey." Dick came right around to lean against his desk. "You just got back from work. Can't whatever it is wait until after supper?"

"Uh-huh. I'm just taking my boots off." Eventually.

"It doesn't usually take you fifteen minutes to take your boots off."

He chuckled. "Right. I had a long damn day is all." He held one foot out. "Gimme a hand?"

Dick grabbed the heel and ankle of his boot and began to tug. "You look pretty tired. We were a total pain in the ass, weren't we?"

"Not at all." Maybe a little.

Dick snorted, sounding for all the world like Rock. "You shouldn't lie."

"Moi? Lie? Bite your tongue."

Dick met his eyes, grinned wickedly. "I'd rather you bit it."

"Oh, ho!" He laughed, leaned in. "Does that mean I get kisses again?"

"I sure hope so. I brushed my teeth and everything." Dick met him halfway, lips pressing, tongue sliding into his mouth.

Oh, nice. He hummed, sliding closer, landing almost in Dick's lap.

Dick's hand slid along his thigh, tugging Rig right out of his chair so he was in his Pretty's lap. "Fuck, I've missed this."

"Your dinner's going to get cold." He pushed close, rubbing on Dick's belly, moaning nice and low.

"Like food could compare to this. Besides, it's keeping warm in the oven."

"Good plan." Dick gave him another kiss, then another, making his head swim. Dick's fingers tugged his shirt out of his pants and then pushed beneath it, sliding on his skin. "Mmm." That felt good. It had been a week since either of his boys had felt up to playing.

Dick groaned, one hand staying at Rig's belly, stroking over his abs, while the other headed straight for his nipple ring. His nipple went tight and hard, begging for the touch. Dick's finger slid into the ring, tugging on it, the tip of Dick's finger rubbing his hard flesh. He felt that, deep in the pit of his belly, his balls drawing up tight.

"Rig..." Dick moaned and dove back into more kisses, feeding him all those sweet noises as his skin was explored.

"Uh-huh. More." He was all about the "more".

"Yeah." Dick's hands slid down to cup his ass. "Couch," his Pretty muttered, standing and half dragging him the few steps to the leather couch that graced his office.

They plopped down, hips nudging together, cocks sliding. Rig moaned low, hands sliding over broad, strong shoulders. His baby green Marine. Dick kept one hand on his ass, squeezing and stroking, while the other one pushed back under his shirt, playing with his bare nipple and then the ringed one. He cried out, hips rocking a little.

"Fuck, love that sound." Dick tugged the ring again and again.

"Dick!" The sound rang out, and he let his head fall back, caught in it.

"Hey." Rock stood in the doorway. "This isn't fetching Rig for supper."

Dick grinned. "No, but it's infinitely more fun."

"You stopped." Rig thought it might be important to point that out.

"Oh, we can't have that." Dick licked his lips. "There's plenty of room on the couch, Rock."

Rock grunted and came to sit down.

Rig leaned until his head was in Rock's lap. "Mmm. Hey, Rock."

"Oh, now, don't be lying like that unless you mean it, Rig. It's been too fucking long." As if to back up his words, Rock's cock had begun to harden beneath his cheek.

"Hmm? You have something for me?" He hadn't had that cock in days.

"You fucking know it."

Dick moaned at Rock's words, hand right there, fingers tugging at Rock's zipper.

"I can smell you." Rig's cock throbbed, battering against his zipper.

"Lucky you. I still can hardly smell a thing." Rock's fingers stroked through his hair as Dick freed Rock's prick from his jeans.

"Good thing you don't have to breathe through your nose for me to do this, huh?"

Rock chuckled. "No, it's a good thing you aren't stuffed up." Rock gave him a wink, and then shivered a bit when his cock was exposed to the air.

"You sure you're feeling up to this?" He licked from base to tip.

Rock rumbled—shit, it had been even longer since he'd heard that particular sound. "Does it look like I'm up?"

"Mmm. I'll have to focus..." He licked again, loving the salt and musk of Rock on his tongue.

Rock groaned, legs spreading wider. Dick's fingers slid over Rock's thigh, his ass, his belly, touching him as he worked on Rock's cock. He sucked in to let Dick open his pants, let that hand in. Quick as anything, Dick had his pants undone as soon as he'd sucked in, fingers stroking over his cock.

Rig grinned, arched up, and sucked Rock right in.

"Fuck!" Rock's hips bucked, pushing that fat prick in deeper.

Rig turned over, offering Dick his ass, taking that pretty cock in all the way.

"Oh, fuck." Dick said the words like they were a prayer and suddenly his pants were tugged down, Dick working them right off.

"Fuck" worked for him. Very well. Extremely well. He was a motherfucking fan.

Rock's fingers slid through his hair as Dick spread his legs and rubbed against him. Rig hummed softly, moaning, tongue sliding over the silken skin covering Rock's prick.

"Fuck, yes. Rig." The words drifted down to him, Rock adding a moan at the end. "Been for-fucking-ever."

"Too long," Dick agreed, fingers slick now as they slid over Rig's crack.

They were all spoiled now. Used to having access to each other whenever they needed, whenever felt good. God, they were lucky.

Dick played with his ass, fingers sliding along his crack and teasing in and out, not going very deep, not deep at all. He found the rhythm, head slowly bobbing over Rock's prick, humming at the taste. Rock's low moans and happy rumbles joined his Pretty's noises, turned them into the best symphony. Dick's fingers pushed in further, two twisting and spreading inside him, finding and poking his gland. He jerked a little, squeezed Dick. Oh, good.

"Fuck yes. You found it, kid."

"Yep, I know." Dick nudged that spot again, and again.

Oh. Oh, fuck yeah. Rig started groaning, sucking harder, working out his pleasure around Rock's prick. Rock's hips moved in little thrusts, thrusting the hard cock into his mouth.

Dick rocked behind him, fingers slipping and sliding inside him, cock rubbing along his thighs, hot and leaking. Rig thought he could do this forever.

Dick's fingers slid away, his Pretty shifting, moving to settle between his legs. That long prick nudged at his hole. He arched, making sure the offer was clear. Please.

"I've got you," murmured Dick, cock head rubbing over his hole, spreading the hot liquid dripping from

Dick's cock.

Rock hummed, hand stroking Rig's head, encouraging him to keep going. Like he needed the encouragement.

"Mmm." Rig closed his eyes, let them fill him up, let his men have him.

Dick pushed in slowly, filling him so deep. His Pretty stilled, cock buried deep inside. "Oh, fuck, Rig. You feel amazing. I'd almost forgotten..."

He chuckled, squeezed Dick, welcoming his Pretty back home.

Dick whimpered for him. "Oh yeah, too damn long."

"You said it." Rock's fingers tightened in his hair, the thick cock pushing deeper into his mouth.

He took Rock to the root, swallowing hard, holding his breath as he sucked.

"Fuck!" Rock held his head still, beginning to thrust into his mouth, hitting the back of his throat again and again.

Dick found the same rhythm, picking it up, pumping into his ass with matching thrusts. This was familiar, good, the place he fit the best, and Rig rode it like a champ.

"Not gonna be long," Dick warned.

Rock grunted agreement. "Too fucking good."

It worked for him. Especially after Dick's fingers wrapped around his cock and started tugging. They moved faster together, Dick's hand squeezing him tight as the long prick filled him, Rock's cock going deep into his throat.

Fuck.

Fuck, yeah.

He grunted, sucking hard, so tired, needing to come, to have his Marines come for him.

"Fucking now," growled Rock.

"Yes!" His Pretty's hips snapped, heat going deep inside him as Rock's cock throbbed on his tongue.

Rock filled his lips, and Dick worked the tip of his cock, sending him over the edge. They all shuddered and shook, come spurting all over the place.

Groaning, Dick lay down on top of him. He leaned against Rock's thighs, suddenly exhausted. Hell, not suddenly. He'd been exhausted all fucking day. His eyes closed, body relaxing.

It only took a couple of heartbeats before he was sound asleep.

Rock was feeling pretty good. He'd taken the week off and was looking forward to the weekend. To Rig being home for a couple days and things starting to get back to normal. Tonight was pizza and beer and whatever happened to come up. He knew exactly what he planned to have come up. All they needed was for Rig to get home.

The phone rang, Helen's number coming up.

Rock picked it up, glancing at his watch. Damn it, he didn't want to hear how Rig was running late. "Hello?"

"Hey, Rock? Did Doc make it home yet?"

"No, he's not here yet. Don't tell me there's some emergency he needs to go back for?" He tried not to growl, because he liked Helen, but it had been a hard week and he was ready for them to be altogether, for more of what they'd had last night.

"No. No, in fact, I just wanted to let you know that Doctor Phillips was making some noises about calling Rig and asking him to be on call this weekend. Turn Doc's cell off, huh?" Oh, Helen was a queen.

"I read you loud and clear. Thanks for the heads-up, and you have a nice weekend, Helen. Don't let those kids of yours drive you too nuts."

"I won't. Take care of my boss."

"Yep, that's my job, Helen." Grinning, he said goodbye and hung up the phone.

Dick wandered in, fresh from the shower. "Who was that?"

"Helen. Wanted to warn us one of the other doctors is

looking for someone to take his weekend on call."

Dick shook his head. "Oh, no. Not Rig. We only just got better. Rig hasn't even had a chance to give us our lecture about taking care of ourselves, yet."

"I know. When he comes in, I'll hold him down and you grab the cell phone, get it turned off."

"It's a deal."

The dogs started barking, howling, welcoming Rigger home. He grinned, and Dick grinned back. They broke for the door, calling the dogs off even as the front door pushed open and the beasts crowded around Rig.

"Hey, y'all. I'm home." Rig looked tired, but the man was grinning for them. Just about the time the man put his briefcase on the floor, the cell started ringing.

"No! Don't get that, Rig. Helen just called. You need to let it go to voicemail and then turn it off."

Dick nodded, taking Rig's hands so they couldn't get to the cell.

"Huh? Helen?" Rig looked a little confused, so Rock took the phone, held it in one big hand, and leaned in to take Rig's mouth. No way was his Rabbit taking anyone's on call shift this weekend. Rig had been working himself to the bone between full days at the clinic and doctoring him and Dick all week.

The phone stopped ringing, but he didn't stop kissing, his tongue pushing into Rig's mouth. Rig didn't argue, those sweet lips opening for him, hips nestled against his own. Groaning, he grabbed hold of Rig's ass, squeezing that perfect little cowboy butt. Rig arched, pushed right into his touch and started rubbing. Dick pushed up behind Rig, arms sliding over his shoulders. Oh yeah, it was about time they'd had a proper hello and welcome home around here.

"Mmm. Hey y'all." Rig moaned, smiled for him. "Happy Friday."

"You fucking know it."

Dick tilted Rig's head, taking a nice, long kiss of his own. Fucking sweet.

Rock got the cell turned off, tossed away. No phones for them, not this weekend. He focused on tugging Rig's shirt up and off.

"Couch?" Dick suggested.

Nodding, Rock moved backward toward the couch, not losing contact with Rig. Rig let him strip the shirt off, Dick had Rig's belt undone before they got to the couch.

"Come on, kid. You get those pants off before we're sitting and we'll have broken the dressed to naked record."

"There's a record?" Rig looked a little fuck-dazed.

"Yeah, and we own it." Rock gave Dick a wink and took Rig's mouth again.

Rig moaned, hands reaching for him, wrapping around his shoulders. Rock slid his fingers around Rig's waist, thumb rubbing one bony hip.

"Mmm." Rig stepped closer, body moving against him, dancing to some music in his cowboy's head.

"More naked," muttered Rock.

"On it." Dick laughed, fingers working his T-shirt out of his jeans.

Rig moaned, hands sliding down to play against his belly. "Mmm... what are you looking for?" He waggled his brows as Dick pushed his T-shirt up over his head.

"Sex. Hard, sweaty, deep sex," Dick said.

Rig laughed. "You came to the right place."

"Hell, yeah." Dick's fingers worked his button open, his zipper down, and then his jeans were yanked off his hips.

Rig sat on the sofa, stubbled cheek rubbing his cock, his belly, his balls.

"Fuck. Yes." Rock groaned, fingers carding through Rig's curls.

"Blue. You feel so fucking good." Rig nuzzled some more, licking the tip of his cock.

"I do. I mean what you're doing is. I... yeah."

He got a low laugh, a nod, Rig's stubble scraping his skin. "Yeah."

Dick pushed up behind Rock and kissed his neck. Oh, hell yes. Rig wasn't in any hurry, kissing and licking, nuzzling his prick. Dick's mouth was hot as it slid along his spine. Oh, he must've done something special to deserve this.

Dick's fingers slid on his back, fanning out across his muscles as the kid sucked and licked and bit. Rock found Rig's shoulder with one hand, holding himself steady. Gray eyes flashed up toward him, happy and warm. Then Rig sucked his prick right in.

Fuck. He'd been in this position countless times and it never, ever got old.

Ever.

Dick's fingers played at the small of Rock's back, making him push forward and deeper into Rig's mouth. His Rabbit took him down to the root, deep-throating him like it was nothing. Easy. That strangled noise came from him, but he didn't give a fuck, as long as Rig never stopped.

Those lips wrapped around the base of his cock, swallowing gently, the suction sweet and steady, giving him what he needed. Dick sank down behind him, lips replacing fingers at the base of his spine. He moved between both mouths, little back and forth movements.

Rig reached between his legs, and he felt Dick's moan as those hands found the kid. Dick's hands spread his ass, tongue working his crack, his hole. The two of them were going to blow his fucking mind.

Soft moans vibrated along his cock, making him grunt, push deeper into Rig before pushing back against Dick. Dick teased him, tongue flicking at his hole, slapping it but not pushing in. Rig wasn't teasing, though, Rig was sucking him like it was the only thing his Rabbit wanted to do. He slid his fingers through Rig's curls, cupped Rig's scalp and encouraged the movements of Rig's head.

"Mmm." That sound made his eyes flutter shut, made him swallow hard.

Dick began to tongue fuck him after that, and

everything snapped into focus, the three of them working toward the same goal. Making him shoot was a fucking fine goal.

"Don't fucking stop." Like they would. Rig snorted, tongue-slapping his cock. Groaning, he jerked and muttered, "Fuck."

"Mmmhmm." Rig did it again, working his prick.

The kid's tongue was just as busy, and Rock tried to hold on, he really fucking did, but it was too much.

"Rig." The word was little more than a growl, a grunt, and he was coming hard.

His cowboy drank him down, pulling at his cock and sucking good and hard, making the pleasure last and last. Dick moved on from tongue-fucking him to sucking on one of his ass cheeks. The kid was going to leave a fucking mark there.

"Welcome home," he growled at Rig.

"Mmm. Happy Friday."

"Yeah. Happy fucking Friday. Let's get horizontal." There were a pair of hard cocks to take care of.

Rig's laugh felt fucking good against his belly, those hands reaching up to him. Rock pulled Rig up, opening Rig's mouth with a kiss. He fucking loved the taste of him in that mouth. Dick pressed up against his back, the kid's prick hot against the back of his thighs. There was a matching cock against his balls. Rig was moving, nice and steady, rubbing on him.

"Couch," he muttered, pushing Rig down, following, feeling Dick come down with them.

"Fuck, yeah." Rig spread for him, spread nice and wide, arms sliding up his arms.

"Gonna let me do you while you do the kid?"

Dick groaned in his ear, clearly a fan of that plan.

"Sounds like a plan, Rocketman."

"It does. Like a good plan."

He kissed Rig again, searching the cushions for the lube. Rigger opened right up, focused on the kiss, on his mouth. He came up with the lube, waving the bottle in triumph. Rig, slut that he was, didn't even fucking notice. The kid did, though, grabbing the tube from him before pushing into the kiss.

"Mmm." Rock chuckled as Rigger hummed and smiled, tugging the kid closer.

Dick's slick fingers were soon everywhere, smearing lube on Rig'scock and balls, his thighs. That had him chuckling harder.

"You're in a good mood," Rig hummed for him, gaze warm.

"You fucking know it. Friday evening, my men, lots of lube. What more could a man ask for?"

"Sex. Chocolate pie. Beer. Pool."

"Well, yeah. But you just blew me and we're about to get to the sex part. The rest is fucking details." He gave Dick a look. "Will you get that lube where the sun don't shine, already?"

Dick started to laugh.

"Ah, romance." Rig grinned, eyes dancing. Asshole.

"Hey, I don't work for fucking Hallmark."

Dick's fingers finally worked their way into Rig's ass.

"Nope. Oh. That's good. Deeper."

Rock pushed one of his own fingers in with Dick's, adding to the stretch. That got them a gasp, Rig pushing down on them, riding them hard. That was his sexy slut. He pushed in another finger, Rig taking four now, two from each of them. Dick groaned, leaning against him as they worked Rig's ass.

"Fuck. Fuck, yeah..." Rig braced himself on the sofa, moving on them, flying.

"Lube up my other hand, kid, and I'll get you ready, too."

"Two hands, no waiting?" Dick ducked his swat, fingers pushing in deep enough to make Rig gasp.

"F...focus, y'all."

Rock pushed his fingers hard and deep, proving how focused he was. Rig's cry rang out, that fine prick bobbing and leaking.

"Like I wasn't focusing." He gave Dick a wink, the kid's cheeks nice and flushed, eyes hot.

Without him having to ask, Dick shifted so his ass was in easy reach, and Rock spread the little hole with two slick fingers. Dick groaned, and the kid's fingers stuttered inside Rig. Rock set the same pace in both asses, though, and soon enough Dick was back with him, riding and finger-fucking like a pro. Rig was close, eyes closed, cheeks flushed, lips parted.

Rock bent down and licked Rig's cock from the base to the tip as his fingers pushed hard against the sweet little gland.

"Fuck! Fuck, Blue!" Oh, yeah. Real close.

He smacked his tongue across the tip of Rig's cock, and then took one of Rig's balls in his mouth, sucking it, rolling it with his tongue. His Rabbit cried out, shooting hard, spunk spraying over his tanned, flat belly. Humming, he took the other ball into his mouth while Dick bent to clean Rig's belly.

His fingers popped out of Dick's ass as Dick bent over, and Rock slapped the sweet ass. "Are we ready for fucking yet?"

"Yeah, yeah. Rig, you wanna go on your hands and knees and I'll get under you?"

"You think I can get it up again? I'm old."

"You're not as old as Rock and he got it up again."

Rock smacked the kid's ass. Hard.

"He's a fucking machine." Rig chuckled, then moaned a little as Rock nibbled at the tip of that half-hard cock.

"You can get hard again for the kid's tight little ass." He slid his tongue across the tip again and rolled Rig's balls in his hand.

"Can I?" Rig hummed and stretched, right there with them.

"Mmmhmm." He wrapped his lips around the head of Rig's cock and sucked hard.

"Oh, fuck." Dick moaned. "That's so fucking hot."

"Yes. Blue. Fuck. Don't stop."

He hummed, sucked more, making Rig hard again. Rig pushed up into his lips, rocking, taking his mouth. He hummed, tongue flicking at Rig's slit. Rig moaned and bucked, hips rocking, cock stiffening, swelling for him. That was it, that's what he was looking for. They were going to make a fucking chain.

Dick groaned. "Okay, come on. I want."

"Uh-huh. Smell so good, Pretty." Rig was so fucking easy.

"Like sex," Rock growled.

Rig shifted to his knees, and Dick quickly lay back on the couch, legs splayed like a two penny slut. Rig leaned down into Dick, whispering something that made the kid whimper, buck, and drag Rig closer. He put his hands on Rig's ass, guiding it as Rig slipped between Dick's ass cheeks.

"Mmm. Want." Rig moved into Dick, arching and pressing in.

Rock watched for a moment, Dick arching, bearing down on Rig's prick, that cowboy ass pushing back and forth as Rig thrust. Look at that fine pair. Rig moved sure and steady, muscles clenching and relaxing. Dick made all those noises of his, fingers sliding around to grab Rig's ass and spreading his cheeks.

He growled a little, testing that little hole with his fingers. Rig slowed down, pushing back toward his touch, over and over. There came a point when he had to be inside that tight heat, and Rock tugged his fingers away, lining up and pushing in, all the way.

"Blue." Rig squeezed him, pulling him in deep.

"Yeah, right fucking here."

He met Dick's eyes over Rig's shoulders, smiled into the glazed over gaze. Yeah, they were all right where they needed to be.

With a groan, he set the pace, moving nice and slow, his thrusts pushing Rig into Dick. This was what fucking Fridays were supposed to be like. Just this.

Rock's hand met Rig's as he wrapped his fingers around

Dick's cock, and he chuckled into Rig's neck, staying there to lick and nuzzle as they worked Dick's cock together. Dick started moaning, whimpering, crying out and filling the air with noise. They almost covered up the sound of their skin all slapping together. Almost, but not quite. Rock started moaning, adding his own vocalization to it. Under it all, there was Rig's little moans, little sounds.

They stayed right there as long as they could stand it, and then all of a sudden, he and Rig squeezed Dick's cock as the sounds of their flesh coming together got louder. Harder, faster, more, now. Fuck it didn't get better than this.

"Good. Harder, Rock." Rig shivered against him.

"You got it." He pounded into Rig, letting his Rabbit really feel it, knowing his thrusts were pushing Rig into Dick with more force.

"Yeah. Yeah, fuck. So good." Rig was crying out, grunting.

Dick didn't say anything, just made those great noises. Because they'd already come, they could go all fucking night. It worked for him, balls to bones.

"Oh, fuck, gonna..." Dick's back arched, the kid's prick throbbing and then shooting hot come over his and Rig's hands.

Rig's ass clenched down on him, working his prick good.

"Yeah, come on now. You next."

"Me?" Rig gasped, squeezed again.

Laughing, he slapped Rig's ass and thrust in harder, nailing Rig's gland. "Yes, you."

"Butthead." Rig chuckled, gasped a little, all in the same breath. "There, Blue."

"Right here?" He slammed in again, loving the way Rig went tight around him.

"Right. Right there. Again."

"I know." He rocked hard and fast, his hips sawing back and forth.

He knew Rig was close when the words stopped, dried

up, the only sound their skin slapping together and the kid's groans.

"Come on, Rig. Show me how fucking good it is."

"Uh-huh. So good." Rig rippled around him and shot hard, spunk spraying against Dick's belly.

"Fuck, yes!" Rock gave one last hard thrust and came, filling Rig.

"Damn..." Rig slumped down against the kid, panting hard.

Rock let them have a little of his weight, humming happily, his hands wandering on skin.

"Mmm. Tell me it's really Friday, huh? We have the weekend off?"

"It's fucking Friday and me and the baby green are healthy and we have the weekend off."

"Baby green? Really?" Dick popped him on the ass.

Rock laughed. "You'll always be our baby green, kid."

"Mmmhmm. Just like Rock will always be my Blue-Eyed Marine."

"You know it. You fucking know it."

Dick turned the bacon and poured out coffee, whistling some song he'd heard on Rig's radio station. He grated cheese into the bowl of scrambled eggs and then turned the bacon again. He figured the smell of food should have Rig and Rock joining him about the same time it was done.

Toast popped and he grabbed it, buttering the two slices and adding them to the pile on the kitchen table.

"Mmm. Smells good, kid." Rig wandered by, took a mug, drank deep. "Thanks."

"You're welcome." Dick smiled over.

Rig kissed him, reached around him to turn the bacon again. "You look happy."

"Uh-huh. It's a great morning. Gonna be a good day."

He leaned in for another kiss.

"Mmm." Rig settled against his hip, cock soft and warm against him.

He slid an arm around Rig, hand resting on one ass cheek as they shared another kiss and then another.

"Don't burn the bacon, Pretty."

He leaned back, glancing over to make sure he didn't burn himself, and turned off the stove.

"Mmm." Rig took another coffee-flavored kiss. "Good job."

"Don't wanna burn down the house." His prick began to fill.

"No. I like our house." Rig grinned at him. "Like bacon, too."

He giggled and sucked on Rig's lower lip.

"That doesn't suck either." Rig smiled, relaxed, moaned.

"I do, though." He slid his fingers down over Rig's belly, headed for Rig's cock.

Rig's laugh was soft, warm, lazy. "We should build a fire today. Spend the day relaxing."

"Works for me." He licked Rig's collarbone and then nibbled his way down to one nipple.

"Mmm. Dick." That little bit of flesh perked up.

"Yeah, that's me." Dick grinned up at Rig as he slowly dropped to his knees to rub his cheek against Rig's prick.

Rig groaned, lips parting as those gray eyes stared down. Dick licked his own lips and then licked at Rig's cock, tongue playing softly around the head.

"Oh, damn." Rig leaned a little, lips open, breath panting out.

He took his sweet time, licking delicately, looking to drive Rig a little bit nuts with it.

Rig panted for him, staring down at him, throat working. "Oh, Dick. That's fucking sweet."

"Mmm..." He slid his tongue against Rig's slit, his fingers finding Rig's balls and gently rolling them.

Rig's fingers tangled in his hair, the touch careful, gentle. He smiled, nuzzling into the touch before focusing back on Rig's prick. He traced the veins with the point of his tongue, up and down and all around.

"Good." Those long thighs spread wider, letting him in and in.

He tickled Rig's balls with his tongue as his fingers slid back to tease the wrinkled skin around Rig's hole.

"Anything you want." Anything either of them wanted.

"I want to make you feel good." Dick took the head of Rig's cock in, sucking lightly, his tongue sliding back and forth across the tip as he did so.

He knew how Rig felt about that. Hell, that was one of the very first things Rig had taught him about making love, so long ago. Work the tip, Kid.

He looked up, meeting Rig's gaze. Those gray eyes were hot, watching him. He hummed, sucking harder now.

"Yeah. Yeah, just like that." Rig's voice was low, rough. "Such a fine fucking mouth."

His finger pushed into Rig's ass as he took Rig's cock a little deeper. He swallowed, creating even stronger suction.

"Oh, yeah. I want you. I want your cock, your fingers. Everything." Oh. Oh, shit. That was hot.

Head bobbing, Dick pushed his finger deeper, wiggling it.

""Fuck. I could ride your cock. Your hand. Oh, fuck." Rig groaned low, hips bucking, cock pushing in deep.

He swallowed around the tip and then pulled back, his moan vibrating from his lips to Rig's cock.

"More." Rig encouraged him to do it again, tugging on his head a little.

Dick made another low noise, his head bobbing forward and then pulling back slowly. He crooked his finger inside Rig's ass, twisting it, trying to find Rig's gland. When he found it, Rig shoved in deep, humping his lips. He kept working that spot with his finger, mouth tight around Rig's cock. He let Rig go for it, eager to have the taste of Rig in his mouth.

"Fuck!" Rig's free hand slapped against the counter as heat poured into his lips.

He swallowed it all down, taking Rig in. When Rig had stopped coming, he softened his suction, using his tongue to love on Rig's prick and clean it.

"Damn. Damn, Pretty. Thank you." Those long fingers were petting him, now, stroking him.

He nuzzled into the touches, still sucking idly on Rig's cock. It finally slipped from his mouth and he smiled up at Rig. "Better'n bacon."

"Mmhmm." Rig looked all lazy, dazed.

He stood and kissed Rig for quite some time before he pulled away. "You wanna help me dish up and take the plates to the bedroom?" There were ways to persuade Rock to eat in bed.

"Sounds perfect. You finish off the eggs."

"I can do that."

He gave Rig another quick kiss and turned back to the counter. The eggs just needed another quick whisk and to be dumped into the pan. It took no time at all for them to scramble up, the cheese melting right into them.

Rig topped off coffee cups and fixed three plates, boom-boom-boom. "Let's go wake up the Rock, man."

He dumped the scrambled eggs onto Rig's plates and nodded. "Scrambled eggs and blowjobs—he'll be in a good mood."

"Yep. Hell, Pretty, we're offering him lazing on the sofa, movies, and weekend sex. He'll be fine."

"Mmm... it's been too long since we've had a lazy weekend like this."

He snapped a piece of bacon in two, popping half into his own mouth and half into Rig's.

"You know it." Rig nodded, smiled. "Let's hasta."

Dick grabbed one of the trays. "After you." He wasn't stupid. He knew the best view in California was that ass. Or Rock's muscles. And he was about to indulge in both.

Lord help him, he was tired.

Rig stopped and sat at the shore, staring out at the water. They'd had a nice weekend, goofing off and playing and all. It'd been cool, up until about an hour ago. The guys had gone to nap, the dishes were done, and he was restless as all fuck.

So he'd left a note and headed out for a walk.

All cool, except...

He was tired. Like heavy-duty, bone-deep, Jesus help him he had to sit a spell tired. Like he was sorta thinking about calling and seeing if the boys wanted to walk back with him.

Right on cue his phone started ringing. Dick's cell number showing on the call display.

"'Lo?"

"Hey, Rig. Where'd you get to?"

"I took a walk, Pretty. What're you up to?"

"It's a long walk... Hey!"

"You coming home soon?" Rock asked. He could hear Dick grousing about people grabbing other people's phones without asking in the background.

"I..." He chewed on his lip, pondering, going between pride and pure exhaustion. "Do you think you could walk down the beach and walk back with me? I'm about worn to the bone somehow." And if Rock made a deal out of it, Rig would scream.

"If it'll get me laid one more time before we have to call the weekend done, you bet. We going left or right off the deck?"

"Left." He grinned, nodded. "Thanks, Rock."

"Uh-huh. You'll show me how thankful you are later."

He could hear that grin, knew exactly how those blue

eyes would be dancing. Rig chuckled, let the phone click shut, and stretched out, waiting.

The sun was beginning to set, the sky beautiful, when his Marines rounded the corner, coming into view. He got up, groaning a little under his breath. Damn, he was getting old.

"You get a little stiff sitting out here in the cold?" Dick asked him as they came up, one arm sliding around his shoulders.

"Yeah, I think so." He nodded, leaning some into Dick's arms. "Y'all have a good nap?"

Rock grunted. "It was restful." Those blue eyes looked him up and down. "You should have joined us."

They started heading back, and if he was still leaning into Dick, well, his Pretty didn't say a word. They wandered, nice and slow, heading for the house, the sand seeming to suck as his feet. Rock's arm went around his waist from the other side, both his boys supporting him now, but it didn't seem to be getting any easier. Maybe he needed some coffee. Or something.

Lord.

It had gone dark before they got to their place, the lights on the deck shining brightly, welcoming them home.

"Wanna get a shower?" Dick asked, hand sliding down to feel up his ass.

"I do. A shower, a cup of coffee." He pushed back into the touch, half-heartedly.

Rock grumbled and began hustling them up the deck and into the house. "Y'all go start the water, and I'll make a pot."

"No, you'll come with me," Rig said. "Dick can make the coffee."

"Sure I can do that." Dick kissed him and then Rock before moving to the coffee machine.

Rig blinked a little, then followed Rock. Rock got the water started and then began stripping him down.

"Thanks for walking out, Rock." He headed into the

shower as soon as he could, lifting his face to the water.

Rock climbed in behind him, hands landing on his shoulders and beginning to work his muscles.

"Mmm." Rig groaned and leaned forward, eyes dropping closed.

Rock didn't say a word, just worked his shoulders and then his back, a solid warmth behind him.

"Mmm." He leaned his head against his hands, eyes closing.

Rock finally broke his silence. "You're awfully wiped."

"I am. I feel like I've been beaten."

Growling, Rock dug in harder.

"That's how I felt before getting sick," Dick noted, popping his head around the shower curtain.

"Me, too," grunted Rock.

"I'm not going to get sick." He'd been taking his vitamins and everything.

"I'm down with that plan." Rock moved the massage down along his spine.

Dick climbed in. "Maybe you should have juice instead of coffee."

"I need some caffeine, though. In the worst way."

"Or you could, you know, take a nap."

"Kid's right." Rock's slow massage made it to his ass, fingers digging in.

"I don't nap." Oh, that felt nice.

"Okay, be a lump on the couch with us. We can channel surf, or body surf..." Dick's fingers slid up along his sides.

"Mmm. I could do that. I could just sit for a minute."

"Yeah, after the shower."

"Uh-huh." Rock's lips slid over his shoulder, heading for his neck.

"Oh." His breath stuttered, his knees buckling a little.

"So fucking easy," whispered Rock, lips closing over the sweet spot on his neck.

"Uh-huh. Y'all's." This wasn't news.

Dick chuckled and shoved past him and Rock, getting in front of him. His Pretty picked up the soap and began to wash him down. Rig leaned back into Rock, head back, throat working a little. Dick took his time, hands sliding all over Rig, washing him thoroughly. Rig moaned, let Rock hold him. Those big muscles cradled him, Rock's hands wandering after Dick's.

"Feels good, y'all."

"Good." His Marines answered together, and they laughed.

Rig laughed with them, surprised at how it ached.

Dick went to his knees, soapy hands cupping Rig's balls, rolling them.

"I don't know if I can get it up, Pretty."

Dick smiled up at him. "Does that matter? This feels good, right?" The slick, soft touches continued.

Yeah." He nodded, then closed his eyes, leaning back and letting Rock take his weight.

Rock cupped his balls while Dick's hands slid along his legs, finishing the job of soaping him up.

"Nobody loves me like y'all do."

"Nobody had better try," growled Rock.

That tickled him, set him to laughing. "No?"

"No." Rock sounded very sure. "And it's no joke."

Dick grinned up at him, rinsing his hands off and encouraging the water to rinse Rig off as well.

"You mean you aren't thinking about renting your old boy out?" He couldn't resist.

Rock growled, and Dick rubbed a cheek against his cock.

"Mmm. No, y'all have to keep me." He swayed a little, sighed. "Let's take this to the sofa, y'all."

"Sounds like a plan." His Blue did like his plans.

Dick turned off the water and grabbed some towels. Rig stepped out, slip-sliding a little before wrapping up in a towel and moving to help dry his boys. Dick and Rock dried him off, too, and before he knew it, he was bundled between them on the couch.

He was three-quarters through a glass of cranberry juice before he remembered his coffee. "Man, wasn't there going to be caffeine?"

"No," growled Rock. "You can have juice or water."

"Huh?" He finished his juice, frowning over the top of the glass.

"You don't need caffeine, you need juice and shit to make sure you're not getting sick."

Dick patted his hand. "I hate to say it, but Rock's right."

"Wait. Did the world just stop?" He chuckled and settled against Rock's side. "I'm not going to get sick. I'm just tired."

Rock's arm settled around him, holding him close. "Then you need sleep and not caffeine. See how well that works out?"

Dick grinned and grabbed the first season of 24, which he'd picked up on Wednesday, putting the first one in the tray and cueing it up.

Rig was asleep before the credits rolled.

Rock had to admit, after being out with the flu as long as he had been, it was nice to be feeling healthy and whole and back at work. He wandered through the gym, giving out tips here and there, helping spot one guy and showing another how to change the weights on the machines.

He was helping a regular get the proper technique going on her leg curls when his cell rang.

"Excuse me a moment." He stepped away and flipped open the phone. "Hello."

"Rock? Rock, it's Helen."

He frowned. She sounded worried. "What's wrong?"

"I wouldn't call, but I really don't think Doc should be driving, as sick as he is. He's being all stubborn about it, and he's still got another couple of hours of paperwork and calls to make, but..."

He growled. "I'll be there in half an hour and he'd better be ready to go." Damn it, Rig had said he wasn't getting sick.

"Don't be mean to him, now. He looked okay this morning, but he's wilting."

"I won't be mean. I'll make sure his stubborn ass gets home and into bed. Thanks for calling, Helen."

"Well, you know, I like the guy. I'll have someone call in cough medicine. Have Dick pick that up with some chicken soup, juice, Sprite, Tylenol. You know the drill."

"Yeah, a little too well, actually." They'd just been through all this with him and Dick. "Make sure you don't get it and bring it home to your kids—it's a nasty one," he warned her.

"Already happened. I was down with it when you two were. It sucked."

"Yeah, it sure did. Okay, I've just got to make sure we're covered here and I'll come get him."

"Okay, thanks." The phone went dead.

He hung up, made his apologies to the lady he'd been helping, and headed for the office. He stopped by the reception counter out front to let the new guy on duty—was it Zimmer? Something crazy like that, anyway—know that he'd be gone for the rest of the day, as would Dick. "Call on the cell if you need anything."

"Why am I off for the rest of the day?" Dick asked, coming up behind him.

"Rig's sick."

"Aw, fuck. I'd been hoping he'd avoid it."

"Yeah, well, he didn't. You go get the chicken soup and shit. Oh, and the 'scrip Helen had someone call in. I'm going to go get him from the clinic."

Dick nodded. "I just have a bit of paperwork that absolutely needs to get done or we're going to have unhappy employees come payday. I'll see you at home."

Rock nodded, mind already on Rig and which route would get him there faster this time of day.

A little over a half hour later found him walking into the clinic.

"Rock." Helen came up, holding Rig's briefcase. "He's in the bathroom. Throwing up. No blood, he just started coughing and blorp."

"Fucking shit. Sorry, Helen." He took the briefcase under one arm and headed for the little row of bathrooms.

Dr. Sam was in there, frowning over Rig. "Let's get you to the hospital. You're burning up."

"I am not going to the fucking hospital. I'm going home. It's the flu."

"Yes, but..."

"But, nothing. They're capable of giving me water and juice and making sure I'm good."

"More than. Don't worry, Doc, we'll keep him in bed and stuff him full of fluids." Rock was gonna tie Rig to the bed if he had to.

"Rock?" Rig blinked over at him. "What're you doing here?"

"Come to fetch you home." He was trying very hard not to growl, but it made a fist sit in his belly when Rig was sick.

"Yeah?" That fist eased a little when Rig relaxed, smiled. "Okay. I wasn't looking forward to the drive."

"Come on, then. Let me get you home. The kid and I'll take care of you."

"Oh, you don't have to fuss." Rig headed back toward his office, looking like his feet weighed a thousand pounds.

He grabbed Rig's arm to stop him. "I have your briefcase, Rig. Let's go."

"Huh?" Rig swayed, fell against him. Jesus, Rig was burning up.

"Come on, Rabbit. I know you don't want me to carry you." He put his arm around Rig's waist, supporting Rig as he walked the man to his car.

"No. No, my ego would never recover." Rig started

coughing again, body shaking with it. "I felt pretty good this morning."

"Well, you weren't feeling great last night. I should have insisted you stay home." Right, like his stubborn Rabbit would have gone for that.

"No. I felt okay. I did. Jesus, it's cold out here."

"I'll put the heat on." He got Rig bundled into the car, threw Rig's briefcase in the back, and settled in the driver's side. "Warn me if you're going to puke again."

"I'm not queasy. I just coughed too hard. There's nothing left to toss."

Rock turned the heat on and nodded. "We'll be home soon and you can go to bed. Dick's getting your meds and stuff."

"Stop at Mongo's and get me a cup of coffee?"

"With stuff like cough medicine and chicken soup and what the hell all else we have, what do you need a cup of coffee for?" If Rig thought he was going through paperwork instead of resting, he had another think coming.

"I want coffee. I'm cold. I'm tired. My throat hurts. I want a coffee."

"You can have juice." He turned the heat up.

Rig grumbled. "I don't want juice."

"Too bad. You're the sick one now—I get to play doctor."

"That sounds way naughtier than it's going to be."

Rock chuckled. "Yeah, it does, doesn't it?" He reached over and ran his hand along Rig's thigh. "Don't worry, we'll take care of you."

"I'm not worried."

No. No, but Rock was. "Looks like all those movies are going to get another workout."

"Nah. I'll be back at work in the morning."

Rock snorted, but didn't say anything. Rig muttered as they zoomed past Mongo's and Starbucks. And Java's. And The Steeping. God, people drank a bunch of coffee around here.

He parked the car and headed around to help Rig get out. "You want a shower before I put you to bed?"

"No. No, I'm cold. I want a fucking cup of coffee and I'm not sleepy. I just..." The coughing started again.

"Uh-huh. Nice hot shower and then we'll see where we are." He all but carried Rig up the stairs and inside.

The dogs were barking, bouncing up, Miss Susie-Q fighting desperately to get to Rig. "Back off, beasts." They weren't stopping to play.

"I need to spend more time with them..."

They were spoiled rotten.

"Uh-huh." He got Rig down the hall and into the bathroom.

Then he took out the thermometer and shoved it under Rig's tongue. Rig muttered and grumbled, the thermometer moving in his lips. Rock ignored the grumbling, turning on the shower and staring to strip Rig. Rig's skin was flushed and dry, hot to the touch.

"How much longer do I leave that in?" he asked, pointing to the thermometer.

Rig held up one finger.

"Another minute. Okay." He started stripping himself down as well.

Rig's hands were hot where they touched him, helping. As soon as he got naked, he took the thermometer. 102.5.

"Fuck. Tylenol for fever, right?" He opened the medicine cabinet, looking for the right bottle.

"Yeah. Tylenol." Rig stumbled into the shower.

He filled a glass with cold water and grabbed a couple of pills from the bottle. He climbed on in after Rig and pushed the pills into Rig's mouth, holding up the glass.

"Thank you." Rig drank deep, throat working.

"You're welcome." He put the glass out of the tub and took Rig into his arms. "You warming up any yet?"

"Yeah. A little." Rig cuddled in, moaned softly. "Hey, Blue."

"Hey." He relaxed a little, holding onto Rig. He had

his Rabbit home now. It was going to be okay.

"Mmm. You're tense."

"I'm fine." Rock slid his hands down along Rig's back. "Just fine."

"I don't think I am. I think I got the bug."

"Yeah, Rig, I think you did."

Rig started coughing again, shaking hard against him.

"Shit, I hope the kid gets here soon with the cough medicine." He rubbed Rig's back, hoping he wasn't about to get barfed on.

"Yeah. Yeah, me, too. I need to sit down some."

"Well, if you're warm enough we can move on to the lounging around being waited on hand and food portion of the day."

"I have some paperwork to do and stuff before tomorrow, Blue, but I could lounge a little."

Right. Like Rig was going to be going in tomorrow. And if Rock knew Helen, she'd have arranged for someone else to deal with anything that needed immediate attention.

He nodded and turned off the water, getting Rig wrapped in a big, fluffy towel. Rig let him dry and rub and touch without complaint, which proved to him how goddamned sick the man was. He would have growled, except that he had Rig home now and it would take less energy to just pamper the man.

He led Rig into the bedroom, getting a pair of sweats and one of his own sweatshirts, getting them onto Rig. "How does the bed look?"

"Good. Real good." Rig climbed up into the bed without complaint, curling under the comforter.

Jesus fuck, look at that. Very fucking sick.

He grabbed a pair of sweats for himself and climbed in with Rig, taking his Rabbit in his arms. He was ready for this flu to be done already. The next few days were going to be hell.

Dick picked up Rig's cough syrup at the drug store, then went to Mama Brigit's for a bunch of take-out chicken soup. He hit the video store and picked up the complete series of *Magnum PI* and *Miami Vice*. He stocked up on juice and fruit, crackers and bread, and headed home, working out in his head how to schedule things so either he or Rock were home until Rig was better.

It was probably more important that one of them was home once Rig was starting to feel better, because if there was anyone who was going to overdo the minute he was feeling better, it was Rig.

Dick pulled up behind Rock's truck, grabbed all the bags, and headed in. The living room and kitchen were both empty, the house quiet aside from the pups, so he put all his stuff away, grabbed a measuring spoon, and headed for the bedroom with the cough syrup.

Rig was sleeping across Rock's lap, wrapped in a bunch of blankets. He arched an eyebrow, and Rock shrugged. "He's restless as fuck, kid."

"Coughing a lot, too, I bet."

He set the cough syrup on the bedside table. "You want *Magnum* or *Miami Vice*?"

"*Miami Vice*." About the time Rock got the words out, Rig started coughing, entire body shaking with it.

"Fucking shit." Dick sat on the edge of the bed and shook the cough medicine before opening it. "Hold him up."

Rock sat Rig up, supporting him as he kept coughing.

"I want a cup of coffee," Rig croaked, in between wheezing hacks.

"Yeah, and men in hell want ice water," growled Rock.

Dick smiled and helped Rig swallowed down a tablespoon of medicine.

"How about some fresh squeezed orange juice?" Dick suggested.

Rig shook his head, tossing off the covers and pulling off his shirt. "Christ, it's hot."

203

"You need to keep that on. You've got a fever."

Dick left Rock dealing with Rig and went to fill a glass with orange juice and heat up a small bowl of soup in case Rig was hungry. Then he grabbed the tray and headed back to the bedroom.

A blanket flew through the air as he walked through the hallway. "I said I'm fucking hot!"

Man, Rig was the worst patient ever. And given he was comparing Rig to Rock, that was saying a lot.

"Who wants juice?" he asked cheerfully as he walked in.

Rig was kneeling between Rock's thighs, flushed and panting and shaking. "What?"

"Fuck, Rig. You look like hell warmed over." He glared at Rock.

"Hey, don't blame me—you know what he's like when he's sick."

"Quit talking about me like I'm not here!" Rig blinked over. "Can I have the juice?"

"Man, I didn't think I was." Dick handed over the juice. "You want some Tylenol or something?"

Rock glowered.

"I don't know." Rig sighed. "I need to get up. I'm hot." The juice was drained down, Rig panting after drinking, like it was a ton of work.

"You need to stay where you are. You know it's the fever making you feel like that."

Dick climbed up into the bed and sat against the wall, spreading his legs. He patted the spot between his legs. "Come on, let me give you a massage."

Rig shifted over, eyes on Rock. "Man, that medicine's making me dizzy."

"You're supposed to stay in bed, Rig. Then it doesn't matter if you're dizzy."

Dick nodded in agreement, hands landing on Rig's shoulders and digging in. Man, Rig was fevered. He looked over at Rock, worried.

"I'll get the thermometer again."

He watched Rock go and asked, "What was your temp when he took it earlier?"

"I don't know. It's up some."

"Did you take some Tylenol?" If it was too high, they were going to have to take him to the hospital.

"I think so, yeah. Don't worry. If it's too high, I'll take a shower."

"Uh-huh."

Rock came back and handed over the thermometer. Rig opened up, then leaned back into him, eyes closing.

Dick kept touching Rig, keeping him relaxed. "You've got to relax and let us take care of you. We know what you're going through."

"Jus' the flu."

"Yeah, the nastiest flu that ever flu-ed. It'll make us feel better if you let us fuss, okay?"

Rig nodded, eyelids drooping. "'M gonna make chili for supper."

Dick met Rock's eyes over Rig's head.

"Get some sleep for now, okay?"

Rock pulled out the thermometer. Rock winced, mouthing, "103."

Rig leaned toward Rock, octopussing around the man, almost asleep.

Dick rubbed Rig's back. "Let's give him some more Tylenol and see if he'll sleep. If it doesn't get better, we'll take him in." Whether Rig wanted to go or not.

Rock nodded, mouth set.

"No hospitals. I just need some juice."

"We'll see," growled Rock.

Dick leaned in to murmur. "Get some sleep and I bet you'll feel better."

"Mmm. Yeah. Stay, Blue. You're warm and I'm fucking freezing."

"I'm not going anywhere, Rabbit."

Dick pulled the covers up over Rig's shoulders and went for more pills and more juice. It was just the flu, he told himself. He and Rock had been as bad during their bout with it.

Still, he hated it when Rig was sick.

Fuck, he was hurting.

Thirsty.

Freezing.

Rig rolled off the bed, stumbling toward the kitchen, trying to figure out why it was dark.

Someone came padding down the hall behind him. "Rig? What are you doing up?" Oh, something had Rock growly.

"I... " Oh, fuck. His throat.

"You need some juice? Some more medicine?"

"Yeah." He nodded. "I think I'm sick."

Rock snorted. "No, shit. Look, go back to bed and I'll bring you shit."

"I'm gonna hit the head first. Wash my face." He patted Rock's arm in thanks and wandered to the bathroom.

Rock followed him there a few minutes later, carrying a large glass of juice and a bottle of cough medicine. "How's your fever?"

"I don't know. I'm hurting, some." He tried to grin, wink. "Feels like you beat me, Blue."

"It was a near thing—you didn't want to just lie down and get better."

Rock pulled the Tylenol out of the bathroom cabinet and handed two pills over. Rig took them and drank half the juice, wincing as his throat screamed.

Rock's hands landed on his shoulders, warm and soothing; the big body warmed him from behind. "You need to come back to bed and get more sleep."

"Okay." He opened the Robitussin with Codeine and swigged back a shot, gagging a little. "Let's go." He was cold, so he must still be feverish.

Rock's arm went around his shoulders, leading him back to the bed. "There's a DVD in if you can't sleep. You are definitely getting back in bed, though, and staying there." Rock said it like he was expecting an argument.

"Okay. My head's killing me." He let Rock move him, nice and slow, toward the bed.

"It always makes me nervous when you agree to rest." Rock chuckled, the sound wry.

"Yeah, me, too. I'll fight you in the morning." He slid into the covers, holding them up for Rock. "Come hold me."

"Always." Rock climbed in and tugged him up against the strong body, so good and warm for him.

"Mmm." He wrapped in close, humming softly, the meds making him loopy and lazy.

Dick snuggled up behind him, still asleep.

Rock patted his arm. "You go to sleep, Rig."

"Yeah. Did you set the alarm for the morning and did someone remember to get the coffee set up?" Those were his jobs, usually.

Rock's arms tightened around him. "You're sick, remember? Fever, coughing until you puked, aching, chills, sore throat. Is any of this ringing a bell?"

"Uh-huh. Sorta. What does that have to do with coffee?"

"You don't need to get up in the morning and you don't need coffee."

"I have patients." His eyelids drooped, his hand was very busy, petting Rock's belly.

"Helen's taken care of everything for you." Rock's lips pressed against the top of his head.

"Oh." Oh, that felt nice. "Okay. Jesus, I'm tired."

"So go back to sleep, Rabbit." Another kiss pressed into his curls, and Rock hugged him close.

"'Kay Blue. See you in the..." He yawned, eyes closing. "In the morning."

"Yeah, I'll be here."

Rock's hand patted his, the touch following him into sleep.

Rock took the first shift with Rig the next day, Dick going in to the gym. Tomorrow they'd switch off. Rock figured he actually had the easier job. By tomorrow, Rig would be feeling a little bit better and he'd be chomping at the bit to go on in the office for "just a few hours."

The kid got off to work, and Rock made himself breakfast and then settled in the living room with the paper, figuring if he went back into the bedroom, he'd wake Rig up.

He heard the coughing about two minutes before the shower started. Man, he knew how shitty that cough felt.

He hauled himself out of his chair and poured a big glass of juice. Oh, look at that, the kid had made up some pudding before he'd left. Cool. He got a bowl of soup ready for the microwave as well. Juice in hand, he headed to the bathroom.

Rig was hanging over the toilet, panting, coughing hard, cheeks red.

"Shit." He bent over Rig, rubbing his back. "You need more cough medicine."

Rig nodded, trying to catch his breath. It wasn't like Rig could afford to not only be not eating, but then throwing up as well. Rock growled a little. He and Dick had done their time; it wasn't right Rig was sick, too.

"'M okay. Thought I was gonna puke, but I didn't." Rig straightened up, panting hard. "Did I see juice?"

"You did." He handed it over, trying not to growl. He wasn't pissed off at Rig, but he could hardly yell at the flu without also yelling at Rig.

"Thanks." Rig drank it all down in big gulps. "God, I'm starving, somehow."

"You hardly ate anything yesterday. I've got soup ready to warm, and the kid made pudding."

"Soup sounds good. What kind?" Rig leaned against him, wheezing some.

"Homemade chicken noodle. Well, homemade by the restaurant. Dick picked it up yesterday."

Rock found the cough medicine and handed it over. Rig sucked some down, then immediately coughed it up.

"Fuck. Okay, if you were one of your patients, how would you get the cough medicine into you?"

Rig blinked at him. "A... a couple of smaller spoonfuls. I'd tell them to sit up under a blanket, try and relax."

"Okay. Then the only question is bed or couch?"

"Couch, so I can visit with you."

"Sounds good." He debated for a half a second and then picked Rig up, carrying him to the living room.

It said a lot, that Rig didn't bitch, just wrapped those long arms around him and held on.

He went via the kitchen, setting the microwave on to heat the soup up, and then took Rig into the living room and settled him on the couch. Wrapping a blanket around Rig, he fluffed the fucking pillows and handed off the remote.

"Daytime TV is a vast wasteland, huh?" Rig looked a little lost.

"Yep. Kid bought some DVDs, though. Or we could just sit."

The microwave dinged. "Be right back."

When he got back, Rig was curled up, sound asleep, mouth open.

Christ.

Rock sat down in his chair. He fucking hated this.

The coughing started again, before he could settle down, Rig looking fragile as fuck.

He got himself settled behind Rig and slowly dribbled the cough medicine in. "Come on."

"Thank you." Rig kept it down this time, going quiet and blinky almost immediately.

"You think you can manage a spoonful or two of soup?"

"Uh-huh. Did you put pepper in it?"

"No, I didn't figure it would be kind to your throat." He offered a spoonful over.

"Oh, yeah." Rig opened up, ate the bite, swallowed.

"Good."

"Good man." He offered another mouthful.

Rig ate three bites, then waved him off. "That's enough."

"You sure? How about some pudding? The kid made you butterscotch."

"Not right now. Thanks, though."

"All right." He wrapped Rig up and tugged him close. "You want a movie or something?"

"Yeah." Rig cuddled in, cheek warm against him, but not burning hot like before.

He flipped on the TV and set the DVD running, not really caring what was on.

Rig was resting quietly, and that was good enough for him.

Dick worked a half day and stopped to grab some Mexican from Rosa's before going home. He pulled up behind Rig's car and headed in with lunch. The dogs milled around, smelling the food.

"Not for you spoiled pups. Rig, I come bearing gifts."

No answer.

No Rig on the sofa.

Office door closed.

Damn.

He could remember Rig's words to him, about how he and Rock needed to take the time off so they didn't relapse.

He knocked on the office door. "Rig?"

"Hmm?" He heard Rig's voice, distracted, lost in the sound of clacking keys.

He opened the door and went in. "Rig? I brought lunch." He waved the bag, running a critical eye over Rig.

"Cool." Rig's cheeks were flushed, dark spots of red

on them - proving that their stubborn cowboy had a fever and had been coughing. Rig was looking skinny, too, which was not going to work.

"Save whatever you're working on and turn the computer off, Rig." Man, Rock was going to hand him his ass if he didn't get Rig back on track. He was going to hand himself his ass. And hand Rig's to him, too.

"Huh? I have a few more things to..."

"No, I think you should save and close it now." He shook his head, going over and trying not to be too Rock-like as he loomed.

"You're really ready for lunch, huh Pretty?" Rig tapped a few more keys.

"Yep, that's right. I bet you are, too." Damn it, he didn't want to have to play the heavy, but if Rig didn't get with the program in the next few seconds, he was going to have to.

"I don't have much of an appetite, but I'll come sit with you for a few."

"You should eat something, Rig. I don't care if you don't want any burritos—I'll heat some soup up for you."

"Ooh. Burritos?" Rig's eyes lit up a little and the man stood, swaying a bit, coughing.

Dick bit back his worried comment and slipped his arm around Rig's waist. "Yeah, the good ones from Rosa's. She made them especially for you."

"Cool." Rig walked around the desk and headed out of the office. "I started the laundry, put a roast in the oven."

"You're supposed to be resting. You remember the lecture about overdoing?"

"Huh? What lecture?"

Dick shook his head, taking Rig's arm and leading the man to the couch in the living room when Rig made to turn into the kitchen. "The one about how Rock and I were going to relapse if we went back to work too early."

"Yeah. Y'all work hard in that gym."

He shot Rig a look, but Rig was serious. "Yeah, well you work hard, too. Between the office and here you work harder than all of us combined and today you've overdone." He took their food out of the bag and handed over one of the burritos.

"Smells good." Rig nibbled, picking idly at the chicken, at the chiles.

"Yeah. There's dessert, too." He could remember how skinny Rig had gotten when he'd been really sick. They were not having a repeat of that.

"Cool." The burrito was put down on the coffee table, Rig coughing softly.

"You need some of that cough medicine?"

If Rig took half as good care of himself as he did everyone else...

"I don't think so. I think it's getting better."

"So eat some more then."

"What?"

He chuckled and handed the burrito back to Rig. "Indulge me and eat."

"Indulge you, huh?" Rig nibbled, eating another bite or two. "It's good."

"Yep, indulge me." He gave Rig a wink and eagerly ate his own burrito. It was good, and there was no reason why Rig shouldn't be able to eat at least one. Except that Rig was dozing off, then waking himself up coughing and not fucking eating.

"I'm going to go get you a bit of cough medicine. Just a little bit, okay?" And some damn Tylenol.

He got the drugs and stopped by the fridge to grab a grape popsicle. The hacking cough had become a whooping wheeze by the time he got back, Rig gripping the edge of the coffee table.

"Fuck, Rig." He went back to the kitchen for a glass of juice and handed that over first to help calm the cough.

Rig had made things worse again by overextending himself today.

"Thanks. Sorry. I'm okay."

Uh-huh. Right. Rock was going to have a stroke.

He watched Rig drink the whole glass of juice and then passed over two Tylenol and the cough medicine, not backing off until Rig had taken both. Then he presented the popsicle with a little ta-da.

"Oooh..." Rig gave him a smile—a real, focused, happy smile—and reached for the popsicle.

Score one for the kid. Grinning, he sat down next to Rig and finished up his burrito.

Rig ate the whole popsicle, sucking and humming eagerly, then actually ate more of the burrito. Dick tried to ignore the way his body tightened as Rig worked the popsicle. The man was sick. Still, that mouth was pure poetry.

"Mmm. That's good." Rig slid closer on the couch, heavy-lidded and lazy, relaxed. That cough medicine worked like a charm. "Hey, Pretty."

"Hey." He put his arm around Rig and tugged him close. Rig wasn't too hot, so if he had a fever it wasn't very bad.

"Mmm." Rig curled up around him, clinging and humming. So sexy.

He stroked his hand along Rig's back, cuddling happily.

"Feels good." Rig's lips found his jaw, his chin, kissing gently.

"Yeah." He supposed a few kisses couldn't hurt anything. He tilted his head, pressing his lips to Rig's.

"Mmm." Rig scooted closer, ending in his lap.

"Just some kissing." He took another one, arms looping around Rig's back.

"Mmmhmm. I like kissing."

"Yeah, it's one of my favorite things to do with your mouth." He grinned and went back to the kissing.

Rig almost laughed, then stopped himself. Dick remembered that—how sore the coughing made you. He hugged Rig tight and gave him another kiss. Rig hummed, settling in, letting him hold on tight.

They kept kissing, lips sliding together, tongues exploring. It was unhurried and unrushed and perfect.

He heard the dogs go nuts, knew that Rock was coming in to check on Rig. The man couldn't not.

He patted Rig's butt. "Your other Marine's coming to make sure you're not overdoing."

"Not. Just working a little."

Dick snorted, but he didn't rat Rig out as Rock came in.

"Hey, you two look cozy."

"Dick brought lunch."

"Burritos from Rosa's. If I'd realized you were coming home, too, I'd have picked a couple for you."

"Nah, I hit the drive-through and got some grease that I ate on the way." Rock sat next to them, putting his hand on Rig's forehead.

"I'm fine. Stop it." Rig leaned up, kissed Rock's palm.

"Are you?" Rock looked at Dick, not Rig, as he asked it.

"He's had his meds, he's eaten, and he's hanging out with me on the couch—he's fine." Now, anyway.

"Mmmhmm. I did laundry and started some supper. Even worked a few hours." Rig leaned down, stretching over both their laps.

"What?" Rock growled.

Man, Rig had to learn to hush sometimes.

"He's been taking it easy since I got home, and I'll be staying. He's fine."

Rock grumbled, but didn't say anything else.

"I took my cough medicine, too." Rig let his hand slide up Rock's thigh.

"Yeah? You feeling okay?"

Dick hid his smile.

"Better. A little goofy, but better." Rig smiled wickedly. "I got to suck off a popsicle."

Rock groaned. "I'd like to have seen that."

"I could get him another one." Dick wouldn't mind watching it again.

"Oh... are there more?" Rig was an addict.

"You want another grape one?"

"Cherry."

Perv.

Grinning, he kissed Rig's forehead and went to fetch another popsicle. He could hear Rock chuckling the whole way. By the time Dick got back, Rock had Rig in his lap, leaning against his arm. Dick handed over the popsicle and settled next to them, resting against Rock's other arm.

"Thanks, kid." Rig smiled at him and started licking the ice pop, tongue sliding up the shaft.

He and Rock groaned together.

"It tastes good." Rig wrapped his lips around the top, sucking.

"Fuck," muttered Rock. "That's got to be illegal."

"Uh-uh. 'S good." Rig licked around the bottom, gathering up the drops he'd missed.

"Fuck," Dick muttered, cock going hard. Rock grunted, eyes never leaving Rig's mouth.

Rig didn't say a word as he sucked that popsicle off.

The minute Rig was done, Rock grabbed the popsicle stick. "Jesus fucking Christ, Rig, my cock is right here."

"Give it over, then." Rig was panting for it.

Rock had his jeans undone and his cock out before Rig could take another breath. Rig scooted down, lips open and dropping over Rock's prick, just like that. Rock's head dropped back, a low rumble coming from him. Yeah, that was the stuff. Dick shoved his hand down his own pants, watching.

Rig wasn't teasing, that head started bobbing, Rock's thick cock disappearing down Rig's throat. Great noises came out of Rock, big hands sliding through Rig's curls. Every few bobs, Dick could see Rig fighting his cough, but Rig wouldn't give up that cock.

He didn't try and stop Rig. Maybe it was fucked

up, but this was the best medicine for their cockhound. Besides, this was guaranteed to get their Rigger to nap.

Rock spread wider, hips beginning to make little jerking motions. Rig hummed, deep in his throat, and Dick knew that sound felt so good. Rock shouted Rig's name and pumped hard and fast a couple times before stilling, pleasure clear on Rock's face.

Rig slowly pulled off, then landed, cheek on Rock's thigh, lips swollen and pink. Now there was a happy man, ready to rest.

Rock panted, still stroking Rig's hair, while Dick worked Rig's cock. Watching Rig give Rock a blowjob still ranked up there as one of the sexiest things in his life. Rig looked over at him, licked the come right off those sweet, swollen lips. Moaning, Rock squeezed the head of his cock, coming over his hand just from that look.

He got a smile and then, boom, Rig was dozing.

"Looks like we're stuck here for awhile." Rock didn't look unhappy about that. Not at all.

Neither was he.

He leaned and Rock met him halfway, the kiss lazy, good. Then he rested his head on Rock's shoulder. A nap sounded pretty good right now.

Rig pulled up into the driveway, wincing when he saw that the guys were home. He'd been hoping to do his shopping and a few hours of work without getting caught.

He was almost better.

Really.

Rock was going to grump, and his Pretty was going to give him those worried looks. Maybe he could leave the groceries in the kitchen and walk down the beach. It would be like a grocery fairy had come. He chuckled, grinned. Rig, the grocery fairy.

The front door opened, both his Marines coming out

and there went his chance to play fairy.

Damn it. He slipped out of his truck, waving. "Hey, y'all. I got groceries."

"You're supposed to be taking it easy," growled Rock as he and Dick came over to grab the bags.

"I only worked a few hours."

"You went into work and then you went shopping." Rock growled and grumbled and stomped up the stairs.

Dick gave him a sympathetic look. "You were going stir crazy at home, huh?"

"I cleaned, did laundry. Washed the dogs. My hands aren't steady enough to work in the shop."

"Rig!" Dick lowered his voice. "Are you crazy? You're only just recovering! If you make yourself sick again, Rock's going to kill you. You need to take better care of yourself."

"I can't just sit and spin, Dick. You know that. Hell, y'all weren't supposed to be back for another forty-five minutes."

"No one's asking you to 'sit and spin', Rig. We don't want anything bad to happen to you." Ever since he'd been really sick, his Marines were hyper-vigilant.

"I'm fine." Of course, that was when he started coughing again. Goddamn it.

Dick's arm went around him, helping get him up the stairs and in the front door, where Rock met them with the damn cough medicine.

"I don't..." He coughed again, groaned. Fuck, that hurt.

"Don't what, Rig? Take the damn medicine and stop trying to be Superman."

He tightened his lips, considering having a temper tantrum and a good hard scream. Then he opened up. He was tired and he wanted Rock to cook him a steak and then possibly go have a soak in the hot tub. He didn't want to fight. He was getting old.

Rig opened up, taking the nasty stuff.

Rock grunted and tipped the spoon into his mouth.

"Better. Now come on in and let us do for you for a fucking goddamned change."

Dick nudged him, grinned. "We play our cards right and he'll grill up the steaks you bought. Maybe even dish out massages."

"That was the plan, huh? There's a chocolate cake from the bakery in one of the bags..."

Dick chuckled. "We may even get a smile out of him."

They headed for the kitchen to help Rock put the groceries away.

Rock handed him a glass of juice and nodded to the table. He took the juice and leaned against the counter. Compromise. Rock grunted, but didn't push. It didn't take his Marines very long to get the groceries away. They left out the potato salad, steak, and salad fixings.

"I suppose you want that green leafy crap with your supper?" Rock asked, making a face at the lettuce.

"If you do the steak, I'll make it up," Dick offered, winking at him.

"I want green leafy crap, absolutely. I hear someone's making a chocolate bar with spinach in it..." Poke.

"What the fuck kind of crazy idea is that?" Rock growled, looking suspiciously at the chocolate cake as it came out of the grocery bag.

"I haven't the foggiest. There's bacon flavored chocolate, too," he teased gently.

Dick shuddered.

"That's not right," Rock muttered.

Rig nodded and got to laughing, which meant coughing, soon enough.

Dick rubbed his back, and Rock handed over a popsicle. "Suck on that, it'll soothe your throat."

"Mmm. Thank you." He did love those stupid things, cold and slick and sweet.

Two pairs of eyes watched him closely. He wasn't the only one who liked them, or at least who liked it when he sucked on one. He did a good job of it, moaning and sucking, working the treat in and out.

Rock and Dick leaned in, moaning as they kissed each other.

Someone really liked that.

A lot.

He licked at the drops that were sliding off the bottom. That earned him more moans and groans, his Marines going at each other's mouths like there was no tomorrow.

"You two are horndogs." He grinned, licked a little more.

They broke the kiss off slowly. Rock grinning over at him. "You started it."

"Me? Bullshit. I was having a snack."

"Uh-huh." Rock came over and licked the corner of his mouth. "Mmm... orange."

He nodded, leaned in for another kiss. "Want another taste?"

"You know it." Rock's lips pressed against his, tongue slipping into his mouth.

Oh, nice. Rig stretched up, tongue sliding against his Blue's. Rock's hand slid into his curls, holding his head in place as the kiss deepened. He opened right up, giving it up. A moment later, Dick's mouth joined the kiss, turning it into a three-way.

"Mmm. Hey." Rig grinned, leaned closer and slid one arm around Dick's waist.

The kisses continued, their tongues sliding together, rubbing. They held him up when his knees buckled, his cock starting to fill. Rock's arms were solid around him, Dick beginning to slide to his knees.

"Mmm." He let himself spread, leaning harder into his Blue.

Dick's fingers worked open his jeans as Rock held him up and devoured his mouth.

"Oh, damn. Damn, y'all. Please." He wanted.

"Dick's got you covered."

"I do." Dick grinned up at him, fingers sliding on his

prick, tugging it out of his pants.

Rig swallowed, nodded, pushing eagerly into the touch. Dick's hand held the base of his cock, hot tongue touching the tip, teasing him. Relaxing, he let himself feel it, let himself ride the slow, sweet build up. Rock rumbled for him, the sound vibrated in the air. Dick kept working the tip, tongue pushing into his slit.

"Oh. Oh, I like that." He blinked up, staring into Rock's eyes. "Remember the sounds, the way you had him hold me."

Rock's eyes went hot, his voice husky when he answered. "I do. And you are feeling better if you're thinking about things like that."

Dick whimpered around his cock, tongue jabbing into him.

"I am. Y'all... you blew my mind." His hips started moving, making little jerks.

"We can do it again," murmured Rock.

Dick sucked harder, head bobbing on his cock.

"Uh-huh." He wasn't even sure what he was agreeing to.

Rock's mouth covered his again, tongue sliding between his lips. One big hand landed on his ass, squeezing. He whimpered, toes curling, digging into the soles of his boots.

Fuck.

Rock encouraged him to fuck Dick's mouth, his Pretty's lips giving him lovely friction, tongue slapping and playing over his cock as it pressed in and out. Low sounds bubbled out of him, pushed into Rock's lips. Rock swallowed each one, moving him faster.

It wasn't going to take him any time; he was close and needing and it'd been a few days.

"Come on," murmured Rock, filling his mouth with the rumbling words as Dick went down all the way on him.

"Uh... Uh-huh..." Rig arched, eyes rolling back. He. Oh. Damn.

Dick swallowed around the tip of his cock, throat tight around him. He shot so hard his teeth rattled, hands opening and closing in Dick's hair. Okay. Okay. Damn. Rock chuckled, grinning at him like Rock had been the one responsible for making him come. The heat around his prick didn't go anywhere, Dick humming and continuing to suck gently.

He groaned, trying to catch his breath, letting Rock hold him up.

Dick slowly pulled off, beaming up at him, looking smug; his Pretty had learned that look from Rock. "You look like you need to sit."

Nodding, he blinked a little. Man. Man, he was light-headed. That was hot.

Rock got him sitting, and Dick got him a glass of water and another popsicle, giving him a wink as it was handed over.

Then his Marines set out to making supper.

Lord, he did have a good damn life.

Bedside Manner

Bedside Manner

13242659R00128

Made in the USA
Lexington, KY
22 January 2012